The groundbreaking, long-running Sharon McCone mystery series, now over two decades old, has seen the intriguingly complex McCone evolve dramatically. Beginning as a '70s idealistic crime fighter, she has become a formidable, battle-tested veteran who has not lost her passion for justice. Now in the newest book in the series, McCone faces a frightening midlife crisis that will truly test her mettle. With her very identity at stake, she confronts an enemy who invades her privacy, disturbs her mind, and threatens to destroy her life.

PRAISE FOR MARCIA MULLER
AND HER NEWEST SHARON McCONE NOVEL
WHILE OTHER PEOPLE SLEEP

"An excellent private-eye tale structured by a master of the form . . . moves smoothly and entertainingly from the first whiff of plot to the big finale."
—*San Francisco Sunday Examiner & Chronicle*

"A rip-roaring conclusion."
—*Washington Post Book World*

"A riveting tale. . . . [Muller is] a first-rate storyteller."
—*Ellery Queen's Mystery Magazine*

more. . .

"Sharon McCone is the new breed of American woman detective . . . redefining the mystery genre by applying different sensibilities and values to it."
—New York Times Book Review

"Reading the McCone novels in order, one can track the astounding literary growth of author Marcia Muller as she hones her skills to scalpel sharpness. . . . A prime example of just how good the noir novel can be."
—Cleveland Plain Dealer

"Marcia Muller launched the present wave of women writing about women as sleuths with Sharon McCone in 1977 . . . [and] quietly keeps getting better and better."
—Charles Champlin, Los Angeles Times Book Review

"One of the most popular female heroines in the genre."
—Los Angeles Daily News

"Pace and plotting are very strong, but it's her characters—especially McCone—who will lure you back."
—Atlanta Journal & Constitution

"Muller has gotten quietly, steadily better. She is building up steam, not running out of it."
—Newsweek

SHARON McCONE MYSTERIES
BY MARCIA MULLER

MARCIA MULLER

WHILE OTHER PEOPLE SLEEP

WARNER BOOKS

A Time Warner Company

WARNER BOOKS EDITION

Copyright © 1998 by the Pronzini-Muller Family Trust
All rights reserved.

Cover design by Diane Luger
Cover illustration by Tony Greco
Hand lettering by David Gatti

Warner Books, Inc.
1271 Avenue of the Americas
New York, NY 10020

Visit our Web site at
www.warnerbooks.com

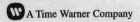 A Time Warner Company

Printed in the United States of America

Originally published in hardcover by The Mysterious Press.
First Paperback Printing: May 1999

10 9 8 7 6 5 4 3 2 1

For the Mourants:
Tom, who won't read it,
Teresa, who will,
Kirsten, who might,
Camille, who might when she's old enough.
And also for Patty and Walt.

Many thanks to:

Peggy Bakker, CFI, for her flying wisdom and expertise
Jan Grape, for her Texas-isms
Erlene Peeples, for her wonderful flying stories
Tim Talamantes, for the story that inspired McCone's
nineteenth case
Melissa Ward, for her help, research, and sympathetic ear

And, of course, to Bill, for everything

PART ONE

•

February 12–24

The hours while other people sleep are the longest for me, and the most uneasy. All that's familiar adopts a vaguely menacing disguise, and the landscape of my life alters. Demons walk beside me, in the form of old regrets and guilts. I'm cut off from those I love. Whether at home and plagued by insomnia or on a long surveillance, I watch the clock and will its hands to move more swiftly toward the time when the darkness will lift and life will once again return to the safe and mundane. But the hands creep slowly, and I'm forced to face what I keep hidden inside.

I'm not as kind as I'd like to be, or as loving.

I'm not as honest as I used to be, and my ethics are eroding.

I'm not as brave as I pretend to be.

I've hurt people, people I care about.

I've killed people, played God.

The list goes on, then replays in an endless loop as

I wait out the night. I feel threatened, but not by anything external.

During the hours while other people sleep, the threat always comes from within.

Wednesday Night

At 11:37 P.M. the interior of Pier 24½ lay in darkness broken only by a few badly placed security lights. The air was cold and damp, redolent of brine and creosote. Rain hammered the flat roof, and directly above it on the span of the San Francisco–Oakland Bay Bridge, a truck's gears ground. Another vehicle backfired, sounding like gunshots.

I paused on the iron catwalk outside my office, watching and listening, my senses sharpened as they always were when I worked alone here at night. The old pier's security was easily breached, there were many places for an intruder to hide, and the waterfront, while undergoing a renaissance these days, was still a potentially dangerous place. Given the right combination of circumstances, most places in this city could be dangerous.

No one was visible on the catwalks that crossed over to the opposite suites of offices; no light seeped through the cracks around the doors. The ironwork threw an intricate pattern of shadows on the concrete floor below, where we tenants parked our cars. After a moment I moved along the catwalk toward the office of Ted Smalley, the efficient and somewhat dictatorial man who keeps both my agency and Altman & Zahn, Attorneys-at-Law, functioning smoothly. The sound of my footsteps echoed off the high ceiling and exposed girders.

A sudden rush of air, and something flew at my head. Reflexively I threw up an arm; my fingers grazed thin membrane and bone.

Jesus Christ, a bat!

Heart pounding, I ran into Ted's office, slammed the door, and leaned against it, clutching the files I carried.

"McCone," I gasped aloud, "you've faced down armed criminals without blinking. Why the hell're you running from a little bat that's probably cowering in the rafters by now?"

I knew the answer, of course: the encounter with the bat had tapped into my old phobia of birds—one I thought I'd long before conquered. Apparently not, though, at least not when I was already nursing a low-level depression and edginess, brought on by the wet and stormy weather that had persisted with scarcely a break since the day after Christmas.

A low-wattage lamp burned on Ted's desk. I used its light to scribble a note, which I then stuffed under the rubber band holding the files together. They contained job applications, background checks, and turndown letters for three candidates I'd recently interviewed. Two of the applicants had been excellent, and my note to Ted asked that he keep the files active, but early last week my friend Craig Morland had finally accepted the position I'd offered him last December. Craig, a former FBI field agent, was just the man McCone Investigations needed; his connections from fifteen-plus years with the Bureau had already proved invaluable to me.

Back on the catwalk, I strode fearlessly toward the stairway. No bat was going to intimidate *me*.

"Hey!"

I froze at the top of the stairway, trying to pinpoint the source of the shout, then dropped down behind the railing and peered through it.

"Hey, Sharon, how come you're hiding from me?"

I let my breath out slowly, recognizing the Australian accent of Glenna Stanleigh, a documentary filmmaker who rented the ground-floor suite next to the pier's entrance. Feeling both foolish and angry, I straightened.

"For God's sake, Glenna! I damn near died of fright."

"You? No way." She came out from behind her Ford Bronco—a petite woman with long, light brown curls and huge, lamplike gray eyes. "Seriously, I *am* sorry. I wasn't thinking."

"No permanent harm done." I started down.

"I wouldn't've shouted like that," Glenna added, "but I've been anxious to see you. To tell you about a bizarre experience I had last weekend."

"Oh?"

She nodded, looking exceptionally solemn for one with a perpetually sunny disposition. When I first met Glenna, I'd found her cheeriness suspect; nobody could possibly be that upbeat—to say nothing of that nice—all the time. But as I got to know her better I realized how genuine she was, and we became friends of a sort. I often sought her out when I was feeling low, and this past rainy month I'd spent a fair amount of time drinking tea with her in her office.

She said, "It's kind of a long story, but I think the sooner you know, the better. Would you like some brandy? I've a leftover Christmas bottle in my desk."

Brandy sounded perfect. "Lead me to it."

While Glenna searched her editing room for glasses, I sat in one of the low-slung canvas chairs in her office and listened to the rain splatter against the high arched window overlooking the Embarcadero. Across the waterfront boulevard, Hills Plaza—a former coffee mill converted to residential and commercial use—was largely dark; the globes of the old-fashioned streetlights along the Muni tracks glowed, highlighting the fronds of the recently planted palm trees. I caught my own reflection in the glass and glanced away, thinking I looked tired.

There was a smashing noise in the editing room, and Glenna exclaimed, "Damn!"

"You all right?"

"I am, but that brandy snifter isn't."

I smiled. The glass had probably been perched precariously, if the editing room contained as much chaos as the office. Framed posters for Glenna's documentaries, on such diverse subjects as Appalachian folk medicine and the ecology of the Great Barrier Reef, leaned at intervals along the walls, where they'd been waiting to be hung for as long as I'd known her.

Glenna returned, a trifle flushed and carrying two plastic tumblers. She poured the brandy, handed one to me, and sat in the matching chair. "Yes, it's a mess in there too," she said, "which is why I broke the last of my snifters. I plan to do something about it one of these days. Or years."

"More likely years."

"You know me—I'm hopeless." But she grinned cheerfully, quite content with her slothfulness. "So what're you doing here this late?"

I shrugged, sipping the brandy. "Paperwork."

"You can't find time for it during business hours?"

"Not unless I chain myself to the desk—and I established the agency to keep from being confined to the office. Besides, I spent most of the afternoon helping Ted sort out what brand of new copier to buy. Leave it to him to suffer a totally uncharacteristic fit of indecision when I have a full in-box. He's been acting weird; it's hell when you can't rely on your most dependable employee."

"Lord, you sound like me: be your own boss and end up working harder and longer than you ever did for anybody else."

"Right." Still, I didn't regret the decision. McCone Investigations was turning a profit and growing; we were steadily earning a reputation for solid, intelligent, reliable work.

"So," I said to Glenna, "what's this bizarre experience you want to tell me about?"

Her small face grew solemn again. "Well, you know that I'm on the board of the Bay Area Film Council?"

I nodded.

"Saturday night we held this positively smashing fund-raiser at the Russian Hill penthouse of one of our patrons. Cocktail party for hundreds. The big money came out in droves. Heavy security, of course, and special name tags so none of the riffraff could sneak in. I networked madly, talking up that Hawaiian documentary I want to do, and somebody told me that a member of the Dillingham family—they're big in construction in the Islands—was in the room where they'd got the buffet set up. So I took myself there and came face to face with a woman wearing a familiar name tag." Glenna paused dramatically.

"Who was it?"

"You."

"What?"

"I am not kidding, Sharon. A woman I'd never seen before in my life was wearing a tag that said 'Sharon McCone.' "

"My God. Did you speak with her?"

"Yes. I went over and asked her if she was the well-known private investigator. She said she was, so I decided to play along for a while, see what I could find out. She knew a lot about you."

I felt a prickle of unease. "Such as?"

"Mainly professional stuff. Nothing she couldn't have gotten from the papers or from that interview in *People* after the Diplo-bomber case."

Agreeing to the *People* interview was one of my worst mistakes; the reporter had made me sound more macho than Dirty Harry, and in the accompanying photograph I looked like someone Harry himself wouldn't want to meet in a dark alley.

"But," Glenna added, "she also knew things that I don't recall seeing in print. Such as what kind of plane you fly, who it belongs to, and what he is to you."

"She knew about Ripinsky?" Hy Ripinsky, my very significant other and the owner of Citabria 77289.

"She did. And she mentioned your cottage. She called it a name . . . Touchstone?"

I nodded, very uneasy now. The small stone cottage on the Mendocino coast, which Hy and I jointly owned, was our refuge when the world became too much for us. We rarely spoke of it by name to others, and we invited only close friends there.

"Did she say anything about the house we're going to build on the property?"

"No."

"Then her information's not completely up to date. So you played along for a while . . ."

"And then called her on it. I told her I had my office here in the pier and knew you. At first she didn't believe me and tried to bluff her way out of it. Then she admitted that she'd been given a ticket to the benefit by a friend who couldn't attend, and she felt outclassed by all the big names and rich people. So she decided to make herself important by impersonating you."

"If impersonating me is her way of achieving importance, the woman's in serious need of a life."

"In serious need of something. Her curiosity about you struck me as unnatural. She peppered me with questions which, of course, I declined to answer. And then the camera-woman I generally use came up and said a potential backer for the Hawaiian project wanted to meet me, and I never saw the bogus McCone again."

"I don't like this one bit. What if she'd gotten drunk and made a spectacle of herself? I have a hard enough time not making a spectacle of *my*self—cold sober."

"Well, if it'll ease your mind any, she was well behaved and attractive. Your reputation's untarnished, at least in the film community."

"What did she look like?"

"Your body type. Nice features, the most distinctive being large eyes and a mouth that tipped down at the corners. Black hair like yours, in a very similar shoulder-length style. Expensive dress—teal-blue silk knit, clingy."

"And I don't suppose you were able to get her real name?"

"I asked; she sidestepped the question. What d'you think of this?"

"A silly prank, probably nothing more than what she said it was. No harm done, and yet . . ."

"Yes," Glenna said, "and yet. That's exactly why I thought you should know about her."

4:11 A.M.

The red digits on my clock radio told me that only six minutes had passed since I last checked the time. I pulled my down comforter higher, snuggled my head deep into the pillows, and shut my eyes. In seconds they popped open. I stared at the ceiling; as a last resort, I'd *bore* myself to sleep.

Cold tonight, and the sheets had felt damp when I first crawled into bed. Into an empty bed, as Hy was at his ranch in Mono County. He'd vowed not to budge from there until he finished briefing himself for an upcoming fact-finding trip to various South American clients of Renshaw and Kessell International, the corporate security firm in which he was a partner. Or until Valentine's Day, Friday.

Not that either of us was sentimental about February 14. In fact, we agreed that it was chiefly a conspiracy among the purveyors of greeting cards, candy, and flowers. The first year we were together we'd felt honor bound to observe the day, and had ended up giving each other the exact same risqué card. The next year he'd been out of the country and sent flowers—coals to Newcastle, since a single rose from him had arrived without fail at my office every Tuesday morning since we'd met. Finally we gave up and took to exchanging cards and gifts whenever the spirit moved us, rather than confining romance to a single day.

However, my friend and operative Rae Kelleher and my former brother-in-law Ricky Savage were still in the throes of romantic delirium, having only been together since the previous summer, and they were celebrating their first Valentine's Day in style. They'd invited a bunch of us to an evening that would begin with cocktails at Palomino in Hills Plaza, progress to one of the city's newest and best restaurants for dinner, and culminate in a flurry of nightclubbing all over town. Dressing up and riding in a limo and ordering extravagantly—all of it on Ricky's credit card, where it wouldn't so much as make a dent in the country-and-western superstar's finances—was more than even Hy and I could resist. And then we'd have the weekend to recuperate before he left for South America on Sunday night.

I tried to concentrate on the weekend's prospects, but my earlier conversation with Glenna Stanleigh kept overriding all other thoughts. A woman had impersonated me at a party. A woman who knew private details of my life, who exhibited an unnatural interest in me.

Why?

Who was she?

Determinedly I channeled my mind to work. Two new cases today, both of them premaritals—singles wanting to investigate the people they were seeing. I'd noticed an upsurge in that type of job over the past year, and while I wasn't completely comfortable with many of the cases, I couldn't afford to pass up the business.

The first client, Jeffrey Stoddard, said that his "old lady" took a lot of business trips, and he was pretty sure she was playing around on him while on the road; they were supposed to get married next month, but if what he suspected was true, the wedding would be off. The second client, Bea Allen, a stockbroker, was seriously considering a marriage proposal, but before she said yes, she wanted a complete background workup on her suitor; he claimed to be heir to a fortune, but he was so cheap that she found the claim suspect. He might be after her money, in which case she'd probably marry him anyway but insist on a prenuptial agreement.

Every week we were hired for at least one premarital—and no wonder, considering the paranoid nature of contemporary society. Sadly, in many situations the paranoia is justified; negotiating the tricky maze of human relationships is at best a scary business. We prey on each other: for money, status, power, and sex. We lie to those closest to us: about our backgrounds, prospects, dreams, and sexual histories. The latter is the most frightening of all; with the spread of AIDS, one evening of carelessness can destroy our lives.

So in the end we eavesdrop and follow—or we hire agencies like mine to do our dirty work.

Paranoia.

Yeah, McCone, that's what's making you stare at the ceiling at—now—4:34 in the morning. Paranoia about a woman at a party whose name tag claimed she was you.

Thursday

Catch!" I tossed the file on the Bea Allen investigation at Mick Savage.

My tall blond nephew reached up from where he lounged in his swivel chair, feet propped on the wastebasket, and made a great one-handed catch.

"You've missed your calling as an outfielder," I told him.

"Nah, I put the talent to use in better ways." He was making an off-color allusion to his relationship with Charlotte Keim, another of my operatives.

I didn't respond to his conversational gambit, just got down to business. "I need a preliminary background check on this subject ASAP."

He opened the file and scanned the sheets stapled inside. "How soon is ASAP?"

"You call it."

"Fifty-five minutes, in your office."

"See you there."

"If I'm early, you spring for lunch."

"Deal."

What had begun as a game with us—him naming the amount of time it would take him to come up with what I needed, and me making concessions if he finished the work in a shorter period—had proved to be a particularly effective way of motivating him.

I left his office—which was also a storage room for the books, files, and spare furniture that neither I nor Anne-Marie Altman and Hank Zahn could find room for—and went along to the more spacious one occupied by Rae Kelleher and Charlotte Keim. Rae was in the field on a retail-pilfering job, but Charlotte sat at her computer, gazing fixedly at the screen as she moved the mouse. She didn't hear me come in, and when I got closer I saw she was playing solitaire.

"Put the eight of hearts on the seven of spades," I said.

She jumped and swiveled around, face coloring as she realized I'd caught her. Keim was a petite, curly-haired brunette in her mid-twenties—too worldly for nineteen-year-old Mick, some would say, if they didn't know my precocious nephew. But Mick had been raised in a showbiz milieu and sometimes made *me* feel like an innocent; he was more than a match for Charlotte.

She tried to cover by going on the offensive. "So you've finally got something for me. Good thing, because I've been goosey as hell." Whenever she was excited or embarrassed, the Texas accent she'd worked to lose ever since leaving Archer City surfaced—as well as what I'd come to think of as her Texas-isms.

"Yeah, it's a premarital." I handed her the folder. "And it involves some traveling."

"Cool."

"Subject's leaving this afternoon for L.A. Don't worry, though; it's only an overnight trip, so you'll be back here for Valentine's Day. If you get something concrete there, we'll wrap it up. If not, you'll be going to Chicago on Monday."

She nodded, studying the file.

I headed for my office and another stack of paperwork, envying her.

*   *   *

Mick sat down across the desk from me in fifty minutes, laden with a stack of downloaded documents, and prepared to give me an oral report.

"I want to have lunch at Miranda's," he announced, referring to our favorite waterfront diner. "A burger and some onion rings don't sound too bad."

"We didn't set a dollar limit; how come you're not after a more upscale place?"

"I like Miranda's. Plus we're gonna get enough upscale with Dad and Rae on Friday."

"True. So what've you got for me?"

"Well, this was the original no-brainer. The dude is so rich and old-money that he's probably got a closet full of tuxes and a garage full of Mercedeses. The bucks go back to Gold Rush days, when his great-great-granddaddy and some other robber barons got together and decided to rip off practically everybody. It's all there in that stuff from *Forbes* and the *Journal of California History*."

I paged through it, nodded. "Go on."

"Okay, real estate is his thing. Office parks, shopping centers, condo complexes, and a big chunk of land smack in the middle of the Nevada desert that ain't never gonna be worth nothin' nohow. The deal is, the guy's got so much money it'll never run out, but he's unlucky as hell."

"How so?"

"I'll give you one example, you can read about the rest. He's got this office park in Milpitas. About a year ago one of his tenants, a Nigerian cab company, declared war on the Arab sanitary-supply service and the Cuban package-delivery firm. Seems they were tossing their trash in the Nigerians' Dumpster. Insults were exchanged, trash was dumped at each other's doors, and it all ended up in a shoot-out in the parking lot. The Nigerians won, but then they got busted, and the guy was out three tenants."

"International intrigue, no less."

"You got it. Anyway, from here on out the news gets worse.

Dude's done time in the bin—nice private hospital for the outrageously insane. What put him there was holding his ex-wife out a seventeenth-story window at the Beverly Wilshire and threatening to drop her unless she gave him custody of the kids. An LAPD negotiating team put a stop to *that* caper. And there're indications that lunacy goes at a fast trot throughout the entire family."

"Poor Bea Allen!"

"Yeah. If you want my opinion, the client should either marry him and keep the knives locked up or run like hell. Whatever, she should definitely stay out of the parking lots at his office parks."

At four-thirty I was sitting in the armchair by the arching window at the end of the pier, watching the bay vista grow increasingly gloomy as the rain pelted down. A sudden heavier spate thundered onto the roof, and I glanced up, looking for leaks. None so far.

A tap at the door. I looked around and saw Neal Osborn standing there. Neal was Ted Smalley's significant other: a tweedy, rumpled, bearded, bespectacled secondhand bookseller whose thinning ginger-colored hair frequently stood up in peaks because he finger-combed it while perusing the tomes in his Polk Street store. Neal had once confessed to me that he would rather crawl through somebody's dusty garage or attic in pursuit of a rare first edition than do almost anything else on earth; frequently Ted, also a book lover, joined him on those forays.

"Hey, there," I said. "If you're looking for Ted, he left early for a dental appointment."

Neal came all the way into the office. "I know. Actually, it's you I'm looking for."

"Oh? Well, pull up a chair."

He moved one over by mine and sat.

"So what's on your mind?" I asked.

"I need to talk to you about Ted. Have you noticed that he's been behaving strangely the past few weeks?"

"I have, and it's getting worse. Yesterday he worked himself into a state of complete indecision over which model of copier to buy. He insisted on my help, even though I can't change the toner in our old one, and went on and on about this feature versus that feature. We'd get it all decided, and then he'd say, 'But maybe we should reconsider . . .' It wasn't like him at all."

"What else?"

"Well, he's been distracted and very short with everybody. On Monday, Rae told him he was being bitchy, and he said, 'Why don't you just come right out and call me a bitchy fag?' None of us knows where that was coming from; nobody's sexuality has ever been an issue around here."

"D'you have any idea what's causing this behavior?"

I shook my head. "One day, maybe three or four weeks ago, he came in here with some letters for my signature, and I sensed he wanted to talk to me about something but didn't quite know how to get started. I'm afraid I wasn't encouraging, either; I was in the middle of a complicated report that the client was picking up within the hour, so I put him off, told myself I'd talk with him later. But then I forgot, and by the time I thought to approach him, he put *me* off."

"Those're the same kinds of things I've noticed. I've asked him what's wrong several times, and he denies there's a problem. But there is: Most of the time it's as if he's thinking of something other than what we're talking about. And he's taken to calling me at the store for no particular reason—four or five times a day, yet. A lot of the time he's not where he says he's going to be, or when."

I reviewed the possibilities. "Do you think he's cheating on you? Or that he thinks you're cheating on him?"

"No. In either case, he'd bring something like that right out in the open. It's the nature of our relationship."

"What about drugs? When a person's as irritable as Ted, you've got to consider the possibility."

"I've considered it, as well as other physical problems."

We both fell silent, our eyes meeting. The unspeakable lay between us: AIDS.

"No," Neal said after a moment, "that's one thing we can rule out. He'd tell me immediately, so I could get tested."

Yes, he would. Nothing angered Ted more than infected people who put others at risk. "Well, maybe it's just . . . some weird phase he's going through."

"I wish I could believe that, but I can't." He hesitated. "What I was wondering, Shar . . . Could you look into it, on an informal basis?"

"You want *me* to investigate *Ted*?" It seemed an extreme solution to what was, after all, a purely personal problem.

"Not really, but maybe you could observe him, try to talk with him. You know what to look for, how to ask questions."

"I don't know, Neal. Ted's watched me operate for a lot of years; he might guess what I was doing, and that would put a strain on our friendship."

Neal ran long fingers through his unruly hair. "I understand what you're saying, but . . . Okay, there's more. Ted's not just short-tempered and strange. He's afraid."

"Afraid?"

"Yeah, I can feel it. Sometimes I wake up at night and . . . You know how you can lie in the dark and know the other person's awake, even if he breathes regularly?"

"Uh-huh."

"Well, almost every night I wake up and realize Ted's awake too. But if I say something, he pretends not to be. He's thinking, thinking hard, and there's a feeling of fear in the room."

I was silent, remembering times when I'd felt that kind of fear in a dark room.

"Has anything unusual happened to Ted recently that might account for this?" I asked.

"Not that he's told me. Up to now, ours has been a some-what staid and boring household—not that that's necessarily a bad thing. You get into your forties and you start to appreciate a life where the biggest event is a signal-jumper almost running you down in the crosswalk."

"Ted was almost run down?"

"No, me. Crossing to the parking garage from the store last week. No big deal; it's a wonder that on any given day Polk Street isn't littered with maimed pedestrians. So how about it, Shar—will you see what you can find out about all this?"

I considered. The behavior Neal described and I'd observed certainly was strange for a man who had always been among the most consistent and levelheaded people I knew. And Ted was my friend as well as my employee; whatever he was going through, I wanted to be there for him. There, if need be, in spite of him.

"Okay," I said, "what I can do is observe him more closely for a day or two. If that doesn't give me some idea of what's going on with him, I may have to establish a surveillance."

"One other thing I wish you'd do . . ." Neal hesitated.

"Yes?"

"I . . . I've actually snooped through his things, mainly looking for evidence of drug use, but I realized I don't know what to look for. Would you?"

"Go through your apartment?"

"Uh-huh."

Now I hesitated. Prying into Ted's personal effects struck me as going too far. But then I caught the worried look on Neal's face, and a memory from my college days that I'd largely suppressed came to mind.

One of the residents of the rambling old house on Berkeley's Durant Avenue that I'd shared with an ever-changing group of fellow students had been a woman called Merrily Martin. When she first moved in, the carefree, somewhat ditzy blonde was living proof of a name being destiny, but within six months she became moody, irritable, depressed, and withdrawn. Hank Zahn, who also lived there at the time, suspected drug use and argued that we ought to search her room; I contested the notion hotly, citing Merrily's right to privacy, and Hank gave in. Several weeks later we found Merrily dead in bed of a heroin overdose; a suicide note on the nightstand asked, "Why didn't any of you help me?"

I'm still a champion of the individual's right to privacy, but I've never again put it ahead of a friend's welfare.

"Okay," I said to Neal, "it's one possible way to find the answer quickly."

"Thanks." He took out a case and removed one of the keys. "Here. I've got a spare in the car."

I took it and tucked it in my pocket. "Are the two of you coming to Rae and Ricky's Valentine's Day celebration?"

He nodded.

"Then if I don't find anything at the apartment, I can check him out tomorrow night and decide where to go from there."

Neal punched me lightly on the upper arm. "Thank you, buddy. I feel better already."

"Try not to worry. It's going to be okay."

He took my hand and held it for a while as we watched the day turn into night.

Thursday Night

I returned to the pier at close to eleven for a meeting with a prospective client.

At around five-thirty Rae—who was working overtime on the report on her investigation of pilferage from an expensive Fillmore Street boutique—had buzzed me on the intercom. "There's a guy on line one who says he's now sure his partner is embezzling and wants to take you up on your offer to get evidence that'll stand up in court."

"What's his name?"

"Clive Benjamin."

The name wasn't familiar, but I supposed I'd spoken with him at some point. "Set up an appointment for tomorrow, would you?"

"He wants to see you tonight. Apparently he's co-owner of an art gallery and they're having a showing, so he's tied up most of the evening, but he said he could come over here around eleven."

An unusual time to sit down with a client, but not unheard of. "Okay," I said, "tell him I'll be here then."

At a few minutes after eleven Clive Benjamin, a tall man in formal dress, with a shoulder-length mane of blond hair and angular features, strode through my office door, both hands extended. When he saw me he stopped abruptly and pulled them back, confusion replacing his warm smile.

He said, "I asked to meet with Ms. McCone personally."

"I'm Sharon McCone."

"No, you're not."

"I'm sorry?"

"What's going on here?"

"Mr. Benjamin, please sit down. Perhaps there's been some mistake; we'll sort it out."

He remained standing. "There's been a mistake, all right. If Sharon doesn't want to see me again or work for me, why didn't she just have her secretary tell me so?"

"You know . . . Ms. McCone?"

"I met her at an opening at my gallery last Friday. She gave me one of her cards. Here." He fished a card from the inside pocket of his suit coat and held it out.

The card was a duplicate of mine but on cheaper stock. I'd never seen this man before in my life, certainly hadn't been to his gallery.

Oh, God . . .

I said, "Mr. Benjamin, let's sit down."

This time he complied. I went around the desk and sat facing him. This situation had a familiar ring—one I didn't like at all. I'd humor him till I got the facts.

"As you were saying, you met Ms. McCone at an opening at your gallery last Friday."

"So you admit you're standing in for her. What does she do, screen all prospective clients, even the ones she knows?"

"There's obviously been a failure of communication somewhere along the line. As you were saying . . ."

"She came to our opening. An exhibition of papier-mâché animals by Jesse Herrera. She was interested in purchasing one—a *Tyrannosaurus rex* with a Dalmatian's face and praying hands. Herrera combines animal species with the human in unusual ways. Anyway, that's how we met, when she admired the piece."

A piece I wouldn't give houseroom to. "And?"

"Well, she was undecided about the piece, so I asked her to dinner in the hope of convincing her it was a good investment. In the course of the evening I mentioned my problem with my partner, and she offered to look into it. Better to know now than be sorry later, she said. I understood what she meant, but Travis has been my best friend since prep school, and I didn't like the idea of having him investigated. So I told her I'd think about it, and after she left the next morning, I decided to take a closer look at the books—"

"After she left *the next morning?*"

He realized his slip, and his lips pulled tight with annoyance. "Ms. . . . I don't know who you are or what your position here is, but your employer's personal life is none of your business."

I got up and went to where my purse hung on the coatrack, took out my identification folder, and spread it open on the desk in front of Clive Benjamin.

"Jesus Christ," he whispered after a moment, "who the hell did I sleep with?"

The woman, Benjamin told me, was around ten years younger than I but fairly similar in appearance. Same body type, same hairstyle and color, but her facial features didn't reflect Native American ancestry, as mine do.

What were hers like? I asked.

Sort of cute.

Could he compare her to anyone, an actress or other public figure, perhaps?

Maybe Susan Dey, who had played on *L.A. Law.*

I'd heard the name, but never watched the show. Having worked closely with attorneys throughout my career, I can't get into courtroom dramas that so seldom approximate real life.

"Okay," I said, "how was she dressed?"

"She wore a teal-blue silk outfit—clingy. Expensive; I noticed its label was from one of the designer collections at Saks."

Teal-blue silk, the same as the woman who had impersonated me at the film council fund-raiser the next night. A color I love but can't wear successfully; it turns my skin tone to mud.

"Mr. Benjamin, how did she look in that shade of blue? Did it suit her?"

"She looked sensational."

So did Rae, a redhead. And Charlotte Keim, with her rich dark hair. But most women with my coloring . . . "Her hair, could it have been dyed? Or a wig?"

Benjamin thought, then nodded. "Now that you mention it, she was very . . . picky about her hair. Didn't want me to run my hands through it or even touch it. It was strange—a passionate woman like that worrying about getting her hair mussed."

The situation with Clive Benjamin was sufficiently embarrassing that I ended up referring him to Joanna Stark, an acquaintance in Sonoma who was a sometimes-active partner in a city firm that specialized in security for art galleries and museums. Stark, a sharp investigator who spoke the language of the art world, would be of more use to Benjamin than any of my operatives. In return for the referral I extracted a promise from him that, should he hear from the bogus McCone again, he'd contact me immediately.

After he left, I remained at my desk for a while, listening to the rain on the roof and pondering this latest turn of events. A prank at a party was one thing, but claiming to be me and then sleeping with a casual acquaintance was another. To say nothing of offering my professional help and card to him . . .

And what if Benjamin wasn't the only one? There might be men all over town who thought Sharon McCone mixed business with pleasure!

I had to put a stop to this masquerade before she destroyed both my peace of mind and my reputation. Before she did incalculable harm to the agency. I'd have to find out who she was, why she'd fixated on me—and quickly.

When I got home I found a message on my answering machine: "Sharon, this is Jeff Riley, over at North Field in Oakland. I caught a woman who looks a lot like you prowling around the tie-downs this afternoon. When I asked what she was looking for, she said she wanted to know where Two-eight-niner was and if it was you or Hy who had it. Claimed to be a reporter doing a story on women pilots. I told her to do it on her own turf and escorted her off airport property. Anyway, I thought you ought to know."

In dreams I'm sometimes two people at once—within myself, yet standing to the side, watching.

Tonight I'm in a strange light-filled room where people in formal dress mingle. Above them float colorful, grotesque animals—mixtures of many species, including the human. I shrink against a wall, avoiding a horse with a vulture's face and a man's hands that try to grab my breasts. But I'm also over there by the Tyrannosaurus rex *with the Dalmatian's face and human hands that appear to pray. My other self is dressed in teal blue that clings to my body.*

I can't wear that color. Why have I?

The animals move on a sudden breeze. I watch myself—the one over there—staring up in amazement at the rex. *And then I'm inside her, going up on tiptoe to move closer to the monstrosity. Its spotted face inclines toward mine, and we kiss. I feel nothing.*

Finally I pull away from the creature. Turn. And I—the self by the wall—realize she's not me at all. She's a woman with hair and a body like mine, who looks beautiful in teal blue.

I want to ask her why—why me? But as is usually the case in dreams, I can't speak.

friday

Ted and Neal lived on Plum Alley, a narrow half-block off the part of Montgomery Street where it dead-ended below the Disneyesque battlements of Julius' Castle restaurant, high on the northeastern slope of Telegraph Hill. The rain had stopped this morning, and now, at close to noon, I glimpsed blue sky when I glanced up at Coit Tower.

I drove along the lower level of Montgomery, where it divided around a retaining wall, but found no parking space, so I hung a U-turn and climbed the upper level till I spotted one. This was a congested area, with not enough garage or curbside space for the residents' cars, much less for the vehicles of tourists visiting the tower; I was lucky to have to walk only a block.

In the alley cars were pulled up on the narrow sidewalks as well as nose in to the retaining wall at its far end, beyond which the waterfront was still shrouded in fog. The short block contained an eclectic mixture of nineteenth-century frame cottages and twentieth-century architectural mistakes, the exception being Ted and Neal's wonderful Art Deco apartment building. As always when I approached it, I admired its streamlined contours, the rounded glass-block elevator enclosure at one corner, and the facade dominated by a series of vertical art-glass windows with a boldly colored design that reminded me of peculiar sea creatures.

I crossed the tiled entry courtyard and took the elevator to the third floor. As the cage rose, the rippled effect of the glass blocks made me feel as if I were underwater; the sensation was heightened as I walked down the hallway behind the etched windows. Ted and Neal's apartment was at the rear on the bay side; I let myself in with Neal's key.

I'd been there many times since they moved in the previous spring, but always when one or the other was home, and usually in the midst of a dinner-party crowd. Now the apartment held a thick silence characteristic of empty places. I shut the door behind me, then hesitated, reluctant to venture farther. The part of my work I dislike the most is prying into people's homes and possessions; it was bad enough with strangers, but to probe a friend's life . . .

Then I reminded myself that probing could save a friend's life and moved down the hallway that opened into the living room. The apartment was a dramatic one, with high ceilings and a wall of windows overlooking a balcony that faced the bay. The living room furnishings were in keeping with the building's era: 1930s-style salon chairs and bulky ottomans and other Moderne pieces. To my left a staircase curved up to a second level, and behind it was tucked a small but well-appointed kitchen; a carpeted, chrome-railed catwalk connecting the front and rear bedrooms spanned the dining area.

Chances were that if Ted had anything in the apartment that would give me a clue to what lay behind his uncharacteristic behavior, he'd hidden it in some private place. Still, I checked the kitchen and living room thoroughly, coming away with only the new knowledge that he and Neal were addicted to cookies 'n' cream ice cream, took a lot of vitamins, and subscribed to the *National Enquirer.*

Next I climbed the staircase and went into the smaller of the bedrooms, which was set up as a combination library and office. I gave it close attention, but learned only that they owned a great many first editions of novels by a diverse group of authors. The desk contained correspondence and bills in orderly files; none of it told me anything more than that both men paid their credit card balances on time and in full every month.

I crossed the catwalk and entered the master bedroom. Its furnishings were also period pieces, or good imitations. Here I searched more slowly, checking the contents of the night-stands, bureaus, closets, and then going over the adjoining bathroom. Nothing unusual there, and certainly no evidence of drug use; in fact, the medicine cabinet held nothing stronger than Tylenol.

There are numerous places where people typically hide things, thinking they're being clever, and I know most of them. Feeling the inside pockets of suitcases and the undersides of drawers, checking the toilet tanks and objects in the freezer, looking for places where the carpet had been pried up or a baseboard removed and replaced—all of it took time. When I finished, it was nearly two o'clock and I had nothing to show for my efforts. Discouraged, I started across the catwalk.

A sound came from below—a key turning in the front-door lock. Footsteps clicked across the entry.

I darted for the library and slipped behind its door.

Who? Neither of the occupants. Neal had promised to take Ted to a long lunch today, so he wouldn't unexpectedly turn up here, as he was sometimes wont to do.

I waited. Silence from below; the plush carpeting muted footfalls. Then I heard a rustling, probably in the dining area. I moved from behind the door, intent on catching a glimpse of the intruder. Too late, though: whoever it was had already crossed the entry and left.

So what had the person been doing?

A large, heart-shaped box sat in the center of the glass-topped dining table. Of course, it was Valentine's Day. I wouldn't have taken either Ted or Neal to be a candy-and-flowers kind of guy, but you never knew.

I went downstairs and crossed to the table. Ten-pound box,

red foil with white lace. Good God, did either of them have *that* much of a sweet tooth?

An envelope lay next to the box, plain white with nothing written on it. Why wasn't it addressed to either Ted or Neal? An oversight, perhaps, by the employee of the candy store who'd taken the order?

Since when did candy stores deliver like florists? And use keys to enter the places where they deliver?

I picked up the envelope and slipped the card from it. Block printing, probably done with a straightedge: "This could be yours."

Your *what?*

I set the card down and studied the box. It was neither encased in plastic wrap nor sealed. The lace was mashed down in places, the foil torn near the bottom. I recalled some hate mail Ricky had received—how it had radiated weirdness. This box was doing the same.

Quickly I yanked the lid off and looked inside.

"Yuck! What the hell—"

A dark, bloody mass, obscene against a white doily. It glistened wetly, gave off the scent of incipient rot. I'd seen its counterparts in the supermarket.

A beef heart.

This could be yours.

I stared at it for a moment, then went to the phone.

"You're kidding," Neal said.

"I wish I was. It's pretty disgusting, and the implication is downright scary. Is there any chance of this being a joke on Ted's part?"

"If it was, I'd be laughing. Besides, this isn't funny, and his jokes are."

"Who else has access to your apartment?"

"Nobody, other than you."

"You don't have a housecleaner? Or somebody who comes by, say, to water the plants while you're away?"

"We do our own cleaning, and you know we don't have any plants."

"What about the building manager?"

"Mona Woods? No. We had the locks changed when we moved in, and since she didn't ask for a copy of the key, we didn't give her one. It's not that we don't trust her, but we don't like anybody in the place when one of us isn't there; the book collection is quite valuable, and somebody who isn't a collector might mishandle the volumes."

"And Ted wouldn't give anybody a key?"

"No. We agreed on that from the start."

"What about the key you keep in your car?"

"I never leave the car unlocked. And my other keys're in my pocket when I'm here at the store. Maybe somebody got hold of Ted's at the pier?"

"Not likely. I've never seen them lying around."

"But possible."

"Anything's possible. What should I do about this disgusting gift?"

"Just leave it where you found it. I'll close up early, be there when Ted gets home. Seeing it might make him tell me what's going on. Or at least give some indication."

I'd been thinking of taking the box and note to an investigative laboratory I use, but Neal's idea was better. Chances were an analysis would turn up nothing; given the proliferation of crime novels, films, and TV shows, the average individual has become as savvy in ways of avoiding detection as your typical street criminal. "Okay, I'll leave it. Now, if seeing it doesn't make Ted confide in you, here's what I want you to do over the weekend: write down the details of his behavior; note anything unusual or out of character, no matter how minor. I'll stop by your store on Monday and pick up the list."

"List? More likely it'll approximate a volume of the *Encyclopedia Britannica*. His every action has been unusual and out of character for weeks."

* ** *

"You get very fast results," Bea Allen said. She sat in one of my clients' chairs—a slender woman with very short brown hair and narrow features. Her fingers played nervously at the briefcase she held on her lap.

I handed her the report on the background investigation of her suitor—which Mick had written in his own inimitable style and I'd then edited to make it more palatable to the client.

Allen opened it and began reading. I swiveled around to give her privacy, taking in the blue sky and the sunlight sparkling on the bay. It seemed the weather gods knew this was a day for lovers, since they'd allowed San Francisco to shine at its romantic best. The respite from the string of storms that we'd all needed to maintain our sanity had finally arrived; I hoped it would last at least through the weekend.

I heard a noise behind me. Oh, God, I thought, she's going to cry, and looked to see if Ted had replaced the empty Kleenex box on top of the file cabinet. But, no, that hadn't been a preliminary to a sob; Bea Allen was now laughing.

"I didn't know he was part of *that* family," she said. "It must be on the maternal side. And this stuff about his business dealings—the man is such an *idiot!* He *needs* me!"

I swiveled to face her again. "He needs someone with good business sense, yes, but did you get to the part about the history of mental illness? It's not encouraging, and the incident with his former wife is alarming."

Allen dismissed my words with a wave of her hand. "I don't care about the family history; I'm not interested in having children. As for the rest, I'll handle it."

She asked for a final invoice, and I said I'd have it mailed to her. "So do the two of you have Valentine's Day plans?" I asked as I walked her out.

"Now I do. I'm going to set the wedding date." Waving the report at me, she walked away, but not before I caught the keen acquisitive glint in her eyes.

I went back to my office, constructing a profoundly depressing scenario: Bea Allen would circumvent a prenuptial agreement, marry the man, and within the year inveigle him into giving her power of attorney so she could properly handle his affairs. Then she would provoke an incident that would force her to commit him to a mental institution, leaving her free to do what she wished with the remainder of the robber baron's fortune. Her husband would escape, of course, and come after her.

WOMAN DIES IN PLUNGE OFF ST. FRANCIS HOTEL
HEIR TO FORTUNE SAYS, "THE BITCH DESERVED IT!"

And I'd often accused Rae, an aspiring writer, of having a lurid imagination!

The intercom buzzed as I sat down at my desk. "Yes, Ted."

"Jeff Riley, from Oakland Airport, on line two."

"Thanks." I punched the button. "Jeff, thanks for returning my call. I wanted to ask you about the woman you came across in the tie-downs. Can you tell me anything more about what she looked like?"

"Well, like you."

"Native American features, too?"

". . . Uh, no."

"What kind, then?"

"Uh, I don't know. Normal? Pretty? Yeah, I guess she was pretty."

I was asking the wrong person for details. Jeff was a good lineman and a good pilot as well, but his powers of observation seemed mainly limited to aircraft. Too bad the woman hadn't had an identification number tattooed across her forehead.

"What was she wearing?"

"Jeans? A sweater? Probably."

"And she said she was a reporter from which publication?"

"She didn't say, and I didn't think to ask. But she was pushy like reporters are."

Big help. It seemed that every other person I met these days was pushy.

"Thanks, Jeff. Has Ripinsky landed yet?"

"Nope. You expecting him?"

"Of course—Valentine's Day."

"Jesus Christ, I forgot! You've saved my ass! I owe you big-time."

Friday Night

Outside the windows of Palomino restaurant in Hills Plaza the loops of lights on the Bay Bridge shone cold and hard-edged against the black sky. Inside the bar, all was mellow wood and brass, soft illumination and warmth. Waiters moved around the long table that had been assembled for our party, taking drink orders. Other patrons cast surreptitious glances at us or frankly stared; Ricky Savage was a celebrity, and the rest of us seemed to interest them almost as much.

I leaned against Hy's arm where it rested on the back of my chair, tipped my head to look up at him. It continually amazed me that my lanky, hawk-nosed, mustached lover was as much at home in a handsome dark suit and tie as in the jeans and tees he wore while tinkering with aircraft or riding fence on his ranch. He returned my look, his gaze sliding from my face to the low V of the clingy red dress I'd pulled from my closet and dusted off for the occasion. When his lips curved in a slow smile, I knew I'd made the right choice.

A waiter leaned over my shoulder and I gave him my drink order, then directed my gaze to the end of the table where Ted and Neal sat. Ted was elegant in one of his brocaded frock coats, but he fingered his goatee nervously and his dark eyes darted around the room; Neal, less rumpled and more tweedy than usual, looked at me and shook his head slightly.

"What's that about?" Hy asked, his lips close to my ear.

"I'll tell you later. Actually there're quite a few things I need to discuss with you." He'd arrived at my house with only minutes to spare to change before the limo Ricky had hired was to pick us up; there hadn't been time to talk at any length.

"Oh?"

"Later."

He squeezed my shoulder.

Charlotte and Mick were seated between Neal and Rae. Mick was telling a joke—long and involved, and he'd forget the punch line, but that didn't matter because Keim would supply it. He wouldn't care that she upstaged him, because he was besotted with this older woman who shared his fascination with cyberspace.

Keim completed the joke, burst into bawdy laughter, then waved toward the entrance. I looked that way, saw that Anne-Marie Altman and Hank Zahn had just arrived to complete our party. She'd had an afternoon court appearance in L.A. and then fallen victim to overbooking on the shuttle; he'd had to deliver their foster daughter, Habiba Hamid, to a slumber party. In spite of the relative lightness of his duties, Hank looked harried, his tie askew, his trench coat collar turned up on one side. Anne-Marie, airline delays notwithstanding, was cool and collected in gray-blue silk that brought out the sheen of her ash-blond hair. As they came over to the table, Ricky flashed Hank a sympathetic look and signaled for a waiter.

Of all of us, though, it was Ricky and Rae who stood out. He'd always had star quality, but now it had matured into something more than good looks and presence; lines that reflected the pain and unhappiness he'd recently suffered gave his face more character, and there was a new self-awareness in the way he spoke and moved. New gentleness and content-ment in his crooked smile, too; Rae was good for him.

And he was good for her. The striking woman in emerald

green whose reddish gold curls fell to her shoulders scarcely resembled in appearance or manner the insecure, often depressed, always needy little person whom I'd hired as my assistant at All Souls Legal Cooperative years before.

Tonight they both seemed unusually excited. They held hands under the table, exchanged occasional whispers. She smoothed back a lock of his thick chestnut hair; he said something into her ear that made her blush and then laugh. I glanced at Mick. He shrugged and grinned, but I sensed he knew something the rest of us did not.

After a while Ricky raised a questioning eyebrow at Rae, and she nodded. He tapped on his glass, and we all grew silent.

"Red and I asked you all here tonight," he said, "because you're very special to us and we wanted to share our first Valentine's Day with you. You accepted our being together when an awful lot of people didn't, and you accepted me for who I am rather than as the guy you'd read about in the tabloids. We both thank you." The man who regularly performed for crowds of many thousands paused, at a loss for words. "Red, how do I do the rest of this?"

"Just wing it, darlin'."

"Okay." He took a deep breath. "There's another reason we asked you here: to invite you to our wedding—date and details to come." He raised the hands they'd had linked under the table and displayed the emerald-cut diamond on Rae's finger.

Rae had her eyes fixed on me—not anxious exactly, but looking for approval from the friend who had once been the harshest critic of their romance. I put any lingering misgivings aside for the moment and raised my glass to them. She and Ricky smiled and toasted back. When I looked at Mick—who only six months ago had raged at Rae and said he would never forgive her for her affair with his father—he gestured in a manner that said if they were happy, so was he. And Hy whispered into my ear, "I told—"

"—you so. Yes, I know."

The waiters brought out champagne in ice buckets, and the celebration really got under way.

An hour later I was on my way back from the rest room when I ran into Tony Nakayama, one of the architects who occupied the suite of offices directly across the pier from ours.

"Hey, Sharon," he said. "Big doings?"

"Valentine's Day. And Rae's engaged."

"Good for her! Say, did you happen to notice that woman who was watching you guys earlier?"

"A lot of people've been watching us. The man Rae's marrying is Ricky Savage—"

"I know. But this is different. The woman came in maybe five minutes after you did. Sat alone at one of the little tables." He motioned toward the center of the room. "She was wearing a sweater with a hood, and she kept tugging the hood forward and down like she didn't want anybody to recognize her. Then she'd twist around and stare at your table. What struck me each time she turned away was how angry she was."

"Angry."

"Yeah. Real rage around the mouth and in her eyes. Bad body language, too. She had a couple of glasses of wine before she tossed some bills on the table and stalked out."

"What did she look like?"

"Very attractive. Honey-blond hair. I couldn't tell its style or length because of the hood."

"Height and weight?"

"Medium height. The sweater was one of those long ones, and she wore it over a loose skirt. Can't really say how much she weighed."

It didn't sound like the woman who'd impersonated me. "Who was her server, did you see?"

"I didn't notice. Sorry."

"Well, thanks for telling me about her."

"You're welcome. And give Rae my congratulations."

Tony went on toward the rest rooms, and I looked across the bar at our table, focusing on Ricky. Now he was telling a joke, but unlike his son, he wouldn't have to rely on anyone else for the punch line. All his life he'd had a way with words, with music, with women. He'd broken many a heart, my own sister's included . . .

He seemed to feel my gaze on him, because he looked my way; I motioned for him to join me. He excused himself, kissing Rae's hair as he passed behind her, and came to meet me. "Something wrong, Shar?"

"I need to talk privately with you."

"Sure."

"No, outside."

We went past the hostess's station and stepped through the doors into the plaza's courtyard. The night was rapidly turning frigid, and the few people who hurried past were bent on their destinations. Ricky saw me shiver, took off his suit coat, and wrapped it around my shoulders.

"What," he said, "you dragged me out here to ask me if I'll be a good husband to Red?"

"Sort of."

"The answer is yes, and you know it."

"Do I?" Quickly I described what Tony had told me of the strange woman's behavior.

Ricky got my drift before I finished; his dark eyebrows pulled together in a frown, and a corner of his mouth twitched in annoyance. When I stopped talking, he put his hands on my shoulders and looked into my eyes for a moment before he said, "I'll tell you this one time, Shar, and that will be the end of this particular type of discussion forever. Your sister and I married very young and made a lot of mistakes; most of them were mine, and I'm not going to repeat them. I promised Red early on that I'd never deliberately do anything to hurt her. I've kept that promise, and I intend to go on keeping it."

His gaze didn't waver; his voice was low and level. Nothing more to hide, no more lies, no more infidelities.

"I'm sorry," I said. "Given the past, I had to ask. End of subject—forever."

"Good." He relaxed his hold on my shoulders and hugged me. "This woman really seemed angry, huh?"

"That's how Tony described her." But I didn't want to dwell on the incident on such a festive occasion, so I added, "I wouldn't give it another thought. He's prone to exaggeration."

"Could be she was interested in somebody besides me. Or was jealous because we're having such a good time."

"That's more likely. Mick seems genuinely pleased with your news. Chris, too?" Chris was his eldest daughter, a freshman at U.C. Berkeley.

Ricky leaned against the brick wall of the building, one arm around my shoulders. "Yeah, she's pleased. You know, the two of them have done a lot of growing up in the past six months. In fact, Chris would've been here tonight, except for a busted romance. Didn't want to be an eleventh wheel on Valentine's Day was how she put it."

"Have you told the other kids?"

"Of course. I flew down to L.A. on Monday. Lisa and Molly are thrilled; Red's completely won them over. Brian chose to pretend I wasn't there. Frankly, I'm worried about him, and so're your sister and her husband. None of us knows what to do."

"Is therapy an option?"

"Charly's looking into it."

"What about Jamie?"

The way Ricky grinned confirmed my suspicion that fifteen-year-old Jamie was his favorite daughter. "Oh, she growled and scowled and gave a snarl or two for form's sake. And then she said her mom was so happy with Vic that she'd already forgotten she was ever married to me."

"Ouch."

"A mild shot is all. In the end she told me that since her mom was happy, she guessed I might as well be happy too. And finally she gave me her permission to go ahead with the nuptials."

I laughed. "She's something else."

"What d'you bet that within a year Red'll have won her over, too?"

"I'd have to agree with you." I hesitated, then asked, "What about Charlene? How is she with this?"

"You know, for all of her lack of subtlety, Jamie may have a point. When I told Charly, she said, 'That's nice, dear,' and kissed me on the cheek like she would one of the kids who'd scored some minor triumph. Then she asked Vic to make us drinks so they could toast my happiness, and she went to check on a fax that was coming in. She's all caught up in getting her M.B.A. and jetting around to these international financial conferences with Vic, and . . . Well, it's strange. I never thought I'd see the day when Charly and I could feel indifferent to each other, but that's what it boils down to."

More likely, checking on the fax had been Charlene's way of hiding her perfectly natural feelings of regret and loss—just as Ricky's talk of indifference was his. "Things change, Brother Ricky."

"Yeah, they do, Sister Sharon."

Our eyes met, and we laughed. "Well, some things do," I said. "But you and I—we're still family."

That night as I lay beside Hy, I felt colder than the temperature warranted. Pulling the comforter closer, I pressed my back against his and burrowed deep. Sleep was an impossibility; my mind kept skipping from pleasant thoughts of the evening to the angry woman in the bar at Palomino. Contrary to what I'd told Ricky, Tony Nakayama was not prone to exaggeration. If he'd felt compelled to tell me about her, she must have been very angry indeed.

There was always the possibility that she was an obsessed

fan of Ricky's, her rage directed at Rae—and that was cause for considerable concern. Or she could have been someone Anne-Marie or Hank had won a civil suit against—also worrisome. Or a dissatisfied client of my agency. Or . . . well, the possibilities were numerous.

Perhaps Hy . . . ?

No, he was the one person I could rule out. When I told him about the woman, over a nightcap once we got home, he was as concerned as I. If he had any reason to think he was the object of her angry glances, he'd have told me. Hy and I didn't lie to each other; half-truths and silences were more our style—and we seldom indulged in either anymore.

And now I was down to the one potential object of the woman's rage that I didn't want to speculate on—not in these dark, quiet hours, even with Hy sleeping beside me.

Somewhere in this city—or close to it—there was a woman who had asked prying questions about me, impersonated me, made love with at least one man who called her by my name. Had she been close by tonight? Close enough for me to see? Would I have recognized her, or was she someone who had chosen me at random?

And what did I know about her? Nothing, except that she resembled me. I had no other information, unless she again contacted Clive Benjamin and he kept his promise to call me. I had all the tools of my profession and an entire agency of talented investigators at my disposal, but I was powerless until the woman made some move.

And God knew what that move might be.

Powerlessness. It's a state that frightens me more than losing a plane's engine over mountainous terrain in the middle of the night. That situation would quite likely result in my death, but at least I'd be trying to *do* something about it when I died.

Tonight I'm dreaming of a chameleon.
It sits at a small table in a warm, softly lighted room and transforms over and over again—from itself to a version of

myself to a woman in a loose sweater who pulls its hood down over honey-blond hair and casts swift, angry glances behind her.

Behind her—where yet another version of myself sits, thinking she's safe among the people who love her.

Sunday Night

"Two-eight-niner, contact Oakland Approach on 135.4."

I keyed the Citabria's mike and acknowledged the SFO air traffic controller's instruction. Then, as I switched frequencies, I heaved a sigh of relief.

I'd flown into the busy Class B airport many times, both as a passenger and as a pilot, but always on commercial flights or with Hy. Doing so was a tense, no-nonsense proposition; you didn't waste a word or a second, and you complied with air traffic control quickly and to the letter. During the flights when I'd piloted, I'd relied, emotionally at least, on the presence of Hy, a former commercial pilot who held nearly every license, certificate, and rating known to aviation; his concern over my dependency was what had prompted him to ask me to fly him into SFO tonight to catch the red-eye for Miami, where he'd connect with his flight to Buenos Aires. Departing there without him, he reasoned, would show me I could handle the situation on my own.

Well, I'd handled it—keeping my nervousness out of my voice, because even at this late hour the controller hadn't the time or inclination to coddle me. And now I was almost back to Oakland, regretting that the ride was such a short one. It was a beautiful evening, the clear spell that began on Friday having persisted. Below me, the lights of the Bay Area tried to outdo the stars and moon in their brilliance. And compared with landing at SFO, landing at Oakland was, in Hy's parlance, a piece of cake.

Back on the ground, I chained and locked the Citabria and started through the executive terminal to the parking area, intent on my car, home, and bed. But at the last minute I veered over to the lobby desk and asked the woman on duty if Jeff Riley was working tonight. Yes, she said, as a matter of fact he'd just gone into the vending room. I followed and found the short, bearded lineman cursing at a cup of what I call cardboard coffee that had spilled over his fingers while he was trying to wrest it from the machine.

"Hey, Sharon," he said, "somebody told me Ripinsky coaxed you into flying him to SFO."

"Yeah, he did. I could've had him there in twenty minutes by car—not to mention more cheaply, given the huge landing fee. But he wanted me to learn a lesson in self-reliance."

"How'd it go?"

"Pretty well. I was nervous departing, of course, but now I know I can do it."

"And a good thing, because someday you may have to do it—there or at another Class B airport. You're all grown up now, at least as far as flying's concerned." Jeff leaned against the wall, sipping coffee and making a sour face. "I've always figured there're two kinds of pilots: those who deliberately choose to limit their experience, and those who go the whole nine yards. Nothing wrong with either; the ones who limit themselves're smart, recognize the extent of their abilities. But for a long time I've had you pegged as the other."

"Have you? I'm flattered. By the way, that reporter—have you seen her around here again?"

"Nope."

"Will you do me a favor? Keep a closer than usual eye on Two-eight-niner for a while."

"Will do."

"Thanks. Hy and I will stand you to a couple of rounds of beer someday soon."

"Hell, it's a pleasure to help out. I wouldn't want any harm to come to that nice little plane. Or to you or Hy."

Until he said it, the possibility of vandalism or sabotage hadn't occurred to me. But I carried the notion home with me, like a suspiciously ticking package.

Somebody had broken into my house while I was gone.

I felt it the moment I opened the door and realized that in our haste to leave, neither Hy nor I had thought to activate the security system. I glanced at the lock; there were fresh scratches on it—picked.

I drew my gun—a new .357 Magnum—from my bag and shut the door quietly, then stood still, listening to the silence and taking in the signs. The temperature was warmer than earlier; somebody had turned up the thermostat. A light burned in the sitting room, but I distinctly remembered turning it off on my way out. And there was a scent on the air, a perfume that I didn't use. Familiar, though. What? I breathed it in and free associated.

Dark Secrets.

Yes, that was it. One of those new, heavily advertised scents that had emanated from a scratch-and-smell card enclosed with my last Macy's bill.

Appropriate—fiendishly appropriate.

Gun held in both hands, I moved forward and peered through the archway to the parlor. A novel I'd been reading while curled up on the love seat last week had been knocked to the floor. The doors to the guest room armoire stood open, but nothing else appeared to have been touched. I continued slowly along the hall.

In the sitting room, embers glowed in the fireplace; the last time Hy and I had made a fire was Saturday night. A bottle of Deer Hill Chardonnay—my favorite, and one that cost a fortune by my standards—sat uncorked beside a glass on the table next to the easy chair; the bottle was only half full.

I moved to the room I use as my home office. Several of the desk drawers had been pulled open, and the chair was shoved over by the closet, as if someone had stood on it to check the shelf. Thank God I kept my important papers in the safe at the pier!

One of the under-cabinet fluorescents burned in the kitchen; by its light I saw a corkscrew and cork positioned in the exact center of the chopping-block island.

In the bathroom I found that my birth control pills had apparently been flushed down the toilet. The empty pack lay on the floor next to it.

I slipped along the hall, still with both hands on the gun. The bedroom door was half closed; it was hung wrong and had a tendency to do that on its own, but . . . I nudged it with my foot and stepped inside, sweeping the room with the .357.

Empty. But my bedding had been ripped off and tossed on the floor.

One of the folding closet doors was ajar. I took my left hand off the gun, grasped the knob, and pulled.

Nothing inside but my clothes.

The intruder was gone. Not long gone, though; the scent of her Dark Secrets still lingered, as if she'd sprayed it in the air. Well, maybe she had. It was as good as writing a message on the mirror.

I looked down at the rumpled bedclothes, anger flaring. I'd been looking forward to crawling into bed immediately, but now I'd have to remake it—

A noise on the back deck—bumping and scraping.

I raised the gun, stepped into the dark hallway. The outside spot was on, and through the glass I saw my orange tabby, Ralph. He had his nose pressed to the glass, and his yellow eyes pleaded to be let in.

"Jesus," I whispered. What if I'd shot him? Even though I had a carry permit, I shouldn't be toting this gun around; it should be locked in the U.S. Navy ammo box bolted to the floor of the linen closet, where it usually resided with my old .38. But since Friday night I'd felt better with a weapon close to hand.

I opened the door, and Ralphie slipped inside, heading for his food bowl.

And then I thought, Allie—where's Allie?

I leaned out the door and called my calico. Nothing. But Alice always came promptly when called after dark; neither she nor her brother was a night-prowling creature.

I hurried through the house, shouting her name. No response.

"God damn that bitch! If she's done something to my cat, I'll kill her!"

Then I heard a scuffling above my head, followed by an unearthly wailing that came from the home office. I ran in there—and realized the significance of the desk chair being moved: there was an opening to the house's crawl space in the closet.

The woman had stuffed my cat into the crawl space!

I climbed up on the chair, shoved the cover aside, and saw widely dilated, frightened eyes peering down at me. Quickly I reached for Allie, but she wasn't having any of that; she leaped down, leaving a long gash in my forearm.

"God *damn* her!" I yelled again—not referring to the cat.

I climbed down from the chair and went to the bathroom to wash and treat the deep scratch. Then I returned to the kitchen, patted Allie—who was frantically crunching Friskies—and poured myself a glass of wine from an open bottle in the fridge. I loved the Deer Hill, but I couldn't bring myself to drink from a bottle that *she* had opened.

What now? I thought. Call 911? Normally I would have, but this business was too bizarre, too convoluted, too potentially damaging to entrust to just any officer. Call a friend— Greg Marcus on Narcotics or Adah Joslyn on Homicide? No, you didn't bother a friend at this hour. Besides, the assault on my home and privacy had the feel of having been well planned and executed; she'd have been careful to leave no fingerprints, no clues to her identity.

Only a silent challenge.

I was here. I can enter your home. I can take your identity. And you don't know who I am or why I'm doing these things.

Yes, you were here. Yes, you entered my home. But you can't take my identity. I can figure out who you are. I can figure out why you're doing these things.

I can stop you.

Monday

"Your initial assumption was correct," Greg Marcus said. "She probably didn't leave you anything to go on."

The Narcotics captain was a big gray-blond man, heavier now than when I'd first known him, and he seemed to fill up my small sitting room. Years before, we'd been lovers—a relationship destined to fail, given its volatility. But time had mellowed us both and nowadays sparks rarely flew between us; we'd settled into a comfortable friendship, having dinner together every couple of months. This morning when I decided I wanted someone I trusted from the SFPD to check out the scene at my house, it was only natural that I call Greg. And just as naturally he'd agreed to stop by on his way to the Hall of Justice.

"I could send a technician," he added, "have the place dusted for latents. But then we'd have to take prints from everybody who normally visits here."

"And even if you isolated an unfamiliar one, it might not be the woman's. Or her prints might not be on file anywhere." And I'd known that before I even called him.

Greg saw my discouragement and put his hand on my shoulder. "You want me to have somebody canvass the neighbors, ask if anybody saw anything unusual?"

"I already did that. Nothing."

"Well, then, I'll file a report, in case she pulls something else." He squeezed my shoulder, took his hand away.

"Thanks."

Greg studied my face for a few seconds. "You look tired. Losing sleep over this?"

"Some."

"Hy's not in town?"

"No, he's in South America for a couple of weeks."

"Maybe you shouldn't be staying alone here. Why not get out, move in with a friend for a while?"

"Absolutely not. I won't allow this woman to disrupt my life any more than she already has. Anyway, her getting in was partly my fault; I'll have to be more careful to arm the system from now on."

He hesitated, then nodded. "I didn't mean to imply that I doubt your ability to take care of yourself, but with crazies . . . Well, you never know. She seems to be a controlled crazy, though, so she may avoid a direct confrontation. You carrying?"

"I have been, but I'm spooked enough that I'm not sure I should be."

"Which gun?"

"A new one—.357 Magnum, Smith and Wesson. Hy finally convinced me that my old .38 doesn't have the stopping power I'd need in a critical situation."

"He's right. The .357 is a good weapon. You can wound an opponent enough to stop him from a distance of more than twenty feet. I'm glad you got it."

"Well, I hope I don't have to use it, especially in my present frame of mind."

"Trust yourself. You're an excellent shot, and you've got good judgment."

Coming from him, that meant a lot. "Thanks for everything, Greg. I haven't been able to bring myself to tell anybody but Hy about the woman. It helps, talking with you."

He smiled gently, the lines around his eyes crinkling.

"Long ago I told you that I'd always be there for you, and I meant it."

Anachronism Bookshop smelled of old bindings and age-mellowed paper. It was a long space—something of a maze—filled with stacks and nooks where browsers could sink into comfortable old armchairs to read. A narrow mezzanine containing more shelves girdled it on four sides, a wide foot-worn staircase ascending to it at the rear. When I arrived soon after ten, I found Neal perched on his stool behind the high, mahogany-paneled counter to the right of the door, perusing a price guide and smiling contentedly.

Seeing me broke the spell, however; he scowled and reached under the counter, bringing out a small spiral-bound notebook and thrusting it at me.

"The weekend didn't go well?" I asked.

"It's all in there, in detail."

"Why don't you recap it for me? You look and sound as though you need to talk."

"You may be right." He got off the stool and said to a young woman who was shelving books in one of the nearby stacks, "Steffi, will you mind the store for a while?"

"Sure." She nodded and kept on shelving.

Neal led me to a nook under the stairs, where a cart with a coffeemaker and some cups stood. We helped ourselves and sank onto a worn red velvet settee.

"Okay," Neal said, "the weekend was awful. To start, Ted claimed the beef heart was a prank on the part of an old friend, but he hesitated long enough before he came up with the explanation that I didn't believe him. Plus he went white around the lips when he read the card—more angry than frightened, I'd say."

"Did he explain the meaning of the prank or name the friend?"

"No. Just said it was a private joke and rushed upstairs to get changed before Rick's limo arrived."

"Any other private jokes that're off limits to you?"

"No subject used to be off limits. Now it seems most are. Anyway, you saw us during the evening. He was very edgy and withdrawn. Drank more than he usually does. After we got home, he sat up listening to jazz and drinking some more, while I went straight to bed."

"And Saturday?"

"I suggested he go to the farmers' market for fresh produce, but he pointed out that we'd overbought last week and had enough in the fridge to feed the entire building. So I suggested we invite some of the neighbors we're friendly with for dinner, but he nixed that. Didn't want to see people, he said. By then it was time for me to come in to work. He dropped by not long after I got here, but after he'd checked out the new arrivals section he took off and didn't turn up at home till well after I did. When I asked him how he'd spent his day, he was vague."

"And that evening?"

"Old movies on TV."

"Was he drinking?"

"No more than I. But I had a feeling his mind wasn't on what we were watching, even though both films were favorites of his. In fact, I could practically hear the wheels grinding inside his head."

"You ask him what he was thinking about?"

"Yes. He said a problem at work. When I pressed him, he mumbled something about billing procedures."

There was nothing wrong with either our billing procedures or Altman & Zahn's; Ted had refined them to near perfection. "All right—Sunday."

"Sundays we usually go to brunch at Café Freddy's in North Beach. Pick up the paper, read while we eat. Again his mind was elsewhere. He kept staring at the other people, to the point where it made a couple of them uncomfortable. Afterward we picked up fresh pasta and sauce for dinner and went home. And then we got into a stupid argument about who was going to do the laundry."

"D'you usually share laundry duties?"

"No, normally I do it. I've got more patience for that kind of thing. But on Sunday he insisted on doing it all himself, wouldn't even let me go downstairs to move it from the washer to the dryer. So I rattled around the library the rest of the day, feeling put out and useless."

"And that night?"

"Dinner and a movie on TV, and all of a sudden he had to go out. Why? I asked. Favor to a friend. What friend? He named a name I'd never heard—John Evans—and took off. He didn't come home, and finally I went to sleep."

"This John Evans—"

"Made up on the spur of the moment, I think. I checked Ted's address book—no one by that name. Then I did some detective work of my own, called every listing for a John or J. Evans in the directory, asking for Ted. None of them had heard of him."

"Could be an unlisted number. Or outside the city."

"I doubt that."

"Frankly, so do I." I thought for a moment. "Okay, I'll take your notes back to the office and go over them. What're your plans for tonight?"

"Ted claims he's working late, and I—" He paused, looking sheepish.

"Yes?"

"I'm taking my second karate lesson."

"What!" Ted had studied karate for years, was well on his way to his black belt. I knew he'd pressured Neal to take up the discipline when they met, but Neal—a decidedly unathletic type—had declined.

"Yeah, I finally caved in." He shook his head. "There's no way to refuse when you're given ten lessons as a birthday present."

The things we do to each other under the guise of generosity! Once again I was grateful for Hy, who—among other things—has never once pressured me to climb upon the back of a horse while at his ranch, much as he enjoys riding. He knows I hate horses with a passion that is surpassed only by my passion for him.

"Well, that was a nice piece of manipulation," I said to Neal. "How're you liking the lessons?"

"I've only had one, so I'm keeping an open mind. I *am* discovering entire muscle groups I never suspected I possessed."

At four-thirty that afternoon I stuck my head through the door of Ted's office and asked, "How're those letters coming?"

"Why? Are you in a hurry to get out of here?" He didn't take his eyes off the computer screen.

"No. Just asking."

"You'll get them when they're done, all right?"

Taken aback by his harsh tone, I withdrew. No, this was not the Ted I'd known and loved for more than a decade.

I kept going along the catwalk to the office that Hank and Anne-Marie shared. It was similar to mine: spacious, with tan walls rising to high, narrow windows that by day admitted a stripe of soft northern light; Berber carpeting, exposed girders, and an arched window overlooking the Embarcadero, as mine did the bay. But there the resemblance stopped. While my furnishings were spare and contemporary, theirs were traditional: an old-fashioned partners desk, oak file cabinets, leather chairs and a sofa in a separate seating area; Hank's old cigar-store Indian stood by the door, coats and scarves draped over his head, and a World War II recruiting poster of Uncle Sam—"I want *you* for the U.S. Army"—hung opposite.

When I knocked on the door frame, Hank looked up from a brief he was studying and waved me inside.

"Where's your other half?" I asked.

"Conference with Habiba's teacher."

"Problems?" Habiba Hamid was nine years old and had been through a lot of tragedy in her young life.

"Nope. They tell us the kid's a genius, or close to, and are recommending she skip a grade."

"Is that a good idea?"

"We don't think so. She's had to grow up too fast. She needs a chance to be a kid and to be with other kids her own age."

Habiba's mother had been an American poet, her father the son of a diplomat from an oil-rich emirate. Her entire family was now dead by violence, except for distant relatives in the homeland, and in spite of the love and support of all of us who knew her, Habiba often felt alone and insecure.

"So you're telling the school no?"

"We're telling them that Habiba'll decide if and when she needs more intellectual stimulation. If she wants private lessons, accelerated courses, fine. But it's got to be when she's ready."

I studied my oldest male friend. Behind his horn-rimmed glasses his eyes brimmed with affection for his foster child. "You love her as you would your own daughter, don't you?"

"Yes, I do. And so does Anne-Marie—which is really something for a woman who used to refer to kids as 'obnoxious, noisy little creatures.' Of course, she doesn't have to live with Habiba . . ."

Soon after their marriage, he and Anne-Marie had found that they were totally unsuited to living together. His untidiness drove her wild; her meticulous housekeeping drove him wild. Their solution was to occupy separate flats in the two-unit Noe Valley building they owned—with liberal visitation rights, of course. Habiba lived at Hank's, the more child-friendly of the two residences.

I said, "No, she doesn't have to live with Habiba, but she's the one who's conferring with the teacher."

"And the one who taught her to ride a bike, and who helps her pick out her clothes, and who comforts her when she's feeling low. And who will soon become her legal mother."

"You're *adopting* her!"

He nodded, grinning broadly. "Yep. The family in Azad's decided to cut her loose. Tainted blood from the mother's side, you know."

"Tainted by her *mother!* Her father was a sociopath, and that whole family is certifiable!"

"And I thank God they don't want to get their hands on Habiba. I've been meaning to ask you, would it be all right if I gave your name to the social worker handling the adoption, as a character reference?"

"Sure. It'll be a pleasure to help expedite the adoption. More than a pleasure. This is a wonderful turn of events!"

"Thanks." Hank got up and motioned me toward the seating area. "So what's on your mind?"

"Does something have to be, for me to stop in to chat?"

"No, but you seem on edge." He put his hands on my shoulders, massaged them with his thumbs. "Big knots there. What's wrong?"

I dropped into one of the leather armchairs, and he took the other, his eyes concerned. "Is it a legal problem?"

"Maybe. Let me lay it out for you."

When I finished telling him about my impostor, he asked, "You have any idea who she is or why she's doing these things?"

"Not the foggiest, and I've given it a lot of thought. She could be anybody, from a disgruntled former client to someone with a personal motive. Or she could've picked me at random. That's the scariest possibility of all."

He took off his glasses and polished their lenses, thinking. "Greg filed a report on the break-in?"

"He said he would. And I faxed him a log of the other incidents, so they'll be on record when I identify her."

"When *you* identify her?"

"Who else is going to do it? The SFPD has more important things to deal with than some woman who's annoying me."

Hank nodded, grimacing.

"What I want to ask you," I went on, "is if I have any legal recourse against her once I identify her, even if I can't prove she's the person who broke into my house." I didn't feel uncomfortable about asking Hank for advice; I paid Altman &

Zahn a yearly retainer, just as they paid one to me—our way
of keeping our personal and professional relationships hassle
free.

He considered for a moment, slouched in his chair, his chin
resting on steepled fingers. "Sorry, Shar, I don't see any recourse unless you can prove she did the break-in. Other than
that, she's committed no crime."

That was what I was afraid he'd say—and exactly what I
didn't want to hear. "You mean somebody can go around pretending to be me at parties, sleeping with men under the guise
she's me, snooping around the airport for Hy's plane—and
there's no legal way to stop her?"

"Well, we could file a civil suit and attempt to show that
she's damaged you professionally, caused you to lose clients,
but we'd need a whole lot more documentation than the situation with the art dealer. Other than that, it's difficult to prove
damage when you're a public figure."

"A what?"

"Shar, your name and picture have been in the paper how
many times? To say nothing of that *People* article. And then
there were those TV and radio talk-show appearances—"

"I did those to build business!"

"Doesn't matter why. Those things have made you a public
figure."

"But—"

"Listen, I could—with the help of a plastic surgeon and a
wardrobe adviser—stroll across the street to Palomino tonight
and claim to be Harrison Ford. I could drink everybody under
the table, puke on the floor, insult all the customers—and
Harrison wouldn't be able to do a damned thing about it."

"But he's a *movie star,* and I'm just—"

"The definition of public figure varies widely, depending
on who's doing the defining."

"Jesus!"

"Okay, calm down. That's the downside. On the upside:
The woman's seriously angry about something. She's escalat-

ing her activity. She's bound to make a mistake soon. If she does any of the following to you, we'll go after her: if she uses your name in an attempt to defraud someone, if she undertakes an investigation while pretending to be you, if she commits credit-card fraud, if . . . well, you get my drift."

I got his drift, all right. I raised my hands to my face, which was already burning with anger, and rubbed my eyes. "God, I hadn't even *thought* of those possibilities! Oh, Hank . . . !"

"I know, it's a hideous situation. People can harass you and stalk you and try to assume your identity, and you have no real recourse. If you know who they are, you may be able to get a judge to issue a restraining order, but what's a restraining order to a head case?"

Hank paused, his eyes going bleak and sad. "I don't know what to tell you, Shar, except that Anne-Marie and I will be behind you all the way when you need us. It's an ugly, scary world these days, and the good guys all too often don't have enough legal tools on their side to protect them."

"So how do *you* deal with that situation?"

"Me, personally? I watch my back and the backs of the people I care about. I try to be the kind of attorney who protects those in the right, rather than one who turns the scumbags loose on the world. I'll tell you, there was a time when I was in danger of slipping over to the other side; the money was too good, the power too seductive. But Anne-Marie and Habiba have changed all that. My wife's an idealist who'd cut my nuts off if I sold out, and Habiba . . . Well, I want to do my bit to make this world a place where she can grow up unafraid."

Monday Night

Ted had told Neal he planned to work late, but at five-thirty I found him putting his desktop in order. "Going home?" I asked.

"Yeah. I'm beat."

He did look tired, his dark eyes shadowed and the lines around his mouth deeply pronounced. This was the Ted I'd caught glimpses of at the height of the AIDS epidemic when many of his friends were dying; but back then he'd taken pains to hide his distress, putting on a cheerful front while providing comfort for those in need of it. Now his trouble, whatever it was, showed plainly.

On the off chance he might confide in me, I said, "You haven't looked too well lately. Is something wrong?"

He hesitated, face conflicted, then shrugged. "Nothing I can't handle."

"I'd like to help."

"I know. Just let it go, Shar." He pushed the chair up to the desk, raised a hand in farewell, and left the office.

I waited only a few seconds before rushing back to my own office for my purse and the keys to the inconspicuous agency van.

*   *   *

Ted drove his white Dodge Neon straight to Plum Alley but, strangely, did not enter the garage of his building. Instead he backed into a parking space next to the retaining wall at the end of the block and sat there. I continued along Montgomery, found nowhere to leave the van, U-turned in front of Julius' Castle, and drove back on the higher section of the street. A car was just exiting Plum Alley. I sped up, made another U, and entered the alley; the vacated parking space was halfway down the street, behind a Dumpster that would block the van from Ted's line of sight—if he was still in his car.

I got out of the van and crept through the shadows between the parked cars and buildings for a closer look. Yes, I could see Ted's head, backlit by the lights of the waterfront. He appeared to be watching his own building. From behind a utility wagon I watched him as several people entered and left, each causing him to straighten and take notice. He didn't seem concerned with others in the vicinity, however: a man who pulled in to the space next to him bumped his car door into the Neon, and Ted didn't even turn his head; a woman allowed her German shepherd to pee on the car's bumper, and he didn't roll down his window to protest. If he hadn't moved from time to time, I'd have feared him dead. Finally I went back to the van to wait.

The night grew cold and overcast; I wished I had some coffee and a sandwich. And soon images began to haunt me: An open bottle of Deer Hill Chardonnay and a glass under the warm lamplight in my living room. Cold fluorescent light touching the silvery corkscrew where it lay on my kitchen chopping block. An empty plastic compact that had contained birth control pills on the fluffy green mat in my bathroom. Rumpled bedclothes and a half-open closet door—

Stop it, McCone!

I breathed in deeply and thought I caught the scent of Dark Secrets perfume, but no one was there but me.

The rain started around eight-thirty. Light mist turned into a torrent, smacking down on the van's roof. I leaned against the door, listening to the downpour. I don't like surveillances; they're one of the most boring aspects of my work. And I especially didn't like this one, because over and over my thoughts drifted to the woman who had invaded my home.

Had her primary purpose been to trash it? Maybe, maybe not.

Reconstruct her actions. That might tell you.

Okay, she's been watching the place, sees Hy and me leave. She picks the lock, quickly, so the neighbors won't notice. That means she's as good with a set of picks as I am, and I'm very good. She checks the parlor, the guest room, the home office. She lights a fire, goes to the kitchen, helps herself to some wine. Sits down and has a couple of glasses.

All right, at this point what's she thinking?

That she's getting to know me. She may even be pretending she *is* me. Cozy, relaxing in my own easy chair. But then something sets her off. Something that makes her flush those pills, strip my bed. She does damage to things that're associated with sex.

Is that it? No, sex had nothing to do with her stuffing the cat into the crawl space.

The cat . . .

Where was Allie on Sunday night? Out, like Ralph. They wouldn't come in when Hy and I wanted to leave, sensed something unusual was going on and got upset, so we said the hell with them. So how did Allie get in?

Now, *here's* a scenario: The woman makes her way back to the bedroom. Allie's at the glass door, wanting in. The woman's now deep into her role-playing; she lets Allie— *her* cat—in and tries to pick her up, to cuddle her.

And Allie, of course, is the most standoffish cat on the

face of the earth. She won't let anybody but Hy or me hold her, barely tolerates Michelle Curley, the kid next door who lets her in and feeds her when I'm away from home. Sulks or panics when company comes, depending on who it is. So what's she going to do when a total stranger tries to handle her?

Struggle. Hiss. Scratch her.

And what's this particular stranger going to do when rudely yanked out of her personal fantasy?

Pitch a fit.

The bedclothes get dragged off, the pills go down the toilet, the cat goes into the crawl space. And I'm lucky she didn't do more—

The Neon abruptly started up, its headlights flashing on. I slumped low, let it go by. Then I followed.

Half an hour later Ted and I were parked several spaces apart on Van Ness Avenue near Pine Street, across from the Far West Academy of Martial Arts. He seemed to be watching its entrance.

Regardless of what Neal thought, Ted had to suspect him of infidelity.

I squirmed around in the driver's seat of the van, seeking a more comfortable position. Across the six lanes of rain-slick pavement was a four-story building occupied by one of our major electronics retailers, the Good Guys; some enterprising window dresser had turned TVs face out across its entire facade, and now the credits of the local CBS affiliate's news show began to roll. Soon dozens of tiny news clones began smiling and talking and bobbing their stiffly coiffed heads in perfect synchronization high above the sidewalk. I watched, in danger of becoming hypnotized.

At the stoplight behind me brakes squealed and tires shrieked. I glanced back, saw a car that had slid sideways across two lanes. Why was it that the vast majority of San Franciscans forgot how to drive at the first drop of rain?

Weren't they aware that rubber adhered to pavement even when both were wet? What would they do if they lived in Seattle, where it *really* rained? Or in the Sierras, where the roads were now slick with ice and snow?

Mental question-and-answer session, designed to keep my mind alert at this late hour—as well as off the subject I'd begun to label as The Woman.

People were beginning to drift through the door of the academy now. Through the windows of the parked cars ahead of me I saw Ted's silhouette straighten; I did the same, my hand on the key.

Neal came outside, gym bag in hand, waving good-bye to a pair of men. He turned down Pine Street and walked toward Polk.

Ted waited for a break in traffic, then pulled away from the curb. I waited a little longer before I followed. The Neon shot across three lanes, made a left on Bush. I got caught at the light, but when I turned onto Bush, I spotted Ted making another left onto Polk. I duplicated it, saw that he was driving unhurriedly, keeping Neal in sight as he walked along to Anachronism, bypassed the shop, and crossed in mid-block to a parking garage.

Ted pulled over to the curb and idled there. I stopped to let pass a trio of young men who seemed to have pierced every conceivable body surface with metal objects that looked as though they'd been subjected to a few whirls in the garbage disposer, then waved across an elderly couple toting sacks from an all-night supermarket. In minutes Neal's beat-up Honda exited the garage and turned north on Polk. I eased forward, watching Ted follow.

Separated at times by various other vehicles, the three of us proceeded along Polk, through the Broadway tunnel, and ultimately to Tel Hill. By the time I arrived at Plum Alley, Ted had emerged from his building's garage and was entering the lobby courtyard. Neal—who parked on the street, since the apartment was allotted only one garage space and

Ted's car was the more valuable—had presumably gone inside.

I idled a few doors down from the building as Ted checked their mailbox and stepped onto the elevator. Watched him through the glass blocks as it rose to the third floor. When he passed behind the art-glass windows, I realized why I always had the sense of being underwater when I walked down that hallway; Ted looked as if he were drifting among the strange sea creatures.

Submerged, perhaps, in whatever lay heavy on his mind.

When I got home, I found a grocery bag on my front porch. Another unpleasant surprise, no doubt.

Without touching it, I opened the door, disarmed the security system, and turned on the overhead light. Then, cautiously, I brought the bag inside and opened it.

A bottle of Deer Hill Chardonnay—the right vintage, no less. Taped to it was a Post-it note bearing one typed word: "Sorry."

I let my breath out in a hiss that was a combination of relief and rage.

Sorry. She'd broken into my home, drunk my wine, flushed my pills down the toilet, terrorized my cat—and now she was *sorry?*

Yeah, sure she was.

I left the bottle in the bag, picked it up by its top edges, and took it to the kitchen. Tomorrow it would go to Richman Labs for fingerprint analysis and to see if it was contaminated, but I suspected the fee I'd pay the investigative laboratory would be wasted; she'd been careful last night, and she'd have been more careful with this specious gift.

Before I reset the alarm, I gave consideration to asking the neighbors if they'd seen who dropped off the bag, but decided against it; I'd already bothered them this morning, and it was too late to go ringing doorbells.

Both cats were sleeping on the sitting room couch, let in

by Michelle from next door. The light on the answering machine was blinking—one message. I hit the play button and heard Hy's voice.

"Just wanted to let you know I arrived here safely. Buenos Aires is even better than I remembered it; someday you'll have to make the trip with me. Anyway, I miss you. Hope that woman hasn't given you any more trouble, and that you've got the problem with Ted and Neal sorted out. You have my itinerary and numbers, so if I don't get hold of you, call me. Love you."

I'd call him tomorrow. I badly needed the comfort of a talk.

Tonight I'm underwater. Murky water in a dimly lighted aquarium where opaque green plants wave their silky tendrils. The pebbles under my feet glisten and shift with my steps.

How can I be underwater and still breathe?

I watch myself move through the plants, clumsy in contrast to their gracefulness.

Movement at the far side of the tank, whipping the plants to a frenzy. Bubbles rise toward the surface. I draw back into a sandstone cave.

Strange sea creatures appear. They're brightly colored: red, blue, gold, vermilion. They dart and weave among the green tendrils, uttering unworldly cries that echo off the glass.

I watch, both fascinated and afraid.

Now comes a procession that silences the sea creatures. A series of faceless women draped in filmy teal-blue cloth. They drift among the sea creatures but don't touch them.

Each woman carries a bottle of wine and a glass.

Sorry, they murmur as they drift close to my hiding place.

Sorry, sorry, sorry . . .

Thursday

"Keim's on line one, Shar."

"Thanks." I picked up. "Charlotte, where are you?"

"Detroit Airport, about to board my flight home." She'd spent the week shadowing the traveling businesswoman from Chicago to Minneapolis to the Motor City.

"Still nothing?" I asked.

"Nothing at all. This woman works too hard to fool around on the road. The client must be paranoid."

"You call him yet?" The client, Jeffrey Stoddard, wanted oral reports on a daily basis.

"I tried, but he wasn't home. I'll try again on the in-flight phone—"

"No, I'll call him and you can fill him in on the details when you get back." Keim, like so many fans of high technology, loved to talk on the airliner phones and had previously run up her expense account to an unjustifiably high level.

"Okay," she said. "I guess if I get bored, I'll have to call Mick—on my own nickel, of course."

"Don't stand up in the aisle while you're talking." That practice has always struck me as a particularly obnoxious way of calling attention to oneself—"I haven't a minute to waste, even at 33,000 feet. I'm important!"—to say nothing of an annoyance to those who aren't impressed with the airborne dialer's need to stay connected.

"Exactly like last night?" Neal asked.

"Yes."

On both Tuesday and Wednesday Ted had driven directly from the pier to Neal's bookstore, idled at the curb down the block, and tailed him home.

"He must suspect me of something. But what? And what cause have I given him?"

"Does he ever quiz you about where you've been, what you've been doing?"

"Never, but that's no surprise, considering he's been following me."

"Does he display unusual curiosity about your phone calls or mail?"

"No, but . . . lately he's been rushing to answer the phone every time it rings. And my mailbox key disappeared two or three weeks ago; I suppose he could've taken it. He claims the locksmith doesn't have masters for that type of key, so it can't be duplicated."

". . . Right."

"So where d'you go from here?"

"Well, I'll follow Ted one more time, to make sure this is a regular pattern. After that . . . We'll talk about it." The intercom buzzed. "Got to answer another call."

"Ms. McCone, Kelly at Richman Labs. We have the results on the items you dropped off for testing on Tuesday. No latents on the bag, the bottle, or the Post-it note. The seal on the bottle wasn't tampered with, and the wine tested negative for contaminants. An IBM Wheelwriter 1500 was used to type the note."

A common typewriter available for public use in copy

shops and libraries. The results were exactly what I'd suspected.

"Mick, will you come to my office? I've got a new assignment for you."

In a couple of minutes he appeared, carrying a Pepsi and a half-eaten salami sandwich, the former of which he set on my desk. I frowned and shoved a coaster across to him. He then set the sandwich down, smearing mayonnaise all over. "Sorry," he muttered, swiping at it with the side of his hand and eyeing the case file.

I said, "This investigation's for Anne-Marie, so give it priority. One of her important clients is divorcing and suspects her husband has hidden a substantial portion of their communal assets. We're to find out where."

"Probably an offshore or Swiss bank account, in which case it's nearly impossible—"

"Unless we gather evidence that, when presented in court, will tend to show he's misappropriated funds. You'll be going into the field to dig up that evidence."

His face brightened considerably. Mick's computer expertise kept him largely confined to the office, and he relished the occasions when he could—as he termed it—play real private eye.

"Here's the file," I went on. "You'll find the subject's home address on the preliminary information sheet. I've already learned that he's due to fly to L.A. this afternoon for a meeting of one of the corporate boards he sits on. Overnight trip, returning tomorrow around noon. I've also called Sunset Scavengers and found out that his garbage pickup is scheduled for tomorrow morning."

"What's his garbage got to do with—"

I smiled, feeling deliciously wicked. "It has *everything* to do with it. You are to follow him to SFO this afternoon to be certain he makes his flight. Then you are to go to his house and steal his garbage."

"What!"

"After that you will pick through it for clues to the assets' whereabouts."

"Gross!"

"I told you when I hired you—private investigation is *not* glamorous."

"Mr. Stoddard, Sharon McCone at McCone Investigations. Charlotte Keim called me shortly before boarding her return flight from Detroit; she's come up with no evidence that your friend is doing anything on the road but working. Do you wish to terminate the investigation?"

"Hang on a second." Stoddard sounded winded, as if he'd been out running. "All right, now, what did you ask me? Terminate the investigation. No, I don't think so. I *know* she's got somebody on the side, and it's only a matter of time till he shows himself."

"Of course we'll be glad to continue the surveillance, but I must warn you: given your fiancée's upcoming travel schedule, our expenses could be very substantial."

"It's worth it. I'm not going to marry somebody who's being unfaithful to me before we make it to the altar. She's fooling around out on the road, and pretty damn soon she's going to be *down* the road."

Something wrong there, I thought as I hung up. The needle of my built-in lie detector was all over the chart. I'd warn Keim about that, suggest she set up a meeting with Stoddard so she could personally assess the situation; Keim's instincts—she called them "shit detectors"—were almost as good as mine.

"Shar, Clive Benjamin on line one."

"Thanks." Oh, God! The gallery owner wouldn't be calling me unless the bogus McCone had resurfaced in his life. "Yes, Mr. Benjamin?"

"Ms. McCone, I thought you ought to know that the

woman who impersonated you apparently lifted the spare key to my apartment. She was here last night in my absence. Drank some very expensive wine and took one of my pieces of sculpture. She left your card on the coffee table."

Christ!

"The sculpture—is it valuable?"

"Not really. It was a gift from a grateful but not very successful client."

"Did you call the police?"

". . . No. To tell you the truth, this is a very embarrassing situation, and I'd just as soon not call attention to it."

"I hear you. It's embarrassing for me, too. Did you have the locks changed?"

"First thing this morning."

"Good. Will you describe the missing sculpture to me?"

"It's small, perhaps a foot high and a foot and a half long. A supine figure of a woman, with a pedestal supporting her at the small of her back. White . . . well, I won't bore you with the technique the artist uses. The woman's nude, her chest is opened to expose her ribs and organs, and the top of her skull is missing. It's titled *Autopsy*."

I felt a wrenching in the pit of my stomach. "No wonder your client's not very successful."

"The piece is actually one of his better creations."

"Well, if I come across it, I'll see it's returned to you."

Autopsy.

My God. Had she seen it, liked it, and taken it on a whim? Or was there something more? Did she know Benjamin had been in touch with me and returned to his apartment in order to send me a message?

Thursday Night

"What the hell . . . ?" I muttered as my knee banged into something in my front hallway. It was after nine, and I was in a thoroughly bad mood. I'd followed Ted through the same routine, then returned to the pier to eat half a sandwich left over from lunch while clearing up more of my seemingly endless paperwork—with thoughts of Clive Benjamin's grotesque missing sculpture and the woman who'd taken it preying around the edges of my mind. I fumbled for the hall light, looked down as I fiddled with the alarm's keypad.

Packages. A couple of stacks of them. Left by UPS, no doubt, and brought in by Michelle Curley, young caregiver of cats. I examined the labels: Macy's, Crate & Barrel, Williams-Sonoma, Nordstrom's.

I hadn't shopped at any of those stores since before Christmas, hadn't placed any mail or phone orders, either.

"What's the bitch done to me *now?*"

I hauled the packages to the sitting room, where I dumped them in the middle of the floor. Ralph and Allie wandered in from their respective sleeping places, sniffed at the new additions to the household, and sauntered off to their food bowl.

"Nice to see you too!" I snapped.

They ignored me.

I followed them to the kitchen for a knife and returned to the sitting room, sat on the floor, and began opening. From Macy's I'd received a cashmere sweater in my correct size and favorite shade of green. Crate & Barrel had sent a place setting of my flatware. Williams-Sonoma had supplied a trio of wine vinegars in the flavors I most liked. And Nordstrom's mail-order department had somehow divined that I used Paris perfume.

It had all been charged either to my store accounts or to my MasterCard. I'd have to expend a lot of time and effort straightening this out.

Rage rose up in my throat and I clenched my teeth against shrieking. Then a heavy atmospheric pressure seemed to be bearing down on all sides of me, making it difficult to breathe. Get a grip, McCone. This isn't worth hyperventilating over. Besides, she's now committed the kind of fraud you can put her away for.

When I felt better I got up and took myself to the kitchen, where I replaced the knife in its drawer and poured myself a big glass of wine. The cats followed me back to the sitting room, Ralphie lying beside me on the couch and Allie jumping on its back, where she could butt against my head.

"Yeah, sure. You've eaten, so now you can acknowledge my existence."

Ralphie yawned and Allie began to purr.

All right, McCone, concentrate. What do you know about this woman?

She's my height, weight, and body type, but she doesn't have the same skin tone and her hair color is probably honey blond. She isn't shy, isn't picky about sleeping with a stranger upon the first meeting. She's a blatant and convincing liar. She's angry enough that her body language communicates it to a casual observer. She's bold enough to enter Clive Benjamin's and my homes and go through our possessions during an absence whose duration she couldn't be sure of. She's pretended, at least to me, and perhaps momentarily believed, that she's sorry for her actions.

Which probably meant she was subject to extreme mood swings and was emotionally, if not mentally, unstable.

This latest intrusion into my life—how had she accomplished it? The packing slips enclosed with one order indicated it had come in by phone, so probably the others had, too. But how had she gotten the charge-account numbers?

Of course. I kept my credit-card bills in the old-fashioned pigeonhole desk in my home office—the desk whose drawers had been standing open on Sunday night. Easy to copy the information for future use.

But didn't they ask questions that would verify you actually were the credit-card holder when taking a phone order? No, not when the merchandise was to be sent to the address shown on the account.

Well, what about caller ID? Didn't the number you called from come up on their computer screens? Probably, and if so, that was a potential lead.

Okay, the woman had the presence of mind not to leave any evidence; the expertise to break into my home unobserved when the security system wasn't armed; the nerve to remain there for a fair amount of time; the foresight to make note of my possessions and credit-card numbers—

Suddenly I felt cold; my flesh rippled unpleasantly. What else was in that desk?

She'd gotten enough information to throw my life into total chaos: all the numbers without which we can't carry on, but which make us vulnerable if they fall into the wrong hands. My particular numbers included credit cards; Social Security; driver's, pilot's, investigator's licenses; passport; employer's ID; mortgage and PG&E and Pacific Bell and AT&T and CellularOne accounts. Hell, she even had my frequent-flier numbers!

I shook my head, remembering how on Sunday night I'd

congratulated myself on keeping all my important papers in the office safe. By that I'd meant my birth certificate, pink slip for the MG and company van, tax returns, will, and the wills of my mother and brother John, who had both made me executor. But I'd kept my whole life here in the house, where the woman could peruse it at her leisure.

What else?

I opened one of the desk's cubbyholes and saw my personal Rolodex. Oh, God, she probably had the phone numbers and addresses of all my relatives and friends! If so, she had numbers that were unlisted, that I'd promised to keep private.

I tugged at a couple of drawers that had been partially open that night. Inside were letters and cards from people I cared about, letters and cards from Hy. She might even have read the private and intimate things my lover had written me!

What kind of investigator was I? How had I missed the obvious on Sunday?

Well, for one thing, I'd been put off balance by the violation of my home, the traumatization of my cats. I'd just returned from my first solo departure from a Class B airport.

No excuse, McCone. You're dropping the ball all over the field on this one. You've allowed your heavy workload and Ted's problem to get in the way of your professionalism. Start treating yourself the same as you would a client.

I shut off the lights and went to the kitchen for a refill of wine, then thought to check the answering machine. Two messages. One from Hy, I hoped.

On Tuesday and Wednesday there had been brief messages from him, but I hadn't been able to reach him either at his hotel or RKI's Buenos Aires office. Last night's said he would be leaving in the morning to check out a client's facilities in the southern part of the country. "Don't know where I'll be staying yet," he added, "so I'll try to catch you when I can."

Our repeated failure to get through to one another didn't really bother me, even though I badly wanted to talk with him. Hy and I had probably spent more time playing telephone tag than most couples, but from the first, we'd connected on an emotional level that transcended both time and distance. Now, I felt hopeful as I pressed the play button.

"Sharon, Jeff Riley again. One of the other linemen told me he saw a woman who sounds a lot like the one I talked to hanging around Two-eight-niner this afternoon. The plane seems okay, but I'll ask around, see if anybody else noticed her."

"Ms. McCone, this is Cecily at Eddie Bauer Customer Service. The nylon jacket you ordered is out of stock in the tan, but we have the blue. If you'd like to change your color choice, please give me a call at our 800 number."

I'm lying flat on my back, bound at the ankles, waist, and shoulders. My arm is extended to my side and . . . oh, yes, that's a needle stuck deep in the vein, attached to a tube that glows a deep blackish red. Funny, it doesn't hurt at all, but I'm tired, so tired . . .

A nurse in a teal-blue uniform leans down, her face close to mine, and asks, "How are you?"

She doesn't really care; I can tell from her tone. I look up and see a mirror image of myself.

I ask, "What are you doing to me?" and she replies, "Taking a blood sample."

"Blood sample? You're taking my life!"

She smiles and glides away.

friday

... And the guy brings home a lot of takeout, only he never finishes it, so his garbage is full of cartons of rotten Chinese and pizza that— Shar, have you heard anything I've said?"

"What?" I frowned at Mick.

"I thought so. Where're you off at this morning?"

"Another galaxy, I guess. You were saying . . . ?"

"Basically that I've gone through the guy's disgusting garbage and come up with a couple of promising leads."

Oh, right—the hidden-assets case. "Such as?"

"Envelopes from CBIC Bank & Trust in the Cayman Islands and Swiss Bank's private banking department here in the city."

"Just envelopes?"

"Yeah, but they've given me two places to start. Almost made it worth pawing through used Kleenexes and food with green stuff growing on it."

"I hope you wore rubber gloves."

"You bet I did."

"Listen, why don't you talk with Keim about this? She might be able to give you some insight—"

"I already tapped into Lottie's financial expertise, and I think I know where to go from here. I should have my report on your desk by Monday noon, latest."

"Good."

Mick looked disappointed. "Make that eleven fifty-seven."

Automatically I said, "Eleven fifty-seven will earn you a steak sandwich at the Boondocks."

"I'd rather it earned me a talk with you about what's wrong."

His concern over my distracted state both surprised and touched me; sometimes I felt I'd spent years giving to Mick and receiving little in return. Now, apparently, that was changing. For a moment I was tempted to tell him exactly what was going on.

But I couldn't bring myself to do that. In the past Mick had displayed a tendency to go off on irresponsible and potentially dangerous investigative tangents, and given this new concern for me, he might do so now. So instead I said, "There's nothing wrong. You have a good weekend, and I'll see you at eleven fifty-seven on Monday."

"Renshaw and Kessell International," the accented voice said.

"Hy Ripinsky, please."

"I am sorry. Mr. Ripinsky is out in the field."

"Do you know where he's staying?"

"I do not have access to that information."

"May I speak with the office manager?"

"Mr. Rivera is in the field with Mr. Ripinsky."

"And you've no way of reaching him?"

"He will be calling in."

"Is there anyone else in the office who can help me?"

"I am sorry, no."

A small office, most likely, like many of RKI's overseas branches. Small, and not terribly well run. I left a message for the man to pass on to Hy, asking that he call me at any time and saying it was important I talk with him. Too many days had gone by; I needed to hear his voice. Needed to tell him about the woman who was rapidly stealing my identity. Needed . . .

* * *

"Well, you're right; there's definitely something wrong with the client." Keim had just returned from a breakfast meeting with Jeffrey Stoddard.

"You able to get a handle on what?"

"Maybe. And I've got a pretty good idea of how to confirm it."

"Then work that angle for a while."

She frowned. "Don't you want to know what it is?"

"No, I trust your judgment. Go with it."

"Are you okay, Shar?"

If I didn't plan to confide in Mick, I certainly couldn't tell Charlotte anything; the two were too close to keep secrets. "Sure," I said. "Why shouldn't I be?"

"You don't seem yourself today. Any more than Ted does."

"What about Ted?"

"He damn near tossed me out of the supply room this morning. All I was trying to do was save him the trouble of making a couple of copies for me, and he blew higher'n a caprock gusher."

I waited till Ted had gone on his lunch break, then went to the supply room behind his office. It was quiet in there, save for the erratic hum of the old Xerox machine that would soon be replaced by the new Sharp we'd ordered; the room seemed almost pathologically tidy.

Now, what could be here that Ted hadn't wanted Charlotte to see?

I stood in the center of the room, taking in the contents of the neat shelves. Every box of pens and paper clips, every roll of fax paper and Scotch tape, every stack of letterhead and envelopes was perfectly aligned and in its assigned place. Had Ted compulsively tidied it while attempting to repel whatever demons were gnawing at him?

After a moment I left and went along the catwalk to the office Charlotte shared with Rae. The two of them were at their desks, eating takeout and chatting. "Charlotte," I said, "when Ted tossed you out of the supply room, did he come in and find you there, or was he already inside?"

"Already."

"Doing what?"

She pursed her lips, thinking. "He was messing around with a carton of Jiffy bags—number fives."

"Thanks." I went back to the supply room and located the carton. The bags were slightly atilt. I slipped my hand between them and the box's side till I came to the place where the Jiffys lay flat, removed the tilted layer, and looked inside the bottom bag.

Cash. A fair amount of it. Tens and twenties. I counted them. Over four hundred dollars.

As the one who paid half of Ted's salary, I knew this was a good deal of money for him to be carrying around, much less secreting in this less-than-secure hiding place. It was also an amount he would not easily part with.

So why was it here—and what did he plan to do with it?

"Shari?"

The voice on the phone was my father's, but I wouldn't have recognized it had he not abbreviated my name in the way nobody else did. He sounded older than his sixty-eight years, and tentative. A chill skittered across my shoulder blades: *Something terrible's happened to one of us, and the family's never going to be the same again.*

"Pa? What's wrong?"

"Nothing's wrong here. But in God's name, what's happened to *you?*"

". . . I don't understand."

"I had a phone call. Twenty minutes ago. A woman who said she was a nurse at San Francisco General. She told me you'd been shot."

Oh, Christ!

"Pa, where are you?" My father and his woman friend,

Nancy Sullivan, spent a good portion of each year traveling in his Airstream trailer.

"The San Diego house, between trips."

The unlisted number of the house where I'd grown up was in my home-office Rolodex.

Pa went on, "The nurse hung up before I could ask any questions, so I called the hospital back; they said you hadn't been admitted. I thought maybe I'd gotten the name of the hospital wrong, so I called a few others. Then Nancy, bless her, suggested I check with your office. The shooting wasn't serious?"

"There was no shooting." I gripped the edge of my desk, felt sweat breaking out on my forehead. "Hold on a second, Pa."

Oxygen in, carbon dioxide out. Clean air in, poisonous air out.

It was a stress-management technique a friend had taught me and, mercifully, it worked.

"Shari?"

"I'm here. Listen, Pa, there's this woman who's trying to stir up trouble for me. She got her hands on the phone numbers for the whole family, and she's probably pulled this with everybody."

"This woman, why—"

"I can't talk about it now. Will you do me a favor? Call the others, tell them I'm okay and to ignore anything like this in the future?"

"I'll call your brothers and sisters, but I will *not* call your mother. If this woman has told her the same story, she'll be carrying on like one of those . . . What do they call them, Nan?"

In the background Nancy said, "Berserkers."

"Right. Like one of those berserkers. We went to a lecture on Scandinavian legends during that cruise we took in December, and I finally learned the right name for your mother when she's on a rampage."

I rested my forehead on the palm of my hand and said,

"Then ask Nancy to call the berserker. Or you call Melvin."
Melvin Hunt was the man my mother lived with.

"I do not converse with the person who stole my wife. And
I see no reason that Nancy should be subjected—"

"Put her on the phone, please."

"That Nancy should be subjected to a conversation with—"

"Pa—please!"

In a matter of minutes Nancy—knitter of hideous
sweaters, baker of wonderful pies, and a woman who, by
virtue of putting up with my father, had a good shot at saint-
hood—agreed to resolve this latest McCone family crisis.
And a good thing for me, because by the time we ended our
call, messages from my brothers John and Joey and sisters
Charlene and Patsy were stacked in front of me by Ted.

I swept them aside, put my head down on the desk, and did
my clean-air-in, poisonous-air-out thing all over again.

At four-thirty someone from Crate & Barrel customer service returned my call of that morning to tell me that the number from which the order for a place setting of my flatware
had been placed was that of my own cellular unit.

Impossible! Or was it? I rushed over to the coatrack,
checked my purse. The phone was there. How, then . . . ?

Mick might know.

I rushed to his office, told him what had happened without
mentioning I was the individual it had happened to. "How
would somebody go about doing that to my client?"

He smiled expansively and motioned for me to sit down on
one of the moving crates that we'd never gotten around to
unpacking. I flopped there, feeling limp and disoriented.

"Okay," he said, "the cell phone's been in the client's possession the whole time?"

"Yes."

"They've used it how many times recently?"

"I don't know, a fair number."

"How many times a day, on the average?"

"I . . . she didn't tell me. Maybe ten?"

"That'd be enough. It's obvious to me that somebody cloned it."

"*Cloned* the phone? I thought that's something they do with sheep!"

Mick sighed dramatically, as he often did when confronted with what he called my dinosaur tendencies. "The way it works, criminals use radio scanners to get your phone number and electronic serial number. Then they program them into a microchip that can make any phone seem like yours to the cellular network. The cloned phones are sold for around seventy-five bucks if there's a guarantee of a month's illegal service before the real subscriber or the cell company catches on. Without a guarantee, they go for as little as ten bucks. Drug dealers and other small-time crooks love them."

As did a woman who was trying to destroy me.

"What if somebody wanted to clone a specific cell phone—one whose number she knew?"

"Easy."

"And there're no safeguards against it?"

"Providers have started instituting them. There's a system called RF fingerprinting, and it's cut out fraud up to seventy-five percent in some areas. But it's expensive when you have as many cell sites as the Bay Area does, so it isn't fully in place yet. The good news is that the client's provider won't charge her for any calls she claims she didn't make."

He was smiling even more broadly now, but I recognized what I'd previously taken to be self-satisfaction and smugness about his superior knowledge for what it actually was: Mick was pleased to be able to help me. His abilities made him feel valuable—and valued by me.

"Thanks, genius." I gave him a big hug and left him looking both happy and embarrassed.

Friday Night

It was dark and silent in the mist-choked alley between Mission and Howard Streets. Then somewhere ahead of me glass smashed and a man shouted unintelligible words, oiled by booze and scrambled by rage. I crouched beside a foul-smelling Dumpster, my .357 in hand.

Feet dragged toward me. A burly shape moved past, head bowed, shoulders rounded, arms loose. He'd emptied his bottle, destroyed it for offering no more solace, and where was he going to get another at close to midnight on this penniless winter night?

I froze in the shadows, waiting for him to be gone. Heard him sob as he stumbled toward Sixth Street, the heart of skid row and the end of the line for so many like him.

Jesus, what was Ted *doing* here at this hour? Something connected with the cash I'd found in the box of Jiffy bags, no doubt; I'd checked before leaving the pier to follow him through the same routine as the other nights, and the money was gone.

At eleven, long after I'd ended the surveillance and gone home to field further calls from my puzzled family members, Neal phoned. Ted had announced he was going to a special midnight screening of Humphrey Bogart's *Dark Passage*, and, no, he didn't want company. It sounded like a ploy to get away for a couple of hours; Ted was a big Bogart fan and could probably recap the film's plot to back up his story. So back to Plum Alley I went, arriving only minutes before Ted's car pulled out of the garage and headed for SoMa.

He parked at an all-night lot on Mission and walked quickly to Sixth Street. I followed in the MG, concerned because he looked so slight and vulnerable among the city's predators. But Ted moved in an assertive manner that told them not to mess with him, and brushed past the few who homed in without making eye contact.

When he disappeared into the alley I spotted a parking space on Sixth and pulled to the curb. Immediately a tall black man whose flashy attire and abundance of jewelry advertised his occupation came over and ran a suggestive hand over the MG's hood. I got out, showed him a twenty-dollar bill and said, "How about watching it for me?"

"I ain't no doorman."

I showed him another twenty and let the flap of my purse fall open to expose the .357.

He hesitated, nodded, and took the bills. On any given night this neighborhood teemed with undercover cops. Do a cop a favor, maybe she'll return it someday.

And now I was crouched in the alley, breathing noxious garbage fumes and wondering where Ted had gone.

After the drunk was out of sight, I straightened and moved along, scanning the doors of the small businesses that opened onto the narrow pavement. Sutton Overhead Door, Liberty Plumbing and Heating, Nell Loomis Photography. I knew Loomis; she'd once supplied me with evidence that had helped me solve a case. All sorts of people eking out a living in these low-rent spaces, but which one was Ted visiting?

Finally I took shelter at the alley's midpoint, squeezing between a parked van and the wall of a building.

Ten minutes, fifteen. The mist grew thicker, and at the Seventh Street entrance somebody began rummaging through the trash cans.

Nineteen minutes, twenty.

A door opened about fifteen feet away on the opposite side of the alley. Light spilled over the pavement and men's voices murmured indistinctly. Then the door shut and footsteps came my way.

I wriggled farther back, to where I could look through the van's side windows.

Ted, head down, carrying a package. He passed within a yard of me, going toward Sixth. I didn't follow; it was more important to learn whom he'd visited.

When he was gone I came out from behind the van and moved along the alley to the door he'd exited. No nameplate, no other indication of who lived or worked there. The number painted above the bell push was in shadow; I took out my flash and checked it. Then I went to Nell Loomis's photography studio and rang her bell; she was often there at odd hours, particularly when working on a rush job. Not tonight, though.

Trash bins were lined up against the buildings. I eyed them speculatively, found one with a number spray-painted on it that matched the number of the door Ted had come out of. When I lifted the lid, a dreadful smell arose. Oh, hell, I thought, this is what I get for assigning Mick to pick through that guy's garbage!

Then, with expertise born of too many hidden-assets investigations, I reached in and heisted the bag.

When I got back to my MG, the pimp was still there, leaning against it. He smiled, bowed, and ushered me toward the driver's-side door as if I were Cinderella entering the coach that would take her to the ball—a bedraggled, weary Cinderella, clutching a smelly plastic sack of garbage. The fairy godmother had done a lousy job on me.

I was stopped at a light on Duboce Avenue underneath the Central Freeway when my phone rang. I reached eagerly for it, thinking the caller might be Hy. Normally he wouldn't phone the cellular unit from as far away as South America, sticking me with a very costly bill, but we'd been out of contact for so long now . . .

"Sharon?" The caller was whispering.

"Yes, who's this?"

"Rae."

"Rae?" All at once I was wire-tight again.

"I'm in trouble. I need your help."

"Where are you?"

"The Vintage Lofts on Beale Street. Please come right away."

The Vintage Lofts was an unoccupied warehouse currently under development as live-work space.

"Sharon?"

The light changed; I turned right, heading back to SoMa. "I'm here. Tell me what's wrong."

"Can't talk. Come quick!" The connection broke.

The whispering voice had been a woman's, but I'd known from our first exchange that it was not Rae's. I'd have recognized hers, and besides, she and Ricky had gone to his recording studio in the Arizona desert for the weekend. Angrily I snapped the phone shut. How stupid did this woman think I was? Did she really believe I'd fall for such a setup?

My anger hardened to resolve. Tonight I'd settle the score once and for all.

The old warehouse was only blocks from Pier 24½, so I left my car at the curb there and hurriedly walked over, keeping well in the shadows. Most of the buildings in this area were still in commercial use or in the process of being developed as residences; at this hour the streets were deserted, and the only sound was the grumble of bridge traffic.

When I neared Vintage Lofts, I took shelter on a dark loading dock and studied the building. Squarish and unattractive by day, its contours were softened by night; no light showed in any of the narrow windows. The door was in a recessed entry portal in the center of the ground floor, and it looked to be open a crack.

How could I get inside without alerting her? She was probably watching for me, expecting to surprise me when I blundered in calling for Rae. But the element of surprise could work in my favor as well.

I slipped along the loading dock and went down an alley between two buildings. It came out on Fremont Street; from there I circled several blocks till I was behind the lofts. The shadows were thick, and I moved quickly through them, looking for another way inside. Found it when I spied a partially rolled-up garage door hidden behind a semitrailer.

I hesitated, glancing up. There were no windows on this side of the building, no way she could observe me. After taking my .357 from my bag, I dropped down and crawled under the door.

The garage was dank and cold; a faint stripe of light seeped under a door at its far side. I moved toward it quietly, one hand in front of me, the other on the gun. Twice I bumped into concrete support pillars, but by the time I reached the door my eyes had adjusted to the darkness enough that I could make out a stack of Sheetrock leaning against the wall to its left. I grasped the knob and inched the door open.

A hallway, lighted for security purposes. Doors to what must be long, narrow loft spaces stood open on either side. I listened, heard nothing. There was a familiar scent in the air, though—Dark Secrets.

A sudden noise made me shut the door and flatten against the Sheetrock. Then I identified the noise: an elevator, at the extreme end of the hall. Going up.

I slipped into the hall, moved toward the elevator. Reached it in time to see the lighted numbers stop at three. No sound in the spaces around me, and the scent of her perfume was now dissipating. She was up there, all right—but doing what?

Laying a trap?

I went back down the hall and located the inside staircase; a door next to it led to a closet containing the circuit breakers. I went in there and flipped the ones for the hallways and the elevator. Then I climbed the stairs.

On the third floor I waited by the stairway till my eyes adjusted. Cold up there, and clammy. Smells of fresh lumber—and Dark Secrets.

Soon I could make out shapes: narrow rectangular windows a few shades lighter than the blackness around them; more concrete support pillars. None of the walls had been finished; the entire floor was a maze of wood framing and copper piping. Electrical conduit snaked between the studs, and underfoot was uneven concrete, cracked and pitted. Surely a woman's shape would stand out among these sharp angles.

I listened for a telltale sound, heard nothing. Narrowed my eyes, waiting for some sort of motion. She didn't move. She didn't even seem to breathe.

Finally I began to slip through the maze, gun extended in both hands. She gave no reaction to me showing myself; the element of surprise hadn't worked. I'd have to flush her out—

Sudden movement and sound behind me. I whirled. A figure ran up the stairs and a door slammed.

On the roof. So she was going to play a cat-and-mouse game. It was a game I knew how to play too.

I crept up the stairs to the roof, opened the door a crack. The night was reasonably clear for a change, with high scattered clouds and a bright moon. By its light I saw a raised area floored in iron mesh, with a huge kettle-type barbecue in its center—the so-called roof garden that ads for the lofts boasted of. A step down was the composition-covered roof itself, but the elevator housing blocked most of it from my view.

She was somewhere down there. I'd wait her out till dawn, if necessary. Eventually she'd have to show herself—

"So how am I doing, McCone?"

The voice came from behind the elevator housing, loud and demanding.

I drew back into the stairwell.

"I'm good, aren't I? Good as you. Maybe better."

I couldn't tell a thing about her normal speaking voice; the shouting would distort that.

"*Lots* better!"

A chill shot along my spine. Because as soon as I heard those words I realized what they meant.

She'd set this up knowing full well I wouldn't believe it was Rae calling me. And she'd known I'd come anyway. Somehow she'd become so intimately attuned to the way my mind worked that she'd known exactly what I'd do.

Well, I still had the advantage; I was at the top of the stairs, armed. And I'd disabled the elevator.

I shoved the door farther open and yelled, "All right! You got me here. Let's have this out—now!"

Amused laughter.

"The elevator's out of commission. There's no way off this roof except through this door, and I'm prepared to wait you out."

Silence.

"You're in a no-win situation. Come on out."

No response.

Then I heard a scuffling noise at the far side of the roof. More laughter, as if I'd told her a good joke—and coming now from below. I pushed through the door, skirted the elevator housing; behind it a ramp led down to a level midway between the roof and the third story. And on its inside wall a door was swinging shut.

Dammit, I'd bought into her entire plan! She'd led me all over this building as if I were on a leash. The woman was a lot smarter than I'd given her credit for.

So put yourself inside *her* head, McCone. What will she do now?

Go around to the other staircase and come after me?

No, she doesn't want a direct confrontation—at least, not yet.

Simply leave, having had her fun for tonight?

Not that, either . . .

"Oh, God!"

I ran down the stairway, taking the steps two at a time. The building's security alarm sounded as I reached the second-story landing. Panting, heart pounding, I got to the ground floor just as the front door slammed. I skidded around, wrenched the closet door open, hit the breaker for the alarm. The deafening noise stopped instantly.

But I'd worked in security; it wouldn't take long for whatever company monitored this building to arrive to investigate what they'd assume was a malfunction.

I rushed through the garage, slid under the partly raised door, and ran down the alleyway to Main Street.

When I got to my car I found a piece of legal paper tucked under its windshield wiper. Printed on it in block letters was a single sentence: SO WHAT MAKES YOU THINK YOU'RE SO GOOD?

Tonight while other people sleep, I pace. To the front parlor, to the sitting room, to the kitchen, and back again. The house is quiet, too quiet. The cats are awake, wary, feeling my tension. I haven't spoken with Hy in nearly a week, and I sense our connection becoming staticky—emotional static, both his and mine.

The woman even guessed where I would park my car. She's smart, very smart. She's tapped into my mental processes, my reactions, my strengths and flaws. She's been in this house, maybe at the pier, too. I'll have to have both places swept for bugs, get the security code here changed, change the code for my cell phone. I've already spent an inordinate amount of time canceling credit cards and requesting new ones. And then there's all this unwanted merchandise . . .

God, I don't need this! My life is totally disrupted. My identity's being stolen from me.

Identity. What is it, anyway? A name? A physical appearance? An address, phone number, and all the other numerical codes that allow us to function in contemporary society? A profession? An avocation? A personal history? A series of connections to fellow human beings?

Identity is the inner you, the unique way you think and act and respond. When a stranger has such a strong grasp of those things that she can manipulate you, you're losing your absolute essence. Your soul.

Yes, that's what she's doing. She's trying to steal my soul.

Saturday

OPEN TODAY, 10–4: LOFT LIVING AT ITS FINEST

The banner hung limp across the facade of the old warehouse; the building looked as dingy and gray as the sky. I pushed through its door and turned left into a makeshift sales office where three men in suits stood talking and drinking coffee. One put down his cup on a folding table stacked with brochures and came forward.

"Welcome to Vintage Lofts," he said, extending a business card. "Are you familiar with the concept of live-work space?"

"Yes, I am." And he wouldn't be happy if I voiced my opinion. The loft concept has always struck me as a colossal real-estate scam. You pay upwards of two hundred thousand for a relatively small space equipped with nothing more than piping for the plumbing—whose location locks you into a limited number of floor plans—and then either finish it yourself or pay somebody else to do so. And the developers, who have probably bought the property cheap, walk away with huge profits.

The salesman offered a price list. "As you can see, we've

sold a number of units already, but some are still available on every floor."

I scanned the sheet. The third-story units ran close to three hundred thousand. "These top-floor units," I said, "do they have views?"

"Well, not in the sense of bay vistas, if that's what you have in mind. But their windows are large, and the rear units have skylights."

They'd *need* skylights; there were no windows at all at the rear. "And how many of them are left?"

"Ah, most of them, actually."

Meaning the people who'd looked at them weren't as gullible as the developer had hoped. "I'd like to take a look around up there."

"Certainly. The entire building's open today. Just take the elevator and all the time you need. And don't forget to check out our roof garden!"

I intended to.

The third story was shadowy, even with daylight filtering through the windows and skylights. Building supplies were piled near the elevator, but a thick layer of dust lay over them, and the place had an abandoned feel about it. Having both re-modeled and added on to my house, I had a fairly good sense of how construction projects come together, but I couldn't vi-sualize what this one would look like when completed. Not that I cared; I was here to search for some tangible trace of the woman who had led me on a cat-and-mouse chase through this building last night.

I took out my flashlight and systematically began prowling around. Anything at all—a lost button, a discarded tissue—would enable me to believe that the woman was not as clever as I imagined, but I came away empty handed. Next I went to the roof, stepped off the iron-mesh area, and checked behind the elevator shaft. I found two cigarette butts, but I doubted they were hers; there hadn't been any tobacco odor in the air, either here or at my house after Sunday night's intrusion.

When I went downstairs the salesman accosted me, looking hopeful. "What do you think of the building?"

"Very interesting."

"I have a list of contractors we recommend for the finish work—unless, of course, you plan to do it yourself."

Contractors who undoubtedly gave kickbacks. "Actually, I'd like to see a list of people who have already purchased units. Would that be possible?"

"Uh, I'm sorry. That's confidential information."

Bullshit. It was a matter of public record. "The reason I ask, a couple of acquaintances of mine mentioned buying into a place that sounded like this. They had very good things to say about the management company and the contractors."

"If you could give me their names, I can check."

"One's Sharon McCone. The other's . . . Sue Macmillan."

He went to the table and opened a loose-leaf notebook that was lying there. "No, neither has purchased a unit."

"I'm almost certain Sue did. Let me describe her: she's got honey-blond hair, features that I guess you could describe as cute, is about my height and weight."

"Doesn't ring a bell." Turning to the other salesmen, he asked, "Either of you guys close a deal with somebody like that?"

One shook his head. The other said, "If I had, I'd've asked her for a date."

I said, "Are you three the only salespeople?"

"That's right. And we'll be happy to answer any further questions you might have."

Any questions except the important one: How had the woman gained access to the building? The same way I did, or . . . ?

It was only one o'clock, but before I visited Vintage Lofts I'd sifted to no good result through the garbage I'd snatched from the alley the night before; arranged for RKI to sweep my home and offices for bugs; requested that my cell-phone code

be changed; gone to the post office to send back the unwanted
mail-order items; stopped by Nell Loomis's studio and found
her not there again; and dropped off the MG for servicing. It
wouldn't be ready till three, so I decided to go to the pier and
clear up some remaining paperwork—or maybe just sit and
think.

When I got there, I was surprised to see Mick's new mo-
torcycle parked at the foot of our stairs. The sleek black
Yamaha was a coming-of-age statement of sorts, as Charlene
and Ricky had adamantly refused to buy him one for his high
school graduation present, and Mick loved it almost as much
as his PowerBook. My sister was still upset about him buying
it—somehow she blamed me, presumably for paying him a
good enough salary that he could afford it—but once Mick
passed the appropriate safety courses, Ricky had conceded it
was good transportation. And I'd benefited from the purchase,
because the prospect of riding the bike the few blocks down
the Embarcadero from the condo he leased had made him my
most prompt employee.

When I tapped on his office door, my nephew called, "Friend
or foe?" without taking his eyes off the computer screen.

"Depends on how you feel about taking on some extra
work on a Saturday."

"Oh, hell, I thought you were Sweet Charlotte."

"Nope, it's just me—about to complicate your life. What're
you working on, that hidden-assets case?"

"Yeah, I've about got it wrapped up. We'll be going to the
Boondocks for lunch on Monday."

"Great. I love their steak sandwiches. Let's take Charlotte
along. Speaking of her, where is she while you're slaving
away?"

"Hot on the trail of a client who's weird."

"Jeffrey Stoddard. She tell you what's wrong with him?"

"Nope." Mick swiveled to face me, his face earnest and
somewhat perplexed. "You know, when I first came to work
for you, I thought the business was glamorous and cool, but I

never figured out till recently how . . . addicting it is. I mean, Lottie and I could be snuggled up in bed watching rotten Saturday-afternoon horror movies on TV and eating popcorn right now. But instead I'm ruining my eyesight in this stuffy office and she's off God knows where in the rain."

"And you both love it."

"So do you, or you wouldn't be here."

"Well, Hy's not in town, so snuggling isn't an option. You want to tell me what you've got?" I motioned at the computer.

"Documentation of money in a tax-dodge account in the Caymans—in the guy's girlfriend's name. And a down payment on a condo on Seven Mile Beach on Grand Cayman—again in the babe's name."

"You can prove that the funds moved from his account to hers?"

"I can prove it—thanks to Lottie. She's got contacts at financial institutions all over the place."

"Then we'll definitely take her along to lunch. And I'll see your report on Monday. In the meantime, d'you want to take on something else?"

"Sure, what?"

"The Vintage Lofts building on Beale Street. I need to get as many particulars as possible on each person who's bought a unit there."

"Easy. I'll do a search by site address and have it to you within the hour. Which case file do I allocate the time to?"

"None. This is personal."

He raised an eyebrow.

"And private."

Seventeen people had been foolish enough to purchase live-work units at the lofts; nine were women, and their names were not familiar to me. The database gave their current addresses, but three were post office boxes, and it would take time to check out the remaining six for resemblance to the woman. Time, and transportation.

At a little before three I asked Mick to drop me off at All-Foreign Motors in the Mission district. Eager to show off his bike, which I'd yet to be given a ride on, he agreed, but drove there with the kind of exaggerated caution he'd have employed if it was my mother on the seat behind him. I'd have liked to think this was because he wanted to protect the one who signed his paychecks, but I suspected otherwise and kept wishing he'd do something outrageous to reassure me he didn't consider me that old and fragile.

Bennie, my regular mechanic, was just closing the MG's hood when I stepped into the garage. "Hey, Sharon," he said, "that rebuilt engine's in great shape. Was worth the money, even though you accused us of highway robbery."

He'd rebuilt the engine years ago, before I'd even met Hy. "You're never going to let me forget that comment, are you?"

"Nope. I'm guilt-tripping you into bringing it back to us."

"So what's the damage this time?"

He wiped his hands on his coveralls, went to the computer, and started printing out my invoice. "My advice to you is to keep the car a long time, even do another rebuild if you've got to. It's damn near a classic."

I eyed the MG thoughtfully. "I don't know, Bennie. When it starts to go again, a new car might be in order."

Shock furrowed his chocolate-colored face. "No way!"

"Well, by then it might be time." I took the sheet he ripped from the printer and scanned it. Shuddered dramatically.

"It's never time to get rid of a beautiful machine like that," he insisted. "Besides, what would you buy to replace it? One of those nothing Japanese models that all look alike?"

"I haven't gotten that far in my thinking yet." I handed him my American Express card—the only one I was able to use till the new Visa and MasterCard were issued; fortunately, I hadn't yet charged anything on it this year, so there wasn't a receipt bearing its number in my home-office desk.

Bennie slid the card through the machine. "You'd have to

look pretty hard to come up with a car that can hold a candle to the MG. I don't know, though—how about a Porsche?"

"God, no! Rae calls them asshole-creating machines, and she ought to know. Both she and Ricky turn into maniacs behind the wheel of his."

"Speaking of Rae, she hasn't brought the Ramblin' Wreck in lately." Rae's former car, an ancient Rambler American, was one of the few Detroit models Bennie would work on.

"The Wreck has gone to the big auto-salvage yard in the sky. She's driving a Miata now. And getting married."

"Well, tell her congrats, and to skip the dealer servicing on the new car. Miatas and me get on just fine." He frowned at the credit-card machine. "What the hell? Your card's been refused."

"What? Why?"

"It's been canceled."

Damn her! How had she managed that? Oh, right—the folder that had come when the new card was issued, bearing instructions about what to do if it was lost or stolen; that was in the desk at home.

"You got another card?" Bennie asked.

"No, I . . . lost my wallet, and I'm waiting for new ones. I'll write you a check."

"Hey, don't bother. Just bring the new card in when it comes, and I'll run it through. And do me a favor? Keep the MG."

Nell Loomis looked the same as the last time I'd seen her: close-cropped carrot-colored hair, outrageous green eye shadow, and ratty jeans and T-shirt with a rubber darkroom apron over them. At least that was my impression until I noticed she'd gotten her nose pierced a few times and had a small tattoo of a vulture on her right forearm.

She caught me looking at the vulture and said, "So I like them. They're very patient birds. D'you want to come in or just stand there staring, McCone?"

Her disposition hadn't improved with time, but then, I hadn't expected it to.

She led me into her cluttered studio: a large white room with a long light table and a seating area in one corner. Light boxes and rolled-up backdrops and props for the magazine ads that she shot here lined the walls. This week, apparently, the subject was cat food, specifically a brand called Royal Repast.

"Fuckin' critters," Loomis said, motioning at the stacks of cans as we sat down on her shabby sofa.

"Cats?"

"Not all cats—I've got three at home myself—just Royal Repast's pampered darlings. Four of the most spoiled-rotten animals I've ever encountered—including humans. They don't *like* Royal Repast. They're junkies."

"Junkies?"

"Catnip junkies. The food's gotta be sprinkled with the stuff before they'll nibble at it. And then they get so stoned they fall asleep real fast. It's taking an eternity for this shoot. So what the hell d'you want after all this time? Information, I suppose."

"Right."

"You paying?"

"Of course."

"How much?"

"Twenty."

"Sixty."

"Forty."

"Done."

"What d'you want to know?"

"The olive-drab door three to your right—who rents the place?"

Her face went very still. "What're you messing with, Mc-Cone?"

"Why?"

"Why?"

"I don't understand."

"Smart woman like you? I read the papers. Don't think I haven't kept up with you."

"Then you know I can't talk about my cases or clients. Who rents that place, Loomis?"

". . . The guy's name is Sandy Coughlin, and he's into a lot of things."

"Such as?"

"Things that kill people. Explosives, guns—you know."

"Drugs?"

"Nope, Sandy's strictly a shoot-'em-up, blow-'em-up kind of guy."

"How would somebody go about making a connection with him?"

"Come on, McCone! You know how to do that."

"No, I meant how would the average person go about it?"

"Well, he wouldn't walk up and knock on that door. Coughlin's paranoid, and his . . . clients come recommended."

"By . . . ?"

She examined her ragged fingernails for a moment. "This is all rumor, of course, but I've heard that he caters to militant factions."

"Left or right?"

"Doesn't matter. He's what my dad used to call a shit-disturber. Likes to see people riled up and mean. That fire-bombing of the abortion clinic last month? They say the explosives came from Sandy. A couple of the Saturday night specials used to kill that Russian refugee family in the Richmond might've been his. And so it goes."

"He makes a profit and foments divisiveness and hatred as a by-product."

"You got it. Ol' Sandy enjoys manipulating from behind the scenes and then watching innocent people get hurt or die."

Oh, Ted, what's going on with you? *What?*

Saturday Night

Six addresses of women who had bought into Vintage Lofts and thus would have access to the premises. Three of them not home. When I'd dropped in on the others, in the guise of an insurance investigator, I'd found that none bore the slightest resemblance to me or to any of the descriptions of my impostor. Mick was working on getting street addresses for the ones with post office boxes, and I'd check out the others when time allowed, but I really didn't hold much hope for this line of investigation. In fact, I was beginning to suspect I'd again been made victim of a clever plan devised by someone who had figured out how my mind functioned.

Fruitless labor, but at least it had filled a few hours of my otherwise empty Saturday night. I'd run no surveillance on Ted, as Neal had told me they were staying in—something he didn't sound happy about. I had nothing going on socially; all my friends were either out of town or had plans that didn't include me. Hy hadn't called; it was as if he'd been swallowed up by the Argentinian jungle. Hell, I couldn't even fret about being spied on or having my home invaded by a crazy woman; RKI had discovered and removed bugs there—but not at the pier—and also changed the alarm system's security code.

Normally I'm not a person who feels at loose ends. I'm out-going, but I also treasure my private time. I love to read, I am fond of music and films, and I'm a consummate putterer. Left to my own devices, I can amuse myself for days at a stretch. And I like being alone at home, wrapped in the illusion that it's the one place where nobody can get at me. But tonight . . . well, I was twitchy and bored.

I checked the clock on the VCR. Nearly midnight, so why wasn't I tired? I stared at the phone. Why didn't Hy call? True, I'd been unavailable much of the day, owing to a dead cell-phone battery that was still recharging, but why hadn't he left messages on the home and office machines? When we were separated we tried to keep in touch as frequently as pos-sible, and he'd have been sure to call when he got my mes-sage. *If* he got my message. Unless . . .

No, I wasn't going to go there. This was a routine fact-finding trip, not a crisis situation. Unless . . .

No, McCone. Get back to the problems you can—maybe—do something about.

I surveyed the scattered sheets of legal paper on which I'd been attempting to analyze both the problem with Ted and my problem with the impostor, and felt an overwhelming sense of defeat. I was too close to the Ted situation, too involved in my own. On Monday I'd turn them over to a fellow investigator whom I trusted—

The phone rang. Hy, at last! I snatched up the receiver.

"Shar?" Neal's voice, ragged and breathless.

"What? What is it?"

"We need you here. There's been a shooting—"

In the background Ted said something indistinguishable.

"Shooting? Is anybody hurt?"

"No, nothing like that. But I—"

Ted said, "Dammit, give me that phone!"

I asked, "Have you called the police?"

"That wasn't necessary, but—"

"Give it to me!"

There were sounds of a struggle, and the connection was severed.

No police cars in Plum Alley. No crowds on the sidewalk. Whatever had happened, it wasn't critical.

I ran along the sidewalk from where I'd wedged the car on Montgomery, nearly tripping over a low-slung bassett hound that a man was walking. After I let myself into the building with Neal's key, I took the stairs rather than waiting for the elevator. Bursting through the fire door on the third floor, I came face to face with Ted. His lips were bloodless, and his eyes glowed hot with rage.

"Go home, Shar," he said. "You've got no business being here. You'll jeopardize everything."

"Jeopardize what? *What?*"

"Neal had no right to call you. Go home!"

Now Neal came out of the apartment, equally enraged. "I had every right to call her, you lunatic! Better Shar than the cops. You're damned lucky nobody phoned 911."

A door was being unlocked down the hall—someone bothered by the commotion. Ted shoved Neal and me into the apartment and slammed its door.

"All right," I said, "what's going on here?"

Ted turned, headed down the hallway. By the time Neal and I caught up, he was in the kitchen, pouring brandy into a snifter. Behind me, Neal said, "That's not the solution, Ted."

"Shut up."

I considered the situation: Neal was wearing a bathrobe, but Ted was fully dressed. The brandy bottle and snifter had been sitting on the kitchen counter, and in the living room the TV was tuned low to a black-and-white movie. And on the coffee table lay a handgun.

I looked questioningly at Neal. He jerked his head at the wall of glass overlooking the bayside deck. There was a bullet hole in one of the doors, surrounded by a web of cracks.

Ted still had his back to us, was pouring more brandy. I

went over and examined the gun. Twenty-two caliber RG-14, serial number intact, but it wouldn't be registered to Ted. "Well," I said, not bothering to keep the anger and sarcasm out of my voice, "what we've got here is a classic Saturday night special. And guess what, folks? It's Saturday night!"

"What we've got here is a real problem," Neal said. "As well as a costly repair job."

Ted remained silent.

"What the hell were you thinking," I asked him, "fooling around with a gun in your condition?"

He mumbled something.

"What?"

"I said, you don't know the slightest thing about my condition. So shut the fuck up and go home!"

That did it. I stalked over there, picked up the bottle, and set it well out of his reach. Then I tried to wrest the snifter from his fingers; he resisted, pulled back, and it flew from his hand and smashed on the tiles.

He looked down at the spilled liquid and shards of glass, then back up at me. When I saw his eyes I realized he wasn't drunk; probably he was drinking the brandy to get his anger under control. But now it showed white-hot.

"What were you shooting at?" I asked.

"Somebody was on the balcony."

"Who?"

"I couldn't tell."

I went over there and opened the undamaged door. An Adirondack chair was overturned and some barbecue tools were scattered on the deck. I crossed to the railing and looked down into the alley. No one, but the bottom section of the fire escape that scaled the wall beside the balcony had been lowered to the ground.

Ted was watching me, his rage still glowing bright. I went back inside. "Did the person try to enter the apartment?"

"No, he didn't have a chance."

"You shot at him with an unregistered gun when he hadn't yet attempted to break and enter?"

"The guy was on our *balcony*, for Christ's sake! Don't I have a right to defend our home?"

"I'm with you on that, philosophically. The law says differently. And, as I recall, you've never fired a gun before—which makes for a very dangerous situation."

"I can fire it well enough."

"Really?" I gestured at the glass door. "*This* is what Sandy Coughlin's twenty-minute course in responsible firearms ownership got you?"

Behind me Neal made a peculiar sound. Ted's face froze. After a moment he asked, "How do you know about Sandy Coughlin?"

Bad slip, McCone! "I have my sources."

But he'd figured it out. "You've been following me," he said flatly. He turned to Neal. "You got her to spy on me, didn't you?"

Neal was silent, his face etched into lines of helplessness and despair.

"You *did*, damn you!"

"Okay, yeah, I did! The way *you've* been spying on *me!*"

Ted recoiled as if Neal had struck him. He turned away, braced his hands on the countertop, hung his head. His labored breathing was loud in the silence that followed Neal's pronouncement.

Neal added, "You ever hear of the right to privacy?"

"You ever hear of a rock and a hard place?"

"What does that—"

"I want both of you out of here—now."

"Ted—" I began.

"Especially you. Get out of here, before you do any more damage. And, Neal, go with her. Please."

I glanced at Neal. He shrugged and went upstairs to dress. I crossed the living room, put the .22 into my purse, and headed for the door.

"Cooling-off period," Neal said when he joined me in the hall. "Let's go someplace, talk."

Neal knew a small, quiet Italian bar on Green Street in nearby North Beach, so we went there and ordered grappa. Only a few other patrons sat at the small tables, and the faces that I glimpsed in the light from candles in wax-covered Chianti bottles were weary. Saturday night winding down and, at least in our case, a good thing.

We sat in silence till we'd been served. Then Neal said, "Jesus, I feel terrible."

"Me too. It's like he's banished us from his life."

"Maybe he has."

"I can't believe that." I put my hand on his arm. After a moment I said, "When I made that slip about Sandy Coughlin, you sounded as though you know him."

"Slightly. Somebody brought him to a dinner party we were at a while back. Nobody was happy about that, and it made for a short evening."

"But Ted remembered him when he wanted to buy a gun."

"A gun. Christ! He doesn't even know how to shoot."

"He's proved that, and his career as a marksman is over; I've got the twenty-two."

"He can always buy another."

"That he can." I sipped the strong brandy.

Neal pressed a hand to his forehead, leaned his elbow on the table. His face looked tired and deeply lined, even in the gentling candlelight; he seemed far older than his forty-five years. "Shar," he said, "what d'you suppose he meant by 'between a rock and a hard place'?"

"I've been trying to figure that out, but I can't seem to figure out *anything* about Ted these days."

"Me either. And you know what? Maybe I've had enough of trying to understand him."

"Neal, you're upset and tired and hurt. Don't make any sudden decisions."

"No, I mean it. I've got troubles of my own, financial problems with the bookstore. I don't think I can deal with Ted's as well—particularly when he won't tell me what they are!"

"As you said, a cooling-off period's in order. You're welcome to my guest room."

"I'll take you up on that." He punched my arm lightly. "Thanks, buddy."

I'd already gotten Neal settled into the guest room before I noticed the light blinking on my answering machine. Hy, I thought, and pressed the play button.

The first message was from Ted. In restrained tones he said that he hoped Neal was staying at my house, and would I please leave a message on his machine that we were both okay? He'd sleep better knowing that.

Odd, I thought, stopping the tape. Why wouldn't we be okay? Was someone threatening Ted, holding the safety or lives of his loved ones over his head? Was that why he wouldn't confide in us?

For a moment I considered calling him and demanding the truth. But he'd indicated he wouldn't be answering the phone, and besides, I was so tired that my mind wasn't functioning sharply. Better to talk tomorrow. I dialed, left the message he'd requested, adding, "Sleep well, guy." Then I pressed the play button for my second call.

"Sharon, Gage Renshaw. Sorry to phone at this hour, but would you get back to me at our La Jolla office? Any time, no matter how late. I'll be here all night."

I felt as if I'd been showered with ice water. Gage Renshaw was one of Hy's partners in RKI; he would never call me late at night unless something very bad had happened. I punched out the number of their headquarters with trembling fingers. The night operator was expecting my call and put me through immediately.

"Before you say anything," Gage told me, "let me emphasize that Hy's okay."

"What's happened? Where is he?"

"We have a hostage situation with one of our South American clients. Hy's handling it."

"What kind of situation? Where?"

"You know I can't tell you that."

"Well, what *can* you tell me?"

"That he's okay and will be in touch as soon as it's resolved. Actually, he's more concerned about you; he's left a number of messages on your machine in the past few days, and you haven't returned his calls."

"Messages? What messages?"

"I don't know how many or when, but enough to make him worry."

"I don't understand— Oh!"

"Sharon?"

"Nothing." My impostor had obviously found the remote access code for both my home and office machines, where they were noted in the Rolodex. Easy for her to listen to and then erase any number of messages. I began to shake with anger. "Gage, I need to talk with Hy."

"I can't put you in touch."

"Then tell him to call me."

"I'll tell him you're okay."

"This isn't right!"

"No, what's not right is what's going on down there. This is an extremely critical situation, and I'm not going to jeopardize it by allowing Ripinsky to become involved in whatever's bothering you as well."

"Dammit, Gage—"

"Sharon." There was a softness in his voice that I'd never heard before. "You're one of us, in a sense. You can hold it together till the situation's resolved."

"Can I?"

"Yes. I've seen you hold it together under far worse conditions. And I'll be in touch with an update as soon as I've got one." Having made one small concession to humane behavior, Gage hung up on me.

I gripped the receiver, stared fixedly at a crack in the wall. Tried to repair my frayed connection to Hy. It still held, but for how long?

Things were very bad for him—I could feel that. Could he feel how bad things were for me? And if so, would the knowledge distract him, cause him to make an error that might prove fatal?

It was the first time I'd ever regretted the intuitive emotional bond between us.

Sunday

When I wandered into the kitchen at close to eleven the next morning, I found a note from Neal propped against the coffeemaker: "I'm going away for a few days to think things through. Will be in touch when I get back."

I wondered if he'd informed Ted of his decision. Probably not; last night he'd said he wasn't sure he could deal with Ted's problems on top of his own, so he wouldn't have taken the chance of provoking yet another emotional scene.

The coffeemaker's light was on, the carafe full. Thank you, Neal. I poured a mugful, went to the sitting room, and found the Sunday paper lying on the couch. Thanks again.

MAYOR, ASIAN LEADER CLASH AT
SUNSET COMMUNITY MEETING

Good. Real good.

HATE CRIMES ON RISE NATIONWIDE

Now, why didn't that surprise me?

CELLULAR PHONE CLONING PREVALENT IN BAY AREA

Enough, already! I tossed the front section on the floor and went to take my shower.

"Hey, Shar, how y'doing?" Craig Morland sounded excessively cheerful—and no wonder. He and Homicide Inspector Adah Joslyn were off this afternoon on a two-week vacation to Mexico before he came to work for me.

"I'm okay," I said. "You all packed?"

"Packed and ready."

"Is Adah there?"

"Yeah, but she's busy right now—feeding Charley." Charley was Adah's enormous, gluttonous white cat; I fully expected him to explode someday.

"Cat's a basket case, right?"

"Ever since he saw the suitcases. Of course, that doesn't prevent him from tearing into his steak."

"Steak?"

"You got it. Here's Adah."

"You're feeding the cat steak," I said accusingly.

"Don't start, McCone. It's left over from last night's dinner."

"And if there hadn't been any leftovers you'd be giving him hamburger."

"Albacore tuna. So why'd you call? Not just to wish us a safe journey, I suppose."

"No, I need a favor."

"It'd better be a fast favor; I've got to get down there, work on my tan." It was a joke; Adah was half Jewish, half black, with flawless honey-brown skin.

"You know anybody at the department who's an expert on stalkers?"

"Sure. Stacey Nizibian. Girl's got an M.A. in psychology from the University of Michigan, and all that book learning hasn't ruined her yet."

"I need to talk with her."

"No problem, I can set something up." She paused. "McCone, is somebody hassling you?"

"No, it's for a case I'm working on."

"Client report the incidents to us?"

"They're on file."

"Well, I'll call Stace, get back to you. You free this afternoon?"

"Of course. *I'm* not the one who's taking off for a tropical paradise."

"No, and you sure are sucking sour grapes. Get off my phone and I'll call you back in a few minutes."

Stacey Nizibian was waiting for me at a table next to the rain-streaked front window of Lavender Blue Deli Deli on Twenty-fourth Street. The overly cute name—one of many along Noe Valley's main shopping strip—had always put me off, but I loved their Brie and Black Forest ham sandwiches. It turned out Stacey did too; she ordered one with a beer while I studied the wine list. A slender woman wearing jeans that fit like a second skin, she apparently had as efficient a metabolic system as I.

"So," she said, running long fingers through her mop of dark brown curls, "Adah tells me you want to know about stalkers."

"Specifically, women who stalk women."

"Lesbian client?"

"Not a client—me." As Nizibian's face registered concern, I explained what had been going on. "I have no idea who this woman is, so any insight you can give me into that type of behavior will help."

She considered while the waitress delivered our drinks, took a sip before she replied. "Well, there're profiles, of course, but every case deviates from them in some way. Before we talk about the stalker, though, let's talk about you. How're you doing?"

"Not too well. I feel frustrated. Helpless. Angry. Afraid of what she's going to do next. Afraid of what damage she's already done me. I'm distracted a lot of the time and not sleeping well. I have bizarre dreams. And there's another situation that's keeping me isolated from the one person I can talk openly with about this."

"You're not doing too badly talking with me."

I laughed. "No, and it feels damned good."

"Well, feel free to call me any time. And I'll check with Greg Marcus about the report he filed. Now, about stalkers: basically you've got four different categories—those where the victims are celebrities, domestic partners, casual acquaintances, or random targets."

I was all too familiar with celebrity stalking; it had happened to Ricky. And I'd seen enough terrified wives, husbands, and lovers pass through my office door to understand the domestic variety. "I'm pretty sure the woman is a casual acquaintance or someone who chose me at random."

Nizibian shook her head. "Being stalked is always a nightmarish experience, but not knowing who's doing it or why is the absolute worst. A random stalker sees you someplace—maybe on the street—and follows you, finds out where you live and work. Then he or she begins a pattern of repeated harassment. You don't know what you've done to attract the person's attention, but suddenly you're a target."

"And a casual acquaintance?"

"The key word is 'casual.' The stalker could be a co-worker, somebody you met briefly at a party, or a clerk in a store where you shop. In short, anybody. Your contact with him or her is glancing; you may have forgotten all about it. But the stalker hasn't, and pretty soon you're getting plenty of reminders."

"Does this type of stalker typically reveal herself to her victim?"

"Some do, some don't."

"And is the situation likely to end in harm to the victim—beyond the obvious psychological harm, I mean?"

"It can. This kind of stalking is simple obsessional behavior that's usually triggered by a specific event. The stalker perceives the relationship with the victim as having deteriorated—even though there really was no relationship—or feels mistreated in some way. He or she then begins to vacillate between hatred and deep attachment to or love for the victim, and as his advances are rebuffed the stalking escalates to a dangerous level."

Our sandwiches arrived. I looked at mine, realized I'd lost my appetite. My stomach was tightly knotted, and my throat felt closed up.

"You say psychologists have developed profiles of stalkers."

"They've compiled a list of what we call high-risk traits— certain behavior patterns that lead you to believe stalking potential exists. Superficial charm, lack of empathy for others, lack of social conscience. Stalkers are usually sly and manipulative. Can talk you into anything. If you confront them, they'll claim there's nothing wrong with their behavior and they shouldn't be punished for it."

"Sociopaths, then."

"Well, some. Those who suffer from a love-obsessional delusion may also suffer from other delusional disorders— schizophrenia, for example. Others are simply fanatics."

And there was no way of knowing which the woman was. "Any other significant traits?"

"They're very cool in situations that would have you or me climbing the walls. Untruthful—that goes without saying. They lack remorse. Can't sustain relationships. Want instant gratification. Can tip over into irrational or destructive behavior. And they want it all but make no effort to establish and work toward long-term goals."

"Exactly what do they hope to gain by stalking?"

"The victims' attention or love. In many cases, they want their approval."

I thought of what the woman had called to me on the roof the other night: *How am I doing, McCone? I'm good, aren't I?* Hadn't that indicated that in a skewed way she wanted me to approve of her?

After a moment I realized Nizibian was watching me analytically. "I'm okay, really," I said. "In many ways I'm better equipped to deal with this kind of situation than your average person."

"Are you? I'm not sure I would be. There are counseling groups, you know. I could put you in touch—"

"Thanks, but no thanks. I have trouble with groups like that—and counselors."

"Oh?"

"Uh-huh." I grinned wryly. "I went to a psychologist once, about some problems I was having in college. And I . . . lied to her, made things sound better than they were. The poor woman couldn't figure out why I was there in the first place."

Nizibian smiled too. "It happens. Some people are better off coping in their own way."

I steered the conversation away from myself. "What can you tell me about the anti-stalking laws?"

"I can give you an overview of California's legislation. We were the first state to recognize stalking as a crime, you know."

"It's a felony?"

"A first offense can be a misdemeanor, but that's left to the discretion of the D.A. Basically the law defines stalking as willful, malicious, and repeated following or harassing. The pattern of conduct doesn't have to carry an actual threat to the victim; an implied threat causing the victim substantial emotional distress is enough. And the law covers the victim's immediate family as well, since many stalkers threaten relatives."

"I've heard that restraining orders seldom stop these people. Does incarceration do any good?"

Nizibian smiled grimly. "Well, let's see what you think. One provision of the law is that the Department of Corrections is required to notify the victim, the family members, and any witnesses to the stalking no less than fifteen days before the release of the prisoner. And any information relating to those parties and their current whereabouts is to be kept confidential—from the parolee and anyone connected with him."

"So basically the law recognizes that punishment isn't a deterrent to stalkers. The end result of becoming one of their victims is usually either physical harm or a lifetime of fear."

I hadn't been able to keep the emotion out of my voice, and Nizibian heard it. She looked pointedly at my half-eaten sandwich. "You sure you want to pass on those counseling referrals?"

I picked up the sandwich, took a deliberate bite. "If I change my mind, I'll call you."

"Call me anyway. You know, maybe you should back off, put the investigation in the hands of somebody else."

That was what I'd resolved to do last night, both with the Ted situation and with my own, but now I knew I couldn't. I wasn't made to give up—any more than I was made to see a counselor.

Stacey looked at her watch, and I signaled for the check. While the waitress was preparing it, I asked, "What would make a woman stalk another woman, assuming it's not a sexual obsession?"

"We've already mentioned one possibility: the stalker may want your approval. Say she admires you. She's fixated on you, and when the perceived slight or injury occurred, she began to alternate between envy and anger, and the need for attention."

"Does that account for her assuming my identity?"

"Possibly. She could have forged an identification with you that's gradually eroded the lines of separation. The thing you've got to remember about stalkers is that there's no predicting *what* they'll do." She hesitated, brow furrowed. "You know, if I were you, I'd try to isolate the event that triggered the stalking. When you've got that, you'll have most of your answers."

That was all very well and good, but if I couldn't isolate the woman, how could I possibly isolate the trigger?

Sunday Night

I've left the phone off the hook.

Hy won't call. I know that because I talked earlier with Gage Renshaw. No change in the situation in South America, he tells me, so I should just wait it out. Right, Gage, wait it out, as I have half a dozen times before, but then I was in solid shape, had a reserve of strength to draw on. And somehow I thought I could communicate that strength to Hy. But now—

No, I can't dwell on what might or might not be happening with him. If I do, I'll never make it through the night.

Those phone calls, over a dozen since nine o'clock. Always a hangup seconds after I answer. Ted, trying to make sure Neal's still staying with me, hoping he'll be the one to pick up? No, Ted left a message last night, he'd talk with me tonight. They've got to be from that woman.

That woman. I've heard the phrase used so many

times by clients whose husbands were seeing some-body else. Hell, once—long ago, when I was very young and foolish—I even heard it used in reference to me. But now it's taken on such a different, evil significance.

But what else can I call her? I don't have a name.

Call her the stalker. The impostor. The harasser.

No, none of those terms is right. For one thing, they're precise terms, put to people whose behavior, though bizarre, fits a recognizable pattern. This woman's all over the board.

They're also terms put to people whose behavior is subject to legal remedies.

What remedies are there when she eludes my identification?

What remedies are there when her behavior doesn't fit any of the profiles?

What remedies are there when she's gradually draining the life out of me and stealing my soul?

Monday

Ted didn't show up for work on Monday morning, but he called, speaking in a direct manner that failed to conceal an undertone of anxiety.

"Did Neal tell you where he was going?" he asked.

"Just out of town, to think things over."

"That's all he said in the message he left on our machine. Think, Shar—I need to reach him. Did he give you any hint at all?"

"No. He left a note and was gone by the time I got up."

"Damn!"

"Ted, are you ready to talk about your problem now?"

"No—especially not now. I'll explain when it's over. And I'm sorry I can't get in to work today. I'll try to make it tomorrow . . ." His voice trailed off, and he hung up.

I glared at the receiver, then slammed it into its cradle. Ted's refusal to take me into his confidence was wearing thin on me, and besides, I had work to do—

"That Jeffrey Stoddard? Is he a jerk or what!"

I looked up at Keim, who was standing in the doorway; even her curls seemed to bristle indignantly. "What'd you find out?"

"The past couple of weeks, whenever his fiancée's out of town, he's been shacked up *in their apartment* with another woman! Not only that, but he's been making gradual withdrawals from their bank accounts and liquidating other joint investments."

"He's a jerk, all right."

Keim began to pace around the office, waving her hands as she spoke. "My take on the situation is that he hired us to keep tabs on her in case she decided to come home unexpectedly. Why else would he want such frequent reports? Maybe he thought she'd concocted all this heavy business travel so she could catch him in the act."

"Seems an extreme and expensive measure."

"Well, sure, but I know if I were up to his kind of shenanigans, I'd be as nervous as a long-tailed cat in a room full of rockers."

"I take it you have solid evidence of his activities?"

"Lord, yes! A couple of the neighbors tipped me to the other woman. Stoddard tried to pass her off as his cousin, but neither of them bought it. As a rule, you don't get caught snuggling in the elevator with that close a relative. The situation interested them enough that they've been keeping a close eye on it. Since the live-in was off to L.A. again this morning, I decided to run a surveillance on the client; the other woman showed up fifteen minutes after the fiancée left, and after an interval long enough for some romantic fooling around, they paid visits to Wells Fargo bank and Charles Schwab."

I looked at my watch: eleven-twenty. The pair had had a busy morning. "I take it you've already spoken to your contacts at Wells and Schwab." When she'd worked for RKI—from whom, in Gage Renshaw's words, I'd stolen her—Keim had been a specialist in the financial area of corporate security.

"I sure have. The jackass has been bleeding joint accounts dry. My contacts wouldn't tell me where the funds're being transferred to, but I'd bet it's someplace similar to the institutions Mick's hidden-assets guy is patronizing. And get this: the happy couple's planning to make a move soon."

"Oh?"

"Yep. After they left Schwab, they went to a luggage store and bought a bunch of suitcases—big suitcases, like you'd use if you were clearing out everything of value in a household."

"And the live-in's out of town for how long on this trip?"

"Till Thursday."

"That gives them plenty of time. Unless, of course, we do something to stop them."

"But what? We can't call Stoddard's live-in and explain what he's up to. There's a confidentiality clause in our contract with him; he could sue us. Besides, legally he's done nothing wrong; the accounts are joint, only one signature required. If you ask me, the live-in's got two brain cells, and one's out looking for the other."

"Our contract with him is a worthless piece of paper as far as I'm concerned. He probably plans to stiff us for charges over and above the retainer."

"Still, we could get in a hell of a lot of trouble—"

"I know. Sit down. Let me think."

Keim flopped into a chair and stared out at the bay, her eyes still glittering with anger.

"Okay," I said after a moment, "how good an actor are you?"

She smiled knowingly and fluttered her lashes at me. "Why, honey, I can ham it up better'n a dance-hall nightingale."

"And Mick's inherited his daddy's showmanship. He'll be here with his report on the hidden-assets investigation soon; the three of us will have lunch at the Boondocks, and I'll tell you what we're going to do about Mr. Stoddard . . ."

I watched from the agency van while Mick conducted a ridiculously obvious surveillance across from Jeffrey Stoddard's Spanish-style apartment building on Greenwich Street in the bayside Marina district. He lurked behind a parked car, checked his watch, scribbled down notes, and exuded furtiveness. I would have known immediately that it was an act, but it seemed to put the people in apartment 10 on edge; in the hour since he'd been there the curtains had moved and two shadowy faces had looked out several times.

Now the building's door opened and Stoddard came out carrying a couple of suitcases. His eyes on Mick, he took the bags to a Blazer that was parked nearby and placed them inside. Mick nodded and ostentatiously made a note. Stoddard hurried back to his building.

A few minutes later Keim drove up and parked. She walked toward Stoddard's building, spotted Mick, and did a double take. Then she crossed the street and went up to him.

"Well, if it isn't my old buddy," she said loudly. "What're you doing here?"

One of the windows of apartment 10 opened a few inches.

Mick glanced around uneasily, said something to Keim in a whisper.

"Oh, who?" she asked.

Another whisper.

Keim whooped with laughter. That wasn't in the script; Mick must have said something risqué. "Oh, no, honey, you got it all wrong. That man's my client."

Mick shook his head and whispered some more.

"You're kidding me. Who hired you?"

"Can't say."

"Well, they must've been handing you a line of bullshit." Keim whirled and started toward the apartment building.

"Hey, where're you going?"

"To see my client, jackass! And you better be gone when I come back."

Mick stared after her, shaking his head, then made some more notes.

Jeffrey Stoddard—a handsome blond man whose ultra-smooth mannerisms had put me off during our initial meeting—greeted Keim at the building's door. "Who the hell is that?" he demanded, motioning at Mick.

"Another P.I. At least he thinks he's one. Claims he was hired to run a surveillance on you."

"By who?"

"Won't say. Mainly he works for financial institutions. But I wouldn't worry about him if I were you—guy's an idiot."

Stoddard stared at Mick, then looked down at Keim. "Hey, how come you're not in L.A.?"

"That's what I came to talk to you about. I lost your old lady at the airport. She got tricky on me."

"You mean you don't know where she is?"

"No. Like I said, she got very tricky, gave me the slip."

"Jesus!"

"It might be the break we're hoping for. If she sneaked off to meet—"

"Look, I can't talk right now."

"When, then?"

"Later. I'll call you." Stoddard stepped back inside and shut the door on her.

Keim shrugged and walked back to her car, giving Mick the finger as she passed him.

A few minutes after she drove away, an attractive blond woman rushed out of the building and drove off in the Blazer. Stoddard's face appeared at the window, looking toward Mick. Mick took out his cell phone and punched in a number. My own unit rang.

"How'd we do?"

"It's a wrap. Now all we do is wait."

We settled in to watch the ensuing show. It wasn't more than fifteen minutes before a tan BMW pulled over to the curb and another blonde—equally attractive but several years older—got out. She hurried to the building's door and let herself in with a key.

Jeffrey Stoddard's fiancée had taken the advice of the anonymous caller claiming to be a private investigator hired by an unnamed financial institution to run a surveillance on him. The investigator had told her he'd discovered something potentially damaging to her and urged her to return home at the earliest opportunity.

It was a pity, I thought, that after all our careful staging we couldn't witness the drama's denouement. The fiancée was now walking into a partially stripped apartment, and I doubted Stoddard would be able to come up with any explanation that wouldn't make her suspicious. Calls to their bank and broker would follow, and then, as Keim would say, our client would be made to feel smaller than a cake of lye soap after a hard day's washing.

Of course, McCone Investigations would never recoup expenses on this one, but at the moment I didn't care. The afternoon in the field had been such a satisfying and diverting one that I'd scarcely given a thought either to Hy's silence or to That Woman.

Naturally the respite couldn't last.

As I neared Pier 24½ I saw two SFPD squad cars parked at its entrance. I sped up, U-turned where Brannan intersected the Embarcadero, and drove along the inside northbound lane so fast that I nearly missed seeing Hank standing behind a truck that was double parked in front of Red's Java House. He was trying to flag me down. I pulled over and lowered the passenger-side window.

Hank gave me no explanation, just got in. "Keep driving," he told me.

"What—"

"Drive! Don't stop at the pier!" The set of his mouth was grim.

I did as he told me, my mouth going dry. "What're the cops doing there?"

"They've got a warrant to search your office, car, and home for stolen goods. I took a look at it, stalled them for a while, but they wanted to get on with it. Rae's in charge; she'll make sure they don't overstep or damage anything."

"Jesus!" I nearly rear-ended a car stopped for the light at Folsom. "What am I supposed to have stolen?"

"Five exceptionally valuable antique coins from the collection of one Carlton Maxwell. I presume you've heard of him."

Carlton Maxwell: dabbler in the arts, darling of the social set—and insatiable womanizer. "I've heard of him, yes. But I've never met him."

"You sure?"

"Yes."

"Turn left here."

"Where're we going?"

"Glenn Solomon's office."

Glenn Solomon was one of the nation's foremost criminal defense attorneys, Hank's friend from law school, and my occasional client. "Why?"

"Because after I read the warrant, I remembered about that woman who was hassling you. You've been on edge lately, so I've assumed it's an ongoing thing. When the cops started searching, I called Glenn and explained the situation. He says you're not to talk with the police till he can call his contacts in the D.A.'s office and find out the whole story. And he wants you in his office ASAP."

Behind us, somebody beeped.

"Go!" Hank said.

I wrenched the wheel to the left, my body trembling as if I'd narrowly averted a bad accident. "This is an absolute fucking nightmare!"

"I imagine so, and it's about time you confided in somebody who's equipped to handle it."

How many times had I wanted to say that to Ted?

A car edged out of a driveway to the right; I slammed on the brakes so hard that we were thrown forward, seat belts straining.

"Shar, get a grip!"

The only grip I had was on the wheel. I leaned my head against it, breathing hard. After a moment I straightened and pulled the van to the curb.

"You'd better drive," I told Hank. "I don't want to kill both of us between here and Glenn's office."

Monday Night

Hank, Glenn Solomon, and I stepped out of the Hall of Justice into the misty evening. Glenn—prosperously plump, silver haired, and trimly bearded—beckoned for us to stop and move in closer to him.

"You may think the mess is resolved," he said to me, "and it is, as far as Carlton's concerned, but this won't be the end of your troubles."

"I know. The woman's going to keep it up, escalate her activity."

"Exactly."

The woman, wearing her Sharon McCone disguise, had approached Carlton Maxwell on Saturday night at a club owned by the son of one of his society friends; he spent the remainder of the evening with her and took her to his home. There he showed her his valuable stamp and coin collections, and she spent the night; she slipped out early Sunday morning, and it wasn't till noon today that he discovered the coins—which the police this afternoon found in the driver's-side door pocket of my MG—were missing. Since no one else had been to Maxwell's home in the interim, it was obvious who had taken them; the police and the judge who had issued the search warrant gave the matter top priority.

After Glenn Solomon—no stranger to San Francisco's official and society circles—learned about the events leading up to the issuance of the warrant, he called Carlton Maxwell and asked him to meet us at the Hall of Justice. He then called the detective in charge of the investigation and said I'd be willing to come in and talk, provided the media were kept out of it. And the amazed look on Carlton Maxwell's face when Glenn introduced us verified my story.

Now Glenn said, "This is one determined woman. She's not going to stop. And the police—in spite of that extensive report they took from you—are making promises they can't keep."

"I'm aware of that."

Hank asked, "So what d'you suggest she do?"

Glenn spread his arms. "If I could come up with that kind of answer, I'd be rich." To Hank's ironic grin, he added, "Okay, richer." Then he turned to me. "Listen well, my friend. You have to start looking out for yourself. You've got the smarts, you've got the resources—so start using them before this woman destroys you."

I looked into his honest, concerned eyes, and then into Hank's. Yes, I had the smarts and the resources, including the friends and associates to back me.

"Okay," I said, "I'll start using them. First thing tomorrow morning."

Tonight, however, there was a personal matter that needed tending to.

From my car, I checked in with the office, found Keim working late. "I'm glad you called," she said. "You've got an urgent message from Ted; he left it at about six-thirty."

It was after eight now. "What did he say?"

"Just that he needed to talk with you as soon as possible."

"At home?"

"I guess. He didn't leave a number."

I thanked her and dialed his apartment, let the phone ring

seven times before I hung up. Dammit, why wasn't his machine on? Next I accessed my own machine; he'd phoned there also, and his voice was shaky on the tape: "Shar, I really need your help. Please call me as soon as you get this." The recording time was six thirty-five.

Something must be very wrong, because he'd finally come to me.

I called the apartment again, waited twenty rings this time. He must have gone out and forgotten to turn the machine on, unless . . .

I started the car and drove toward Tel Hill.

No lights showed in the windows of the third-floor rear apartment. I let myself into the building, took the stairs two at a time. When I unlocked Ted's door, darkness and silence greeted me. Quickly I moved down the hallway. No lights anywhere downstairs, but a spot on the deck made the bullet-shattered door gleam like fragmented starshine. Pieces of glass had fallen to the carpet, and cold air seeped through the hole.

I hurried up the stairway, poked my head into the library. Nobody. Rushed across the catwalk to the bedroom. Same. The bathroom? Empty.

I let out my breath and sat down on the bed. What had I been afraid of? That Ted had been murdered? Surely matters couldn't be that critical. That he'd taken his own life? No, he was not a man who would do that.

This business with the woman had me so rattled that I took every possibility to the extreme. I wasn't thinking straight, but I'd better start. The important thing now was to find Ted.

On the sidewalk outside the building I encountered Peter Jackson, a friend of Ted and Neal's who lived in a cottage near the end of the alley. I asked if he'd seen Ted, and he told me Ted had gotten into his car around seven. "He looked kind of unsteady—been drinking, maybe."

I didn't think so; something other than alcohol was responsible for Ted's condition. But Peter's mention of drinking made me remember a bar Ted and Neal sometimes frequented. I asked Peter its name and location.

Jimbo's, on Filbert near Washington Square.

The night was fog-warm, and the double doors of Jimbo's stood open. I stopped on the sidewalk, looking inside at the customers. No Ted. Still, he might have stopped in; somebody might know where he was.

Through the doors where no woman was welcome I went.

Several men near the door glanced at me and frowned. The plaid-shirted bartender set down a glass he'd been drying and came forward. "Sorry, ma'am—"

I stopped him by showing my ID. "Ted Smalley works for me. Have you seen him?"

"He was in earlier today, right after I opened up. Wanted to know if I had any idea where his partner, Neal Osborn, is. I didn't. He asked me if I'd check with the other regulars when they came in."

"Did any of them know?"

"Uh-uh. And Ted hasn't called like he said he would."

"Seems both he and Neal are missing. I'm worried about them. Could you ask your customers about them now?"

"You mean make some sorta announcement?"

"Please. I think Ted and Neal may be in trouble."

He shrugged and rang a bell suspended above the bar. The patrons looked around, some checking their watches. Too early for last call.

"Listen up," the bartender said. "This lady's trying to find Smalley and Osborn. Thinks they might be in trouble. Anybody know where they are?"

Silence. Then a bald, mustached man in a cowboy shirt said, "Ted called me at the office this afternoon, asked if I'd loaned Neal my place out at Inverness. I hadn't."

A biker type added, "I thought I saw Ted in his car tonight, stopped at the light at Lombard and Divisadero."

"Going toward the Golden Gate?"

"Yeah."

"What time?"

"Seven-fifteen, seven-thirty."

Leaving the city. Dammit, why hadn't I been available when he called?

I sagged against a stool, and the bartender saw my distress. "Hey, why don't you sit down?" he said. "You look like you could use a drink—on the house."

For a moment I was tempted to refuse; after all, I had no business in his bar. But then the biker said, "Better take him up on it, lady. He don't usually buy."

I got up on the stool and had my first and only drink at Jimbo's.

When I got home I found a dark shape sitting at the top of my front steps.

"Shar." Ted's voice, soft and flat with depression.

"Where've you been? I drove all over the city looking for you!" I ran up the steps and threw my arms around him.

He put his around me and we hugged for a moment. Then he gently disentangled us and stood up. "I went over to Marin on a hunch, looking for Neal. The hunch was wrong. Since I got back I've been sitting here waiting for you."

I looked up, saw his pain-etched features. Felt the same kind of pain reflected in mine.

"Thank God you've finally decided to confide in me," I said. "Maybe now we can help each other."

PART TWO

•

February 25–March 7

The hours while other people sleep are when things come together for me: facts, impressions, nuances, shades of meaning. Patterns emerge—some clear, others like cracks in a bullet-pierced pane of glass. But all are patterns and contain some inner logic.

The clear patterns are well integrated, concise. One detail leads neatly to another. I tend to distrust them; simplicity of structure can hide falsehood. The chaotic patterns interest me more. One crack intersects another, then leads to a third, a tenth, a hundredth. If I allow my thoughts to flow freely along those cracks, a truth may appear.

It's not easy to give myself over to that kind of mental meandering. There's the compulsion to manipulate, create order where none really exists. Or to throw everything into greater chaos and destroy something of value.

In these late-night hours I try to match my actions

to my thought processes. I move about my home—or wherever else I might be—slowly and deliberately. I pour a cup of coffee or a glass of wine carefully, without spilling a drop. I sip measuredly. But my thoughts surge onward.

As they gain speed, the thoughts meld with emotion. Then there's no stopping the process. A conclusion lies ahead—but who's to tell if it's true or false? A conclusion I may have to stake my life upon—and who's to judge its validity?

Not I.

The hours while other people sleep are a fragile balance between truth and falsehood, a time when the scales may tip either way.

Tuesday

The faces around the old oak table in the conference room my agency shared with Altman & Zahn were attentive and solemn: Rae, Charlotte, Mick. Ted sat a little apart, tension and weariness evident in his face and posture. I'd just finished explaining that both he and I had serious problems that needed the entire agency's attention, and now I handed Rae three sets of fact sheets that Ted and I had worked up this morning, detailing his situation. She took one, passed the rest on.

For a moment I flashed back to the hundreds, perhaps thousands, of hours I'd spent at this table when it stood by the kitchen window in All Souls Legal Cooperative's big Victorian; back before the poverty-law firm began its inevitable decline, many of us had frequently gathered there to share triumphs or miseries, to play poker or Monopoly. Sitting at it today reminded me that things hadn't changed all that much since those times; I still had people in my life whom I could count on.

I said, "Those sheets give dates and details of some horrifying incidents in Ted's life over the past month, but before you read them, he's going to outline the situation for you." I motioned to him that he had the floor.

He hesitated briefly, then shrugged as if he was letting go of something that wasn't important anymore. Cleared his throat and said, "Why do I feel like I ought to announce, 'Hi, my name's Ted, and I'm an asshole'? Well, that's what I've been this last month. I've hurt a lot of feelings around here, and I'm sorry. The whole thing started when I came home from work one day and found a folded slip of paper with Neal's name on it stuffed into our mailbox. Normally I wouldn't've read it, but it flipped open and I saw the word 'faggot.' So I took a look. Only one sentence: 'Why don't you die of AIDS, faggot?' "

Rae and Charlotte groaned, and Mick muttered, "Some gay-bashing bastard!"

"Yeah. I decided to ignore it, threw the note out, and didn't tell Neal about it. The bookstore isn't doing well, the IRS is auditing him, and I didn't want him to have to worry about some homophobe on top of everything else. The notes kept coming, though—uglier each time. Finally I filched his mailbox key so he wouldn't see them.

"When you read those fact sheets, you'll see it's obvious that the person's been watching us, following Neal, waiting for the opportunity to harm him. So I started watching our building and following Neal, too. After all, I work for an investigative agency. Even though I'm only the office manager, I should've been able to find out who it was—right?" He shook his head. "Wrong. I didn't accomplish anything except using up a lot of gas and time and working myself into a weird state, which you all paid the price for. Neal, too." His lips twisted wryly. "Poor guy: for his birthday three weeks ago I gave him a series of karate lessons, thinking that they'd at least make him more fit to defend himself. He *hated* the first two lessons."

I looked around at the others; they saw no humor in the situation. Rae was furiously scribbling notes on the back of the fact sheet. Charlotte's and Mick's expressions had grown increasingly grim.

"Anyway," Ted went on, "after a week and a half of notes, a phone call came. Luckily, I picked up, and the guy thought I was Neal. He said, 'Don't go to the cops or tell that private eye your faggot boyfriend works for about me, or somebody's gonna die.' Sounds melodramatic, I know, but something in his voice convinced me he meant it."

Mick asked, "Anything familiar about his voice?"

"No, it was muffled, obviously disguised."

"But definitely male?"

"Yeah."

"Somebody you know, maybe?"

"Maybe."

Rae looked up from her notes. "At that point, why didn't you just tell Neal what was going on?"

"Because by then I was in too deep. I'd hidden things from him, lied; I was afraid it would permanently damage our relationship if he found out. I did think about going to the police, but crimes involving gays always seem to be assigned low priority. A couple of times I came close to telling Shar, but I just couldn't make myself do it."

Rae nodded. "Were there more phone calls?"

"Almost every night, after Neal got home from the store. I took to hovering around the phone, snatching it up as soon as it rang. When I had to go out and he was there alone, I'd unplug the thing. The situation kept getting worse: somebody tried to run Neal down in front of the bookstore; a disgusting Valentine's Day gift showed up in our apartment. So I called a guy I'd met a while back and bought an unregistered handgun off him. And busted a glass door firing at somebody who climbed onto our balcony Saturday night. Neal was freaked that I had the gun and called Shar. I panicked, thinking that the guy who'd been outside might see her arrive and carry out his death threat. And then it came out that Neal had asked Shar to look into my weird behavior nearly two weeks ago." He laughed mirthlessly. "She's been following me while I've been following Neal, who's being followed by—"

"Hey, Ted," I said, "it's okay."

He shook his head, rubbing his hands over his face. "Now that I'm talking about it, it all seems so surreal."

Rae quickly steered the conversation back to a businesslike level. "So what's the status on the situation now?"

When Ted didn't answer, I replied, "Not very good, I'm afraid. Saturday night, Ted told both Neal and me to leave the apartment. He thought if we were together no harm would come to either of us, it turns out. But on Sunday morning Neal took off to think things over, and nobody knows where he went. Then yesterday evening the guy called Ted, said he knew where Neal was, and he bet he could get to him first."

Ted said, "I'd been calling around to friends and acquaintances all day, trying to locate him, but I'd gotten nowhere. I didn't know whether to believe the guy or not, but I was convinced the situation had turned critical. So I decided to finally confide in Shar, ask for her help. When I did, she called the police and had them put out a pickup order on Neal, so he could be taken into protective custody. And we decided to bring you three in on both our problems right away."

Rae exclaimed, "Jesus, Ted, you should've come to all of us right away! Or at least before you went and bought a handgun."

"I know, but at first I thought I could handle the situation. And later I was too ashamed."

"Ashamed?"

"Yeah, because I'd messed up so badly. Because I *couldn't* handle it."

"Well, you silly faggot!"

For a moment everybody in the room tensed as Rae and Ted locked eyes. Then, simultaneously, the two of them burst out laughing. Ted gave her the finger. She responded in kind. Old buddies who, at All Souls, had regularly shared popcorn and beer and late-night movies on TV, were mending fence in their own peculiar fashion.

Mick asked, "So how do we proceed? Are the police investigating this?"

"In a way," I said.

"Which means we'd better get on it."

"Yes. I'm going to head up the investigation, but I'm

putting the entire agency on it as well. After we talk about my problem, I want to hold a brainstorming session to develop a strategy on how to nail this scumbag. Any questions?"

"Yeah," Mick said, "what *is* your problem?"

"I'm being stalked and impersonated. I also couldn't bring myself to tell anybody about the situation, except to ask a few legal questions of Hank and talk with the police. My reason was similar to Ted's: I was ashamed I couldn't handle it by myself. Tough private investigator, got a reputation to live up to. Couldn't ask for help, not me."

Questions flew, and I answered them while Ted passed out the fact sheets on my situation. By the time everybody had skimmed them they were coming up with various strategies, none of which fit my plan.

"Hold on," I said. "Here's what I want to do: First we work on Ted's problem, combine resources to wrap that up. Then I intend to take a leave of absence from running the agency; I'll turn day-to-day operations over to Rae and put all my time and energy into identifying and nailing my own scumbag."

"Wait a cotton-pickin' minute!" Keim exclaimed. "We go full tilt after whoever's bothering Neal, but *you* go it alone?"

"Not exactly. But we can't afford to stop servicing our regular clients, or to turn down new ones. The woman's trying to ruin me personally; let's not allow her to bring the agency down as well. I'll bring all of you in on it whenever I need you, and I'll keep you posted, but the actual field investigation will be done by me."

I paused, looking at each of them in turn. "I want this woman *bad*. She's all mine."

During our brainstorming session we decided that Ted and Neal's building was the logical place to start our investigation. We'd talk to the other tenants, ask if any of them had seen a suspicious person or witnessed any unusual activity. And also examine their responses and the subtexts of our conversations, in case one of them was the perpetrator. Ted said

that we ought to get permission from the building manager,
Mona Woods, so I called for an appointment with her and, a
couple of hours later, set off for Plum Alley.

According to Ted, Mona Woods was in her late seventies,
but if so, she was living testimony to age often being a matter
of mind-set; when I met her at three that afternoon, she'd just
returned from swimming laps at her health club. She looked
me over with lively curiosity as we settled into chairs in her
comfortable living room.

"So you're the woman Ted works for," she said. "He speaks
of you fondly—and often. This business with Neal that you
explained on the phone is very distressing. How can I help?"

"First I'd like to ask you a few questions about the building. I looked at the mailboxes when I arrived. It would be difficult to slip anything inside without a key. Does anyone
besides you have duplicates?"

"No one that I know of."

"What about duplicate keys to the apartments?"

She shook her head.

"Let's talk about the tenants. Ted says one may be gay."

"Well, there's a lesbian couple. But Ted and Neal are the
first openly gay couple to move into the building in the six
years I've been manager. The other tenants are three single
men, two single women, three married couples. I don't know
much about them personally."

"Have any of them exhibited signs of homophobia?"

Mrs. Woods thought, pursing her lips. "Well, it's not a prejudice one openly displays to an acquaintance. Not in this city.
People here are often not what they seem."

And that didn't apply only to matters of sexual orientation.
"I'd like to ask your permission for my staff and me to question the tenants. If one of them is the person who's threatening Neal, our presence here may force his hand."

"Certainly. Of course, it's up to them as to whether they
agree to talk with you." She gave me a list of tenants and

showed me to the door, pausing there, her face grim. "You know," she said, "we San Franciscans pride ourselves on being such a tolerant people, but that's not really true."

She was correct. All you have to do is drive around the city and you see dozens of pockets of self-interest. The gays in the Castro, the Chinese and Russians in the Richmond, the wealthy in Pacific Heights, the blacks in Hunters Point, the Catholics in their various dioceses, the Vietnamese in the Tenderloin. And then there are the homeless, the developers, the cults, even the bicyclers, for God's sake. Nothing wrong with healthy self-interest; it's how we make a better world for ourselves and our children. But when it starts to infringe upon others' rights, the structure of a society begins to crumble.

One of my biggest fears is that it's crumbling already, right here and now.

With such cheerful thoughts on my mind, I met with my staff in the conference room at five o'clock, and we split up the list of tenants. I would take the lesbian couple and the single men; Rae would take the single women and one of the couples; and together, because Mick had little interviewing experience, he and Charlotte would take the remaining married couples. The interviews, barring complications, were to be completed by this time tomorrow. In the meantime I'd asked RKI to put a security guard on Ted's apartment.

After the others went their respective ways, I remained at the table in the gathering gloom for a while. Instead of depressing me, the encroaching darkness had an intoxicating effect, and as night became total I felt a rush of pleasure that was almost sexual. With any luck, I'd soon be free to move through the city in search of the woman who was stealing my identity piece by piece.

I'd soon be free to take back my life.

Tuesday Night

Neal and Ted?" Karen Cooper said. "They're nice guys. We don't socialize all that much, but they've helped us out now and then—stuff like feeding the cat and watering the plants when we're on vacation."

"People in this building respect each other's privacy," her partner, Jane Naylor, added, "but everybody's pleasant. I can't imagine one of the tenants threatening Neal like that."

"Does anyone in the building strike you as homophobic?"

The women looked at each other, then shrugged. Cooper said, "Nobody's treated us any differently because we're lesbians."

"When you get right down to it," Naylor said, "we're pretty congenial, considering what a mixed bag we are. Karen and I are lucky to have gotten an apartment here."

I hoped when this was over Ted and Neal could continue to share in their feelings of good fortune.

"Neal's good people," George Chu told me. He leaned against the wall in the hallway outside his apartment, still sweating from an evening run.

"Well, somebody doesn't think so. Are you sure you

haven't noticed anything, such as one of the other tenants making derogatory comments about him?"

"No, and if I had, I'd've told them what they could do with their comments. Anybody who messes with either of them is gonna have to mess with me first."

Chu's toughness and protectiveness toward Ted and Neal seemed put on, for someone who earlier had admitted to only a nodding acquaintance. Was it a cover-up?

Miles Furth was in his eighties and walked with a carved wooden cane topped by a brass eagle's head. "I'm not comfortable with homosexuality, and I don't like the lifestyle," he told me, "but they've got as much right to be what they are as I do to be a cantankerous old geezer. If I catch whoever's doing this to Mr. Osborn—you see this cane?" He waved it.

I nodded.

"If I catch whoever it is, young lady, the eagle will have landed—on his head!"

"One of the tenants? No way," Norman Katz said. "I'm gay, and nobody's bothered me."

"I notice you live alone. Perhaps whoever it is isn't aware of your sexual orientation."

"Well, I don't post a sign on the door with a picture of a woman in a circle with a line through it, but I don't smuggle my dates up the fire escape, either."

"How long have you lived here?"

"Four months."

"Whoever's harassing Neal may not have turned his attention to you yet."

"Now, there's a cheerful thought."

I handed him my card. "If anybody bothers you, give us a call."

I couldn't have been sleeping very deeply, because it was the unnatural silence in my house, rather than a noise, that woke me. The forced-air heat, which I'd turned up when I came home, no longer hummed. The ailing refrigerator no longer ticked. I'd started the dishwasher before going to bed, but it wasn't sloshing and pulsing. I pushed up on one elbow, looked at the clock. No red digital numbers gleaming in the darkness.

Power outage or . . . ?

I sat up, parted the mini-blinds above the bed with two fingers. Lights showed in the Halls' house next door. I looked through the bedroom door to the window facing the Curley house on the other side; a small mist-diffused spot shone down on the footpath beside it. The entire street was on the same power grid; when my electricity went out, so did everybody else's.

Reaching for my robe, I slipped out of bed. Put the .357 that lay on the nightstand into one pocket and went to get a flashlight. As an afterthought I took my house keys from where I'd dumped them on the kitchen table; no sense in leaving the house unlocked while I went outside.

When I stepped onto the backyard deck, the mist was so thick I could barely see beyond the railing. That could be either an advantage or a disadvantage. I shut the door quietly, stood watching and listening. Nothing moved, and all I heard was a dog barking in the distance. Finally I felt my way across the deck to the stairs and down them. At their foot I ducked under the deck and moved across the uneven ground from support post to support post, stubbing my bare toe once on the stack of firewood against the house's wall and narrowly avoiding piercing the sole of my foot on a rake I'd left there. Finally I reached the opposite corner, around which the gas meter and electrical panel were located.

There I stopped, feeling a presence. The woman could be hiding in the backyard, but more likely she was in the alley between the house and the fence. Mist was trapped there; all I could make out was the diffused glow of the Curleys' spotlight. If I ventured around the corner to the utilities hookups, I'd be placing myself at risk.

So flush her out.

I glanced over at the fence, beyond which the Curleys' German shepherds slept in their dog run. Felt my way back along the wall to where I kept a collection of empty terra-cotta flowerpots. I located a medium-sized one, carried it back to the corner of the house, and heaved it over the fence.

Smash! And all hell broke loose. Growling and bellowing and snarling as the shepherds were up and alert to protect their territory. Within fifteen seconds a window opened and Will Curley, an early-rising trucker who cherished his sleeping time, shouted, "Shut up, you noisy buggers!" The dogs continued to bark, but in spite of them I heard footsteps running down my alley toward the front sidewalk.

I was around the corner immediately, running after her. I couldn't see her, but I heard her feet pounding on the pavement. The sound of our combined footsteps set other neighborhood dogs to barking. Lights flashed on in the house across from me. And then her footsteps stopped and a car door slammed somewhere down the block.

I paused, waiting for its engine to start. Nothing. My neighbor was out on his front porch now. I called softly, "It's okay."

"You sure?"

"Yes." I surveyed the cars parked along the street. She was hiding in one of them—

Roar of an engine starting, and then a car near the Church Street end of the block shot out of a space and around the corner. Dark-colored, possibly a Japanese model, no light over the license plate.

"Dammit!" I exclaimed, saw my neighbor was looking alarmed. "A prowler," I told him. "Won't be back."

He nodded as if he only half believed me and went back into his house.

I retreated into the alley, took out the flashlight, and shone it on the utilities hookup; the cover of the electrical panel was gone, propped against the foundation. The main switch had been pulled to off.

I yanked the switch to on, decided to leave reattaching the cover till morning, and went inside. The heat hummed once again; the fridge ticked; the dishwasher sloshed and pulsed. In the bedroom the digital clock's red numbers flashed 12:17 A.M.

She'd been so close, only yards away while I slept, and now she was gone, her night's mission fulfilled. She'd probably go home and sleep soundly, while I wouldn't close my eyes till exhaustion overtook me around dawn.

I went into the living room and huddled on the couch, watching the dying embers of the fire I'd made earlier. After midnight, close to five in the morning in South America. Where was Hy, and what was he doing? Was he thinking of me?

Our connection was dead, short-circuited by our separate crises. I'd felt alone many times in my life, but never as alone as this.

Wednesday

Charlotte and Mick had found two of the married male tenants at the Plum Alley building somewhat suspect, and I added George Chu's name to the list. Then I asked my nephew to run background checks on all three. After dealing with some routine correspondence, I called Mona Woods for another appointment and set off for Tel Hill to do more digging.

When I arrived at the building I found a heavyset Nordic-looking man tending to the bedding plants under the glass ceiling of the courtyard. In spite of the rain and the cold, gusting wind, he was bare chested and sweating. I introduced myself and asked if he was the gardener.

"Yes, miss." He stood and held out a dirt-caked hand, then thought better of it. "Bud Larsen. I take care of three buildings on this side of the hill."

"How long have you worked here?"

"Going on ten years. It's a grand old place, isn't it?"

"Certainly is. I suppose you know the people who live here pretty well."

"Some of them."

"I'd like to ask you a few questions, if I may."

Larsen frowned, white brows pulling into a straight line. "I don't know. Mrs. Woods, the manager, might not like me talking about her tenants to a stranger."

"I have her permission to ask around; you can check with her, if you like."

"Oh, that's okay. What is this, some kind of survey?"

"No." I handed him one of my cards. "My associates and I are trying to find out who's been harassing Neal Osborn."

"Osborn? Bearded guy, apartment 305?"

"Right."

"Somebody's been bothering him? How?"

"Threatening notes and phone calls, mainly."

"Why?"

"Because he's gay."

Larsen thought that over. "Well, if that's so, aren't they bothering the other guy—Smalley—too?"

"The threats, for whatever reason, are directed only at Mr. Osborn. But his partner's been bothered plenty, believe me."

"Huh." The gardener hesitated, then motioned to a green wrought-iron bench near the elevator. "Let's take a load off. What d'you want to ask me?"

I sat next to him. Up close, he smelled of a combination of freshly turned earth, rain, and sweat. "I'd like your personal impressions of a few of the tenants. Start with George Chu."

"Young Chinese guy, jogger. Works for an insurance company. I don't much like him."

"Why not?"

"Has an attitude. Superior."

"How so?"

"Just in general. Like he knows something the rest of us don't."

"Anything else?"

Larsen shook his head.

"What about Doug and Marlene Kerr?" One of the married couples.

"He's a banker type. She's pretty and shops a lot. He hits her."

"How do you know that?"

"A lot of the time she's got bruises, bad ones. She tries to cover them with makeup and dark glasses, but it doesn't work. People talk about hearing them fight."

"Have the police ever been called?"

"Not that I know of."

"Any other violent episodes on the part of Doug Kerr?"

"No. His wife is the one who sets him off."

"Anything else about either of them?"

"Uh-uh. They keep to themselves, hiding the family secret."

"The other tenants I'd like to ask you about are Al and Doris Mercado."

"I like her a lot. She's a gardener too, has helped to start a couple of neighborhood gardens here on the hill. Him . . . he's okay. Ex-cop. Works in security now. Has a lot of guns. Spent an hour last month showing them to me."

"Responsible gun owner?"

"Yeah. Keeps them locked up but handy. Pity the poor bastard who ever tries to break into his apartment and gets caught, though. Mercado don't like people."

"Any particular kind of people?"

"Most all of them—he don't discriminate."

"Does he get along with the other tenants?"

Larsen thought, shrugged. "I suppose so. The only disagreement I remember between him and anybody else is the time he threw a rock at Karen Cooper's cat because it was prowling around the garbage bins. Karen saw him do it, threatened to call the SPCA. He apologized quick enough. Guess he don't like animals, either."

Or maybe he didn't like lesbians—and gays.

Mona Woods had left a note for me on her door: she'd have to reschedule our appointment because she'd forgotten this was her day to help serve lunch at the San Francisco Senior Center. I smiled at the remarkable energy of the woman, who was probably serving people years her junior. Would I be like her in my seventies? I hoped so.

Since I was there in the building, I decided to check with the guard on Ted and Neal's apartment and took the stairs to the third floor. Tony Casella, a young single father whom I'd used on jobs before, was glad to see me: he'd just received word that his small son had gotten sick at day care and Tony needed to pick him up, but RKI couldn't get a replacement here till three. Could he take off right away? Of course, I told him. Then I let myself into the apartment.

I wasn't sure what I expected to find there. I'd been over it thoroughly, but that was more than a week ago. It wouldn't hurt, I supposed, to take another look around.

In the living room I stood still and did just that. The apartment was orderly and clean, the door that Ted had shot covered in fresh-smelling plywood. A stack of mail addressed to Neal sat on the kitchen counter.

Neal. Neither he nor his car had been spotted here in the city or in any of the nearby jurisdictions. As time passed, Ted had become increasingly withdrawn and silent—poised on the edge of panic, I supposed. And I had to admit I was seriously worried.

A key rattled in the front-door lock. Interesting, so soon after the guard had left. I drew back into the kitchen. Maybe I'd gotten lucky; maybe it was the perpetrator, come to leave another grotesque gift.

Footsteps came along the hall. I slipped my gun from my bag, held it ready.

Neal appeared, a small duffel bag in hand.

"Thank God!" I exclaimed.

He whirled, focused on the gun, and froze. Then he let out a whistle of relief. "Shar! For God's sake!"

"Are you okay?"

"Of course, why wouldn't I be? What're you doing here? Is Ted all right?"

"Ted's fine. Where've you been?"

"Staying at a bed-and-breakfast up the coast. What is this?"

"We've been so worried, and we asked the police to put out a pickup order on you, but—"

"On *me?* Why?"

"It's a long story—"

"Tell me anyway. I need to know what's going on."

"Okay, sit down and I will."

"I can't believe it. I just plain can't believe it." Neal got up from his chair and began to pace. "He kept all of that from me? From you?"

"You've got to understand—at first he didn't want to burden you, and then he thought he was in too deep."

"What does that say about our relationship? Did he think I'd break up with him just because he'd made a mistake?"

"Neal, Ted's not used to making mistakes. He's good at just about everything he does. I suspect he was angry with himself because he couldn't handle the situation, and he projected his own feelings onto you."

"Well, he and I have some talking to do."

"And I'd better cancel the pickup order on you." I started for the phone. "I wonder why nobody spotted your car out at the coast?"

"Because it's been parked over on Greenwich since Saturday. As you'll remember, we left that night in your MG. My car was having carburetor problems, and I didn't want to risk moving it till I could get Triple-A out to take a look. On Sunday I didn't want the hassle, so I called a cab from your house, had it take me to a rental-car place, and picked up this bag and a few things I needed at a Wal-Mart on my way north."

And of course the one place the police wouldn't search for a missing person's car was in his own neighborhood.

When I got off the phone with the SFPD, Neal was leafing

through the envelopes on the kitchen counter. "Bills," he muttered, "and there'll be more at the store."

"Things're that bad?"

"Grim, but I'll survive." He set them down and glanced at the boarded-up door. "At least that's taken care of. While I was at the coast I called a glazier I know who works cheap, but he couldn't come out till tomorrow. Shar, about this guy who's threatening me—what's going to happen next?"

"We're proceeding with our investigation."

"And in the meantime?"

"Exercise extra caution away from home. When you're here, there'll be an RKI guard on the door; one will arrive at three this afternoon."

"All right to call Triple-A and get my car looked at?"

"Sure. I don't think the guy'll try anything in daylight; he doesn't want to get caught. Just be careful."

"I will. I intend to enjoy life for a long time."

After a quick stop for a burger, I drove back to the pier and went directly to Ted's office. "Neal's home," I announced. "I explained everything. He's getting Triple-A out to look at his car, then will phone the store to see how things are, and come here."

Ted looked both relieved and apprehensive. "He's okay?"

"He's fine. The phone call you got on Monday was designed to panic you. Fortunately, it drove you to do what you should've done two weeks ago."

"You're not going to let me forget that, are you?"

"No more than you're going to let me forget *my* past transgressions." I grinned at him and headed for my office.

"Shar, somebody from Get-a-Bug's insisting on talking with you. Line two."

"From *where?*"

"Termite service."

"I don't have termites—that I know of." I pressed the second button. "Sharon McCone."

"Ms. McCone, this is Ellie from Get-a-Bug. I'm calling to see when we can schedule the extermination—"

"Extermination!"

". . . The message you left on our machine said you have pests—"

"I have *one* pest, and it would take more than your services to get rid of her."

"Sharon McCone."

"Sharon, this is Ed."

"Ed?"

"Ed Martin, from Gorilla Destruction. We're here at your place and ready to start breaking up the driveway, but I've got to get your signature on the work order."

"Don't you touch my driveway!"

"But you said our estimate—"

"Don't you let one of your gorillas so much as *step* on my driveway! Oh, Jesus Christ, what's she going to do to me next?"

"Ms. McCone." The voice was low pitched and formal, oily too. Solemnity overlaid a note of great pleasure. "My heartfelt condolences to you and your family."

"Condolences? Family? Who is this?"

"Ah, the person who answered my call didn't identify me to you. This is Bradley Sampson, of Sampson and Sampson Funeral Directors, returning your call."

I ground my teeth, said, "My call."

"Ms. McCone, we know how distracted you must be in your time of need, but Sampson and Sampson is here to help you. Your message, left on our answering-machine tape over the noon hour, says you anticipate requiring our services imminently."

I pressed the point of my pencil into the legal pad I'd been writing on so hard that it broke. "Mr. Sampson—"

"Ms. McCone, I hear the stress in your voice. The loss or the imminent loss of a loved one—"

"Mr. Sampson, do you have the tape?"

"The . . . tape?"

"The answering-machine tape!"

"Why, yes."

"Play it for me, please."

"A most unusual . . . certainly."

Clicks and whirls as he rewound it, and then a voice whose muffled quality could have been attributed to grief: "My name is Sharon McCone. I expect to need your services within a few days. Please call me—"

"Enough!" I shouted. I slammed the receiver into its cradle, got up, and rushed out onto the catwalk. "Enough!" I shouted for all the pier to hear.

Down below, Hank was fetching something from his car. He straightened and ran his hand through his pad of gray-brown hair, frowning. On the opposite catwalk, Tony Nakayama and one of his partners halted their conversation and stared. And Glenna Stanleigh, about to load some film equipment into her Bronco, called, "Sharon? Maybe you could use a cup of that Natural Serenity herbal tea?"

Then we all turned our heads as a car shot through the entrance—Neal's Honda, going much too fast. So fast that if I hadn't already notified the police to cancel the pickup order on him, I'd have sworn they were hot on his bumper.

Neal, Ted, Charlotte, and I stood around the conference room table, staring down at a truly bizarre salad. The wooden bowl that Neal had brought to the pier—one from his own kitchen—contained a mixture of tomatoes, radishes, olives, garbanzo beans, mushrooms—and wilted weeds with dirt clods still attached to their roots. On top of it all was a garnish of dead insects.

The accompanying block-printed note said: HOW'S THIS FOR A GOURMET MEAL, FAGGOT?

"About as yummy-looking as barbecued roadkill," Keim commented.

"Where'd you find this?" I asked Neal.

"On the dining room table, when I went home to call the store after Triple-A gave my car a clean bill of health."

"You see anybody hanging around the street or the building?"

He shook his head, then glanced at Ted, who stood a little apart from us. "You okay?" he asked stiffly.

". . . Yeah."

"We need to talk."

"I know."

I studied the salad, decided it wasn't worth sending to Richman Labs. Their tormentor struck me as equal to mine in leaving no clues to his identity.

Charlotte apparently had followed the same reasoning process. "You ever think there might be a connection between the guy who's after Neal and the woman who's after you?" she asked me.

"No—the M.O.'s too dissimilar. The two of them may be shirttail cousins in the craziness department, but nowadays that's a very big family."

She nodded agreement and picked up the bowl. "I'll clean this for you, Neal."

"Thanks." Neal turned to Ted. "I guess Bud explained that the glazier couldn't come by till tomorrow to fix the door? I called him from the coast, asked him to remove the glass and board it up for the interim."

"Bud?" Ted frowned.

"Bud Larsen."

"Oh. I could've boarded it up and dealt with the glazier."

"Yeah, but I'm the one who usually handles stuff like that, so I went ahead and made the calls."

"Well, Bud hadn't boarded up the door by the time I came

to work this morning. I haven't even seen him in more than two weeks."

"How'd he get in, then?"

At first the men's conversation had simply served as a background to my thinking about the similarities between my position and theirs, but their final exchanges caught my attention.

I asked, "You're talking about the gardener at your building?"

"Not just the gardener," Neal replied. "Bud's an all-around handyman. Works for two or three other buildings on the hill and runs a locksmith service on the side."

"Was he the one who changed the locks when you moved in?"

"Uh-huh."

Bud Larsen: he was smarter than I'd thought. I'd sat on that bench with him this morning and bought into the tales he told about the tenants we'd found suspect. George Chu had a superior attitude; Doug Kerr beat his wife; Al Mercado didn't like anybody. Implying possible prejudice, violence, and hatred. I wondered if any of it was true.

Bud Larsen . . .

Wednesday Night

Our plans were made, and everybody was in place. Soon, maybe, we'd have evidence of yet another hate crime in our supposedly idyllic City-by-the-Bay.

I'd spent the late afternoon at the Plum Alley building, staging follow-up conversations with various tenants within the hearing of Bud Larsen, whom Mrs. Woods—at my request—had asked to touch up the paint on the courtyard walls. Larsen acted as if he wasn't listening, whistling as he worked with his brush, but his body language betrayed him in the same way a cat's does when it swivels its ears. When I announced to Karen Cooper that I couldn't wait to nail the bastard who was bothering my client, he flashed me a quick sidelong look that simmered with rage.

Larsen was the guilty party—now I was sure of that.

I also sensed he was ready to take the bait.

The sidewalk of Montgomery Street sloped steeply from where it intersected Plum Alley, ending in a series of concrete stairways that scaled the side of the hill in switchbacks above the northern waterfront. At one of the landings, the steps turned to the right and passed through an area of low, dense vegetation and cypress trees. It was very dark there, with only footlights to illuminate the cracked pavement, cold and quiet on this damp winter night. And uncomfortable, as Glenna Stanleigh and I were finding out while crouched on the bare ground behind a clump of junipers.

"Are you sure the video cam'll work when it's this dark?" I whispered.

"The tape's made for filming under these conditions."

"But what if—"

"For heaven's sake, Sharon, relax! I've a lot of experience with night filming, you know. And spontaneous action like we're hoping for is my specialty."

The wind rustled the branches overhead; from the street above I heard faint talk and laughter—late patrons leaving Julius' Castle. Car doors slammed, engines started. Out beyond the Gate, a foghorn moaned. Close to midnight now—

My cell phone buzzed. I flipped it open, and Mick's low voice said, "Neal's leaving the building."

"You spotted Larsen yet?"

"No." Fifteen or twenty seconds went by. "There he is. Must've been lurking down by the retaining wall."

"Thanks." I ended the call. To Glenna I said, "They're on their way."

She nodded, busy with her video equipment.

A minute more and the phone buzzed again. Keim said, "Neal just passed me. And Larsen's coming out of the alley."

"Wait for Mick, then follow." I closed the phone, tucked it into my purse, and took out my small flashlight. "Now," I whispered to Glenna as I flashed the beam at the porch of the house across the steps, where Rae had gotten the residents' permission to wait.

Glenna began filming.

Rubber soles slapped on the concrete and a stocky figure clad in jeans and a down jacket appeared. Neal. He skidded to a stop and peered into the shadows, as if to reassure himself that we were really there. I coughed softly. His posture relaxed some and he moved to the railing and stood as if taking in the misted lights below.

More footsteps, stealthy but unhurried. I tensed as Glenna swiveled the camera toward the stairway.

Bud Larsen turned the corner. For a moment he paused on the landing. Then he started down the next flight in a predator's walk: slow, calculating, fluid. He stopped no more than a yard away from Neal.

Neal turned his head, said in an uneven voice, "Bud. You startled me."

"More like I scared you." Larsen moved closer.

"Not really. I don't scare easily."

"Come on, all you faggots do."

"What did you call me?"

Larsen was silent. Beside me, Glenna fine-tuned her focus. Neal turned to face Larsen, his back against the railing. " 'Faggot'—right?"

Larsen shrugged.

"You're the one who's been doing those things."

"What things?"

"The notes, the phone calls. The Valentine's Day heart, the salad. You made a death threat on the phone."

Larsen licked his lips, looked around. For a moment I was afraid he'd stonewall Neal, but his type never can resist boasting of their own cleverness.

"Okay, all right—I did those things. And you shoulda listened to what I told you on the phone. That bitch your boyfriend works for is asking questions. Says she's your friend. You know what a real man'd do if he had a friend like that nice piece of—"

"Shut up!" Neal's voice was controlled, quietly angry.

At any point now I could go down there and break up the confrontation; we had what we wanted—Larsen admitting on video what he'd done. But I was curious to see how this scene would play out.

Larsen laughed. "Oh, the faggot's gettin' tough with me!" Sarcasm, but also a touch of surprise there.

"What I want to know, Bud, is what started this business? And where's it going to end?"

"I told you on the phone—somebody's gonna die. Guess who?"

"You don't mean that. Now, *what started it?*"

"You oughta know."

"But I don't."

"Remember a month ago, in the elevator? When you made that pass at me?"

"I *what?*"

"The day I fixed that leaky kitchen faucet for you. You were leaving, and we rode down in the elevator together."

"Yes, I remember that, but—"

"You gotta remember what you did."

"Honestly, I don't."

"Oh, man, you must come on to a lotta guys! Too bad for you you picked the wrong one."

"Bud, I'm asking—"

"Yeah, questions—like that McCone bitch. All right, you want me to say it, I'll say it. You punched me on the arm and called me Buddy."

". . . Is that *all?*"

"Isn't it enough?"

"Bud, I do that with everybody—male or female, straight or gay. It's just a mannerism I use with people I like. I was thanking you for fixing the faucet."

"Bullshit, man! You perverts're all alike."

"All alike. In what way?"

Larsen hesitated. Looked away from Neal, alert, like an animal sniffing the air. "What is this?"

"What's what?"

"This whole month you never went for a walk alone before. Tonight you're standing here like you're waiting for me."

"I was just looking at the lights."

"No, I don't think so." Larsen shook his head, peering into the darkness. "Uh-uh."

"So what're you saying, Bud?" Neal braced his hands on the railing behind him, ready to push off.

"I'm saying this is a trap. That McCone bitch has you wired."

Before Neal could reply, Larsen lunged at him, got him by the throat. I started sliding down the mat of cypress needles on the slope, and Rae came off the porch. We were equidistant from the struggling men when Neal brought his forearms up against Larsen's wrists and broke his hold.

Larsen grunted and staggered back, grabbing his left wrist. Neal saw his advantage, charged him, and butted his head into Bud's soft belly. As Larsen frantically sucked air, Neal grabbed his forearm, shot one leg out, and flipped him onto his back. Larsen lay still, gasping and moaning.

Rae and I approached slowly, while Mick and Charlotte clattered down the steps. I said to Neal, "I thought you were taking karate, not judo."

"I'm not taking either—anymore. But I'll tell you, rage is a great teacher." Breathing heavily, he stared with narrowed eyes at Larsen.

I went over and took a closer look at Larsen. He'd had the wind knocked out of him, but didn't seem to be badly hurt. When he saw me, he waved his arms and uttered something that sounded like "Scraw!"

"I don't suppose that's a compliment," I said to the others. "Let's go now. Mr. Larsen would probably prefer to be left alone."

"The wire," Larsen muttered. "Wha' the hell you gonna do with the tape?"

"Neal wasn't wired."

"Then why—"

Glenna came out of the shrubbery, video cam perched jauntily on her shoulder. "Smile, Mr. Larsen," she said. "You're going to be a very big star!"

*   *   *

Glenna's film came out beautifully. I stayed around the pier while she edited it, so I could see the finished product. In the morning she'd screen it for Anne-Marie and Hank, and then they'd start the legal maneuverings that would guarantee Bud Larsen would leave Ted and Neal alone forever.

Funny—I'd thought the film was going to be about rage and hate and evil. And it was, in a way. But once you've looked unreasoning hatred in the face, you know not only how evil it is but how sad. That's mostly what Glenna's film showed: sadness.

At after four in the morning I was still in my office, curled up in the ancient armchair under my schefflera plant, the handwoven throw that usually hid the worn upholstery and bleeding stuffing pulled around my shoulders against the damp and cold. The chair was old and ill treated when I found it in the cubbyhole under the stairs that was my first office at All Souls Legal Cooperative. God knows why I had a fit of sentimentality on moving day and brought it along to the pier. But maybe the fit was more pragmatic than sentimental; I'd always done my best thinking in that chair.

So there I was, sitting in the dark and feeling free. A strange way to feel, given that my impostor was still out there and Hy's situation was still unresolved. But I was free to go after the impostor like I'd never gone after anybody before. To-morrow—

But why wait? It was already tomorrow. My mind was clear, and I wasn't the least bit tired. Why not go over my notes one more time?

Initial awareness of her: conversation with Glenna on 2/12. Not a conversation I'm ever likely to forget.

2/13: Clive Benjamin, the art dealer who slept with the bogus McCone. I've always felt I missed something there. What?

We were here in the office. He was sitting across the desk from me. I asked him to describe her.

"She was about ten years younger than you, but very similar in appearance."

"Native American ancestry, perhaps?"

"No."

"What were her facial features like?"

"Well, sort of cute."

"Is there anybody you can liken her to? A public figure or film star?"

"Maybe Susan Dey, the actress who was on *L.A. Law,* you know?"

That's it!

"Shar, you've got to be insane! Neal just got to sleep and now you want him to—"

"You're awake, aren't you?"

"Well, yeah, but—"

"Take his keys and meet me at Anachronism. Please."

". . . Okay, give me twenty minutes. It's the least I can do after what you did for us."

The bookstore was pitch dark, but I didn't wait for Ted to put the lights on, just rushed down the main aisle toward the cubbyhole where Neal stocked film memorabilia. The overhead fluorescent flickered on as I began flipping through the files of studio glossies.

Please be here.

Darnell . . . Darren . . . de Havilland . . . De Niro . . . Dey—

"Oh, my God . . ."

Back at my office I spread the prospective employee's file open on the desk and read it slowly, refreshing my memory.

On January 30 she'd sat across from me, smiling, anxious to please, giving all the right answers. Her references—from

Carver Security, a high-tech outfit here in the city—had checked out beautifully. Lee D'Silva was a fine technician, highly versed in all the latest systems, as well as a whiz with computers and an all-around good employee.

The interview had gone well—so well, in fact, that after I ran out of questions we chatted for at least fifteen minutes, mostly about flying, because she was a student pilot. When she left my office Lee D'Silva must have had every expectation of landing the job. And by all rights, she should have. She was just the sort of person McCone Investigations needed to handle the increasing number of breach-of-security cases that came our way. But then Craig Morland called to accept my still-open offer, and I decided I needed his contacts with federal law-enforcement agencies more than D'Silva's expertise. I'd sent her a turndown letter saying I'd keep her in mind for a future opening. And that was when all my trouble started.

Strange that there had been no hint of emotional or mental disturbance in the background check Mick had run on her.

I went over the file again. D'Silva was thirty-one and single. She was born in the small town of Paradise in the foothills of the Sierras northeast of Oroville, attended school there, and earned her degree in police science at nearby Butte College. She explained a two-year lapse in employment after graduation as time taken off to nurse her dying mother. Afterward she moved to San Francisco and worked for three security outfits, the last being Carver where, presumably, she was still employed.

I should have put this together sooner. After all, it would have taken a knowledgeable technician to plant the bugs in my home, clone my cell phone, and breach security at Vintage Lofts. Why hadn't I remembered her?

I stood, shut off the lights, went to sit in my armchair again. It was dawning gray outside, raining again. The traffic sounds on the bridge had grown louder, and the Golden Gate would be similarly busy; the early commuter ferries would be churning from Marin County toward the city. I watched boats slip by, dark and mysterious with only their running lights showing. And I began to reconstruct what had happened.

February 3: Craig called. Immediately I dictated the letters on tape, and Ted had them on my desk for signature by that afternoon.

At the latest, Lee D'Silva would have gotten her letter on Wednesday, February 5. On Friday the seventh she'd passed herself off as me to Clive Benjamin. The next night she'd assumed my identity at the fund-raiser.

Deliberate attempts to damage me? Or delusional attempts to live my life, now that she'd been denied the opportunity to become part of it?

Didn't matter. I'd identified her.

The hunter was becoming the hunted. I was back in control.

Thursday

On Thursday morning I spent a couple of hours wrestling with a moral dilemma, and in the end personal satisfaction won out over the letter of the law.

Legally I was required to notify the SFPD of Lee D'Silva's identity; otherwise I'd be obstructing their ongoing investigation—an offense that could cost me my license. But I doubted the investigation was really so ongoing, and besides, there was little hard evidence against D'Silva, only my word and that of Glenna Stanleigh and Clive Benjamin. Glenna hadn't witnessed her committing a crime, and Benjamin couldn't prove she was the person who had taken his spare key. Nor was there anything stronger than circumstantial evidence of her theft of Carlton Maxwell's rare coins. Circumstantial cases are only as good as the D.A. who builds them, and a defendant of D'Silva's demonstrated histrionic talents could easily enlist the sympathy of a jury.

So went my reasoning, but deep down I knew I was manipulating it in order to justify what I planned to do. I, not the police or the courts, would be the one to bring Lee D'Silva down.

*　　*　　*

"What, you stole one of my top technicians, and now you're not happy with her?" Mitch Carver said. "Sorry, we don't accept returns."

I'd known Mitch, Lee D'Silva's former employer, since the days when we'd guarded office buildings in the dead of night for low hourly wages and no benefits. In the intervening years we'd both prospered, but neither of us had changed all that much. This morning he half reclined in his swivel chair, booted feet propped on the desk; his sandy hair was rumpled, his tie askew, and his sport jacket looked as though it could stand a trip to the dry cleaner.

"I didn't steal her."

"Then what d'you call—"

"I interviewed her, but I didn't offer her the job."

"Say what?" He lowered his feet to the floor and sat straighter, hitching the chair up to the desk. "She bragged to everybody that she was going to work for you, and one day she just didn't show up. I thought it was tacky of her not to give two weeks' notice, but that's about par for the business."

"When was this?"

"That she didn't show? I'll check." He dialed an extension, spoke briefly. "Three weeks ago tomorrow."

About the time she would have received my turndown letter.

Mitch asked, "So what's the story here? You change your mind about hiring her?"

"Possibly."

"Well, good luck finding her. Her supervisor called her place a few times, never got an answer. And she didn't bother to pick up her final paycheck."

"Did she leave any personal possessions behind—in her desk, for instance?"

"Let's go see. And if you do locate her, tell her to pick up her goddamn check so we can close the books on her."

*   *   *

The items D'Silva left behind in her desk had been packed in a cardboard carton and placed in a storage room. After her supervisor located them, she showed me to an empty office where I could go through them in private.

Chap Stick, nail file and clippers, personalized coffee mug, box of tampons, pair of running shoes, panty hose in their original packaging. Two paperback novels featuring fictional female private detectives, well thumbed; tucked inside one was a copy of an interview I'd given to a local magazine last spring. I unfolded it and saw that certain phrases were underlined.

Q: I understand you're a <u>licensed pilot</u>. Do you use your flying in your work?

A: Mainly I fly for pleasure, or sometimes to get away from what's happening on the ground. Nothing and no one can get to you at several thousand feet.

Q: When and where did you learn to fly?

A: Close to four years ago, at <u>Los Alegres Municipal Airport</u>, where I had a terrific <u>woman instructor</u>. Now I <u>fly out of Oakland</u>.

Q: What kind of plane?

A: A <u>Citabria</u>. It's a type known as a <u>tail-dragger</u>. On the ground, the tail rests low, the nose high, because the third wheel is at the rear. It's— Don't get me started; I'll bore your readers to death.

Q: Sounds more scary than boring. Isn't flying an expensive hobby?

A: It's perceived that way, but most airports have <u>flying clubs</u> that offer <u>discounts</u> on lessons. And aircraft rentals are fairly reasonable: you only pay for the time you spend onboard, and the planes rent wet— meaning the fuel is included. You can rent a plane, fly someplace two hours away, stay a weekend, fly back, and only be charged for the four hours you actually used the aircraft. It's when you own a plane that you get into the heavy-duty expenses.

Q: So you don't own the . . . Citabria?

A: No, it <u>belongs to a friend</u>. I've got a great deal there, because he's also a <u>CFI—certified flight instructor</u>—and once I had the private license, he taught me what I needed for my <u>instrument</u> and <u>multiengine ratings</u>.

Q: I'm impressed.

A: Don't be; it's like any other skill—you learn one thing, and it's a building block to another. When I started out, I thought it would be enough if I could just get the plane into the air and back down again, but now . . .

There wasn't a lot of personal information in the piece, but D'Silva had used what she'd underlined as the kind of building blocks I'd mentioned. Easy for her to come up with Hy's name: Citabrias aren't all that common, and CFIs make up a small proportion of licensed pilots. A computerized cross-referencing of Citabria owners and CFIs must have put her on the way to a wealth of information. And that information, cross-referenced with what she knew about me, must have amounted to a treasure trove.

In spite of the cold rain spattering against the window, the small office seemed overly warm and stuffy. I got up and opened the door to let some air in before I went through the remaining contents of the box.

Calculator, gold pen-and-pencil set, business card holder. I opened the latter and found numerous cards belonging to women in a wide variety of occupations. It isn't unusual for an investigator to possess such a collection—the cards come in handy when operating undercover—but I couldn't think of any reason a security specialist would need them.

Another box, containing checks on an account at Wells Fargo and printed with D'Silva's driver's license number; I ripped one out and pocketed it. Copy of *The Golden Gate Pilot's Guide,* a publication issued by the Oakland Flight Service Station; it looked new and unused. Small bottle of Advil and a larger one of generic aspirin. Box half full of—

Facsimiles of my own business card, like the one she'd given to Clive Benjamin. They'd obviously been printed from a negative shot off the one I gave her at the conclusion of our interview. The box had probably held 250 cards when full. I couldn't bear to think where and to whom she'd passed out the rest.

The last item in the box was a ring holding what looked like extra car and house keys. I pocketed them, too, and was about to box up the rest when something wedged between the overlapping flaps at the bottom of the carton caught my eye. I poked at it with my fingernail and pried loose a rectangular piece of black plastic the size of a credit card; when I held it to the light, iridescent threads of color appeared: blue, silver, pink, purple, green. I turned it over, saw the back side was blank except for a magnetic strip.

Mitch stuck his head through the door. "You want to go grab a bite to eat?"

"Uh, sure, in a few minutes. Does this mean anything to you?"

He squinted at it, shook his head. "A lot of our systems make use of key cards, including the one here in the office. We change them weekly, make them up in the copy room. But none look like that."

"Something I forgot to ask you earlier: is Vintage Lofts one of your clients?"

"Sure. Developer's a golf partner of mine."

"And D'Silva was a technician on that job?"

"One of them. Why?"

"Just guessing, from what I know of her."

Mitch let it go at that and told me he'd meet me downstairs in ten minutes. The man might be good at what he did, but given his lack of an inquiring mind, he'd never have made it as an investigator.

The gray clapboard house on Potrero Hill's Mariposa Street was in poor repair, its paint like peeling skin; the windows of the upper and lower flats reminded me of dark eyes staring reproachfully at the rain. A realty sign hanging crooked above the ground-floor bay window completed the forlorn picture. In Spanish *mariposa* means butterfly, but had any frequented these parts, they'd long since moved on to more hospitable climes.

After lunch I'd driven directly to the address given by Lee D'Silva on her job application. A quick look around assured me that no one was home at either flat, but I decided not to use the spare keys I'd removed from her personal effects just yet. Instead I returned to the pier and set Mick to work getting the make and plate number of her car, as well as the multiple listing on the property.

Two-unit Victorian house, bay view from top flat, potential for third unit. Tenants: Misty Tyree (lower), Lee D'Silva (upper). Monthly rental income: $1,000 (lower); $1,300 (upper). The phone number for D'Silva matched that on her application. Under remarks, the agent described the building as having "two charming units, with a sunny private front garden."

As I stood before it now I shook my head. The front garden was merely a terraced slope overrun by weeds that threatened to claim the steps and tiny porch. As I went up to the door, blackberry vines reached hungrily for my ankles. The wooden steps were rotted, the doors warped. And for this they wanted over half a million dollars?

I rang the bell for the lower flat and received no answer. Rang D'Silva's flat, waited, rang twice more. Then I used her key to let myself inside. A steep, narrow staircase lay straight ahead, the walls to either side painted a harsh burnt orange. As I climbed, a familiar nobody-lives-here-anymore feeling stole over me.

The staircase ended in a hallway that branched to the front and back of the house. More burnt orange, trimmed in lemon yellow. I went toward the front, into a white-walled living room whose only furnishings were a salmon-colored couch, black iron floor lamps, and an unfinished mission-style coffee table. In the center of the table sat a white figure of a nude woman on a pedestal, her chest cut away to expose ribs and organs—*Autopsy,* the piece stolen from Clive Benjamin's apartment.

"Hard evidence," I said softly. Evidence, and a nightmare waiting to disturb one's dreams.

I took a quick turn around the room, then followed the hallway to the next door. A bedroom, with plain pine flooring and white walls like the living room. The low platform bed was covered by a goose-down comforter, and in one corner under a skylight, an old claw-footed bathtub sat, a thick woven rug spread next to it. When I went over there I saw that it had been retrofitted as a Jacuzzi. Fairly expensive improvements for a woman on a security technician's salary. I crossed to a pine armoire and opened its doors, immediately smelled the familiar scent of Dark Secrets perfume. Most of the garments had been removed, but one item hung in the exact center: a teal-blue outfit, soft and silky.

And spooky. Definitely spooky.

Eager now to see what else she had left for me, I went on to the last room. It was large, its walls sky blue, with a minuscule kitchen tucked behind a bar at one side. An overhead grid supported a variety of spotlights; I flicked the switch by the door and my breath caught.

Before me half a dozen chrome-and-leather sling-back chairs mingled with at least nine chrome-and-glass tables. And on each table lay an artfully arranged and lighted display. I began to move about the room, taking in each object.

Guns: revolvers, automatics, rifles, shotguns. The light caressed their well-oiled surfaces.

Badges, antique and recent: sheriff's departments, police, security firms, U.S. Marshals Service, even FBI. They shimmered and glinted.

An SFPD officer's visored hat, displayed on a wig stand.

Handcuffs, nightsticks, walkie-talkies, and all sorts of other law-enforcement paraphernalia.

And a final object, all by itself and intensely lighted: Lee D'Silva's diploma from Butte College, where she'd majored in police science.

I kept moving among the tables, trying to make sense of it all. Bizarre, but less so if you understood the collector's mentality. I don't have that instinct myself; I'm always trying to get rid of unnecessary possessions. But Hy is an avid collector of western novels and Americana, and I appreciate the compulsion that drives him.

But this collection was no normal one; it bordered on the monomaniacal. Nothing else in the flat spoke of another passion or interest—

Motion at the far end of the room. I whirled, going into a crouch, reaching for my .357.

No one. A sliding door to a small balcony had been left open a crack. The wind had shifted, blowing the curtain aside and twirling around an object suspended from the lighting grid in front of the glass. It was a model airplane. A white high-winged Citabria with a blue gull silhouetted on its tail section. A Citabria bearing the identification number 77289.

I felt a moan of protest moving up my throat. Quickly I forced it down and studied the model. It was faithful to Hy's plane in every detail—the product of a skilled and expensive craftsperson. Minutes passed as I contemplated it, the seconds ticking in counterpoint to the elevated beat of my pulse. Finally I continued through the room, ending up in the galley kitchen. A corkscrew and a single glass sat on the countertop next to the refrigerator; I opened the refrigerator door.

Its only occupant was a bottle of Deer Hill Chardonnay.

More showing off, bragging to me of how accurately she could anticipate my moves. But now I was beginning to understand how she did that: she'd been keeping me under partial surveillance, followed me to Carver Security, and realized I was on to her. So she'd cleared out of the apartment, leaving her Sharon McCone outfit and this gift.

I shut the fridge door and went to the center of the room, where I assumed the acoustics were best. Said, "Thanks for the wine, Lee, but no thanks. I hate to tell you, but you've made a big mistake. I don't have to explain what; you know how my mind works. Or do you? Let's see which of us can be the better McCone."

The flat lay in silence, but somewhere, I knew, a recorder was taping my words.

I'd been parked across from the Mariposa Street house for close to two hours before anything happened. Two long hours, which I mainly spent on the phone. Calls to RKI's La Jolla headquarters went unreturned by either Gage Renshaw or the third partner, Dan Kessell. There were no messages from Hy at the office or on my home machine. As early rain-soaked darkness closed in, I began to feel isolated and depressed. Warm lights glowed on in the nearby houses; people hurried to home and hearth. I wondered, as I often did on surveillances, why I'd chosen such a solitary occupation. Wondered why I'd been drawn to a man whose lifestyle demanded long and frequent separations.

Easy answers, of course: Hy and I were perfectly suited to our vocations, were perfectly suited to one another.

The phone buzzed: a friend of Hy's who worked for the FAA at their Oakland Airport office, returning my earlier call. I'd asked him if he could find out whether Lee D'Silva had gotten her pilot's license.

"She's got it. High marks on the written test two months ago. Passed her check ride on the fifteenth."

The day after she'd stared angrily at me in the bar at Palomino—and one of the few good-weather days we'd had recently.

Across the street an old VW bug pulled into D'Silva's driveway, and a woman got out and hurried through the rain to the door of the lower flat. She juggled purse, umbrella, and keys, then let herself inside. Light flared in the bay window.

"Sharon?"

"I'm here. Sorry. Can you give me the license number and examiner's name?"

He gave me the number, said he'd get back to me about the examiner. After I ended the call, I scrambled from the MG and hurried across the street.

The woman who came to the door of the lower flat wore a pink uniform with a prim white collar and cuffs, and her feet were swaddled in fluffy blue bunny-rabbit slippers. Her face was plain to the point of being homely, and her upper teeth protruded slightly, but her hair was a luminous pale blond, arranged in an intricate braided style. She stared at me, said, "Oh, you're early," and glanced down at the bunnies with apparent embarrassment.

"I'm not the person you're expecting." I handed her one of my cards.

"Oh, jeez, I thought you were my six o'clock appointment. I try to look professional for the clients, and these stupid rabbits, they aren't gonna do it."

"They look comfortable, though. What kind of clients?"

"I'm a hairstylist; I work downtown at Finesse, but I take on private clients here at home as well." Now she was eyeing my rain-wet hair, probably thinking that I could do with her services.

"You're Misty Tyree?"

"Yes. And you . . ." She looked at my card again. "You're Lee's boss."

A drop of water from the eaves landed on my forehead and dribbled down my nose. As I wiped it away, Misty Tyree said, "Oh, Lord, I'm sorry! Come inside, please."

I stepped into the hallway, and she relieved me of my damp coat, hanging it on a peg near the door. "Let's sit in the living room," she told me. "I've got the fire on."

I followed her to a comfortable room furnished in what looked to be good secondhand pieces and, at her urging, took the chair closest to the small gas-log fireplace. Tyree went to the window, pulled the draperies shut against the gathering gloom.

"I've got to tell you," she said, "Lee is really jazzed on working for you. I've never seen her so up before."

"She's not usually?"

"She hated that job with the security people, just *hated* it. Not that she didn't give it a hundred and ten percent effort. Lee always gives a hundred and ten percent. But, then, you must know that."

". . . Uh, yes. Tell me, when was the last time you saw her?"

Tyree paused in the process of sitting down opposite me. "Why . . . it's been a few days now. Is something wrong?"

"She's out on an assignment, and we've lost contact with her."

Her face creased with such genuine concern that I felt bad about lying to her. "Jeez, let me think. I guess it's since Tuesday morning that I heard her up there. And now it's Thursday. So three days. But I haven't been home much, so she could've come and gone and I wouldn't've known it."

"Can you think of someplace else she might be staying? With a friend, perhaps?"

Her forthright gaze wavered. "Well, it isn't unusual . . ."

"Yes?"

"This is . . . I'm not sure I should be mentioning it to you, is the problem. You being her boss and all."

"Something about her private life?"

"Uh-huh."

"Please, don't worry. At my agency we respect each other's right to privacy. I would never let anything you might tell me color my feelings toward her as an employee."

She nodded, fingers pleating the hem of her uniform where it lay across her knees, obviously still uncomfortable.

"What concerns me more than anything," I added, "is that she may be in danger."

". . . In that case, well, okay. Lee gets around. She hits the club scene pretty heavy, and she's into the art circuit—galleries, showings, stuff like that—too. Any kind of event where she might meet—"

"Where she might meet men."

"Uh-huh. And she meets them, by the dozens. Stays out a lot of nights. I asked her once, wasn't she worried about all the stuff out there—AIDS, weirdos, you know. She just laughed, said she could take care of herself." Tyree wouldn't meet my eyes now; I could see it distressed her to reveal such intimate matters about a friend.

I moved to put her at her ease. "Lee's guilty of bad judgment, but she's got to be the one to realize that and change her behavior."

Tyree looked up at last. "You won't tell her what I said?"

"It's not my place to. These clubs she goes to—any specific ones?"

"Well, the usual, in SoMa and North Beach. Even the Mission—and that's strictly a bridge-and-tunnel crowd."

Meaning D'Silva had probably picked up suburbanites. "Sharon McCone's" sleazy reputation could easily have spread throughout the Bay Area!

Tyree was looking away from me again. I followed her line of sight, saw she had focused on the flames licking at the gas log.

"Ms. Tyree—what is it?"

"Something worse."

"Than . . . ?"

"Than what I just told you." She took a deep breath. "Lee's mentioned a place called Club Turk a number of times. And a man, Russ Auerbach."

"Who is he?"

"Club owner. He's got a string of four, all over the city, including Club Turk. Three of them are very hip and upscale, but that one . . . there's something wrong about it."

"What?"

She shook her head, eyes still focused on the fire. "I don't know exactly. But in my job, you hear things. Clients talk to you and each other. It's like you're not there or you don't count, so they can say anything in front of you. A few weeks ago I overheard two of my society ladies discussing Club Turk. One said she wouldn't want to get caught there in a police raid. The other laughed and told her the police wouldn't come near the place, because if they raided it they'd end up embarrassing half the city's *and* the state's power structure. When they realized I'd overheard, they stopped talking."

"Where is this club?"

"The back of Nob Hill where it borders on the Tenderloin."

A rough area. "Have you ever been there?"

"Not a chance! The club scene's not for me."

"What does Lee say about it?"

"That she hangs there a lot, and she's got something going with Auerbach."

"An affair?"

"Could be, but I think it's more than that. When she talked about it, she got really excited—more excited than she ever does over a man. In fact, the only time I've seen her that way was about the job with you."

"Did you ask her what was going on at Club Turk?"

"Uh-huh. She said I'd know in good time."

Interesting. I'd have to check out the club scene; with the exception of the evening on the town on Valentine's Day—when Ricky had taken us to two exclusive clubs frequented by celebrities and to one private club—I'd been away from that particular rapidly changing milieu for several years.

Misty Tyree was watching me, expecting some kind of response. When I didn't offer one, she said, "You know, Ms. McCone, I'm kind of a vanilla person. Was born and raised in Marysville and never would've left if my husband hadn't gotten a job down here. We're divorced now, share custody of our little boy; he needs to be near his father, or I would've gone home a long time ago. That side of the city—the one Lee's into—I just can't understand. And Lee, I like her a lot, she's got so much to offer, but this other life of hers . . . I mean—why?"

"But you're her friend anyway."

"I try to be. She doesn't have any women friends except me. But sometimes I get so mad at her for wasting her time on something that's so meaningless—and maybe dangerous."

I wanted to tell her that Lee D'Silva wasn't worth wasting her emotions on, but I couldn't. Against my better instincts I found myself feeling for Lee, too. Maybe that old syndrome was kicking in: prisoner identifying with her captor. D'Silva had held me captive long enough that I was beginning to understand what drove her.

Well, that wasn't all bad. Knowing one's quarry is essential to the successful hunt.

Thursday Night

The sidewalks of the Eleventh Street corridor between Folsom and Harrison in the South of Market area gleamed wetly, reflecting the neon lights of the city's liveliest nightclubbing district. A break in the rain had brought out the crowds, who lined up in front of Slim's, the Paradise Lounge, Twenty Tank Brewery, and the DNA Lounge. Rock music from a live band boomed through the door of Eleven Restaurant & Bar, where they were really packing them in. At ten forty-five, the evening had not yet reached its peak.

I moved through the knots of well-dressed people, keeping my eyes on Russ Auerbach, the club owner with whom Lee D'Silva "had something going." I'd kept him under surveillance for two hours, since he'd put in an appearance at Napoli, his North Beach jazz club, and now he was crossing Folsom on his way to End of the Line, a similar establishment.

After I'd left Misty Tyree's flat, I'd put in a call to my old friend Wolf, who runs a two-person agency, hoping to co-opt him to run a surveillance on the upper flat on Mariposa Street. I didn't really expect D'Silva to return there—not now that I'd visited it—but I wanted it watched all the same. Wolf, however, was about to leave town on another job.

"Anybody you can recommend I use?" I asked.

"As a matter of fact, yes. You've met Tamara Corbin?"

"Uh-huh." Wolf's assistant was a bright young African American whose computer skills were a close match for Mick's. She had brought Wolf, an avowed technophobe, kicking and screaming into the twenty-first century.

"Well, Ms. Corbin has decided that the P.I. business isn't as demeaning as she first thought and that it might be a career option for her. 'A way to scam some of the big bucks' is the way she puts it. Of course, she's looking at the high-tech end, but as I keep telling her, some low-tech fieldwork is necessary for an all-around education."

From his joking tone, I knew Tamara was there and listening to his end of the conversation. "Absolutely necessary," I agreed.

"Besides, you'd be doing me a favor. This job I've got may keep me away for a week or so, and if she's stuck here in the office all by her lonesome, she'll probably do something else to make it impossible for me to find anything around here without her help. As things stand now, it's a toss-up as to which of us is running the operation and which of us is the scut worker."

"Consider her hired, then."

Wolf put Tamara on the phone, and after she made a few kidding remarks in response to his, we discussed the details of the surveillance and settled on a fee. Then I went to Mick's office, where he was waiting for Keim, whom Rae had assigned to a new corporate undercover job.

"What d'you know about the nightclub scene here in the city?" I asked him.

"Everything." He smiled self-importantly.

I regarded him sternly. "How come you're so in tune with it?" Mick was only nineteen—two years short of the legal drinking age here in California—and while he looked and acted older, most clubs carded anyone who appeared to be under thirty.

His grin faded. "I thought you and I had agreed to the principle of don't-ask, don't-tell when it comes to our private lives."

"Only because *you* agreed to don't-take-risks, don't-get-hurt."

"I'm not, and I won't."

Which probably meant he'd come into possession of an extremely good and complete set of fake ID. I sighed and gave up on playing the interfering aunt. Mick had been raised with somewhat loose supervision under conditions that would make most experts on parenting wince, but he'd also inherited his parents' basic good sense. He didn't do drugs, I'd never seen him drunk, and he was his own man in every respect.

"Okay," I said, "first give me a rundown on what clubs are hot."

"Hot depends on what you're after. You've got four areas of the city: SoMa, the Tenderloin, the Mission, and North Beach. You'll find different kinds of people and clubs in each." He began a description of individual ones so detailed that I stopped him before he finished with SoMa.

"Let's shorten the process. Have you ever heard of Russ Auerbach? He owns Club Turk, among others."

He thought for a moment. "Is that the guy . . . Yeah, he owns Napoli in North Beach. Little guy, curly brown hair, his face kind of reminds me of a chipmunk's. Likes to play host, circulates from table to table—oozes from table to table, Sweet Charlotte would say. I think he's got a club in the Mission and End of the Line in SoMa, but we don't go there. And the one you mentioned in the Tenderloin—Club Turk—has a weird reputation."

"How so?"

"Nobody talks specifics, but a lot of movers and shakers frequent it."

"Strange area for the power brokers."

"Strange area, period. We steer clear of it."

"Can you describe Auerbach in more detail?"

"Well, he's really kind of ordinary. Glasses? No. But he

squints, like he might be wearing contacts that irritate his eyes. No facial hair or distinguishing marks. Dresses Italian-casual, lots of jewelry."

"Who does?" Keim's voice asked.

Mick looked toward the door. "About time. We're talking about Russ Auerbach."

"Who?"

"The oozer from Napoli."

"Oh, him. Why, for God's sake?" She came into the office and perched on the arm of Mick's chair, slipping her arm around his shoulders.

"Yeah," he said, "why are you interested in him?"

"A neighbor of D'Silva's says she's got something going with him, hangs out at Club Turk. Can you think of any way I can recognize him?"

Keim said, "Why not go to one of the clubs and ask for him?"

"I'm hoping to establish a surveillance on him, see if he'll lead me to her."

"Well, I don't know where you can get a photo, at least not tonight, but . . . Of course!" She looked at Mick. "You remember that night last month when we were waiting outside Napoli for Jessie and Matt, and Auerbach drove up?"

He frowned, shook his head.

"Well, he did. I remember because you'd just had your hair cut and kept complaining that the fog was ruining an expensive styling job. Anyway, Auerbach left his car with the club's valet parker. Black Porsche—about the same vintage as the one your dad drives. I got a look at its vanity plate— RUSS A 1."

Mick ran his hand over his blond head. "I was not complaining about my *hair*."

"Yes, you were."

"Charlotte, thanks," I said. "Mick, when it comes time for the clubs to open, will you call all four of Auerbach's and ask when they expect him tonight? And then call me at home with the information?"

"Sure. In the meantime, what'll you be doing?"

"Getting ready for a hot night on the town."

Now I watched Auerbach enter End of the Line, then joined the queue waiting for admittance. Conversations swirled around me; from them I gathered that the majority of clubgoers were suburbanites or tourists. The couple ahead of me were describing to friends the great house they'd just bought in Walnut Creek; behind me two women were marveling at how cool this scene was compared to Saint Paul. Many of the younger people expressed concern about their ID standing up to the carding at the door.

I hadn't even thought of presenting ID, should I get close enough to venture inside. I'd never be carded again in this lifetime. The thought made me feel both smug and a little sad.

For reassurance, I glanced down at my clubbing outfit—a form-fitting little silver sequinned dress and black velvet coat that hadn't seen service in so long that they were right back in style. The sadness vanished. They fit as well as they had the last time I'd worn them. Not bad for an old broad of forty, as Mick was fond of calling me.

Behind me the line grew. If Auerbach ran according to the rather loose schedule Mick had put together by calling his clubs, he'd come outside very soon and head for the Mission.

The man in front of me turned, looked me over, and said, "Sure glad the rain's quit." He was handsome, if you cared for the drug-lord look.

"Uh-huh," I replied.

"It's hell when you've got to stand in line in the rain."

"Pure hell."

"Supposed to clear tomorrow, though, I saw it on the news. They're predicting—"

"They can't predict."

"No? Why not?"

"Because the weather gods jam their radar. They send out these rays, similar to what you get when you bounce a signal off a cell-phone site, only more powerful. They hate us, you know."

"Uh, sure." He smiled nervously and turned away.

Sometimes clear evidence of insanity is a great way to deflect a man's interest without bruising his feelings.

At a few minutes before midnight I stood in the dark outside entryway of an apartment building on Guerrero Street, indulging in a largely unwarranted attack of nostalgia while watching the door of Auerbach's Mission district club, Bohemia. The owner had come directly there from SoMa. The club was small, so I'd decided against going inside and calling attention to myself. Auerbach still had one stop left to make—at Club Turk—and if he was to rendezvous with D'Silva, that would be the place.

Newspapers and flyers littered the entry's floor, and the overhead bulb was burned out; several of the mailboxes flapped open, their locks broken. I'd rented a studio in this building near the intersection of Guerrero and Twenty-second Streets from the time I graduated from U.C. Berkeley till I bought my house. One of my first big cases had played out here. I'd walked these cracked sidewalks and dark alleys thousands of times, yet now I was a stranger.

In those days the Mission wasn't the greatest place to live in the city, but parts of it weren't that bad, either; ethnically mixed and solidly working class, they harbored a nice sense of community. At this intersection there was a corner grocery, a Laundromat, a small bakery, and Ellen T's Bar & Grill; I patronized them all and knew their proprietors. Parking was always a hassle, but I felt safe leaving the MG on the street, and on the way to and from it I exchanged greetings with many a neighbor.

But after I scraped together the down payment on my house and moved away, I'd heard that even this pleasant little pocket had deteriorated. Drug deals, which usually went down in the Devil's Quadrangle section bisected by Mission between Sixteenth and Twenty-fourth, went down here as well; winos lurched along the sidewalks and urinated publicly; buildings became blighted by graffiti as gang activity escalated; one by one businesses that had catered to the district's solid citizens closed their doors; and those solid citizens who could afford to move away began a rapid exodus.

But now the character of this intersection had changed again. My old grocery store was still there, but it had changed hands and looked to be ripe for a takeover by the adjoining bar. There was an upscale restaurant on the opposite corner; the Laundromat had been replaced by a gift and card shop. A succession of clubs, the latest being Bohemia, had occupied the space that used to be Ellen T's, since the day when the dreams of the congenial couple who owned it were shattered by a robber's bullet. Tonight I'd felt disoriented and had to take a look at the number to make sure this *was* my former building. And no one had greeted me but a well-dressed drunk who mistook me for a hooker.

The neon lights of the club and the soft glow from the bar and restaurant offered me no false reassurance as to my safety. The establishments catered mainly to neo-bohemians who lived in other neighborhoods or, more often, outside the city, and I hoped they were aware that this was still rough territory where simply making eye contact the wrong way could create a volatile situation.

The rain began—lightly at first, then sheeting down and gusting into the entryway. I retreated, pulling my flimsy coat closer and shivering. A few people who had been talking on the sidewalk in front of the Lone Palm Bar scattered to their cars. Auerbach had been inside Bohemia for a long time; I wished he'd hurry up and leave for Club Turk. One good thing about this weather—it would keep the predators off the streets of the Tenderloin. Most of them, anyway.

The area around Turk and Taylor made the Mission look like a parochial school playground. Even in the now-steady rain, miniskirted hopefuls—and not all of them women—

stood under umbrellas on the corners, calling out to occupants of cars. Derelicts huddled in the shelter of closed and barred storefronts amid a welter of filthy blankets and rags. One block over, I'd passed a squad car and ambulance, their lights flashing; the paramedics were lifting a crumpled figure from the gutter to a stretcher. And scattered among the abandoned buildings and evil-smelling alleys and human misery were clubs that ranged from unadorned dives to glittering establishments where the more adventurous of the city's night crowd flocked.

It was late enough that the patrons of the nearby theater district had dispersed, so street parking was plentiful. I waited at the corner till Auerbach pulled his Porsche to the curb and handed the keys to the valet, then made my turn and parked half a block down from Aunt Charlie's Lounge—a lavender mecca for the cross-dressing set that even I had heard of—and got out, looking askance at a large black man wandering along the sidewalk and muttering to himself. When he drew closer, I saw he was actually muttering into a walkie-talkie and recognized the familiar beret of the Guardian Angels. He nodded as he passed.

That was all well and good, but he didn't look a match for the guy leaning against the burned-out hotel and cleaning his nails with a switchblade; and that hooker who had just given the finger to a cruising john may have been clad in chiffon, but his biceps were on a par with a heavyweight's. I glanced apprehensively at the MG, then thought, What the hell. My mechanic might think it was a gem, but to me it was just a car, and an increasingly unreliable one at best.

I moved along the street, avoiding eye contact with passersby, concentrating on Club Turk. It occupied the ground floor of a narrow, nondescript building like most of the others on this block, and was distinguished only by a large black window shot with iridescent threads of blue, silver, pink, purple, and green, with the name spelled out in purple. When I'd first spotted it, the color scheme had struck me as familiar. Now I reached into my bag for the key card I'd found among Lee D'Silva's office effects.

Yes, the colors were the same.

A limo pulled to the curb in front of the club, and a group of six people in evening clothes got out, the driver sheltering them with umbrellas held in either hand. The black-clad doorman ushered them in, then waited for a couple who were leaving. Late on a midweek night, but—

A woman was walking quickly along the opposite sidewalk, head bent against the rain, her steps staccato in high heels. Making for the club's door. Honey-blond hair lay across her cheeks and forehead, hiding her features. Her wrap, over a long, dark dress, was teal blue.

The doorman appeared to know her, held the door as she went inside.

I angled across the street.

The doorman was tall and muscular—a bouncer, really—completely bald but possessed of a curiously boyish face. He looked at me with eyes that had seen everything and not been surprised by any of it, and seemed to wait for some action on my part. On impulse, I pulled out D'Silva's key card and showed it to him.

He nodded and held the door open.

Private club? No, not according to Mick. Maybe the card was a way of separating the regulars—the people who participated in whatever illegal activity went down there—from the uninitiated.

I stepped into a small space so dark that, once the door closed behind me, I felt as if I'd been swallowed up by a black hole. Then I saw colors leaking around a rectangular shape—the same colors as on the key card and window. I put out my hand, felt velvet cloth, and pushed it aside.

The room ahead of me was dark except for threads and swirls and splashes of the thematic colors. Some came from spotlights, others from metallic substances embedded in the black Plexiglas furnishings, still others from neon tubing running along the walls, ceiling, and floors. It was a typical cocktail lounge arrangement, a jazz combo playing at the far end, enveloped in a multicolored smoky haze.

I walked toward the bar, taking careful note of the patrons. Most wore dark clothing, the spots highlighting their faces and bare skin. The women had that anorexic look termed by the press "heroin chic," and most of the men appeared sullen and bored. The group I'd seen exiting the limo were seated in a large banquette; I recognized a movie actor and a well-known writer. Nowhere did I see Lee D'Silva.

I sat on a stool at the end of the bar, ordered a glass of Chardonnay. When the black-clad bartender brought it, I laid the key card down and he ran it through a charge machine. No bottles or glasses stood above bar level—nothing to mar the effect of the dazzling colors. The mirrored wall behind the bar resembled a giant iridescent spiderweb spun against a midnight sky; its strands shimmered and shifted, distorted perceptions, alternately dulled and excited the senses. I looked through the filaments at the reflection of the room behind me, scanned the patrons once more. No Lee D'Silva.

After a while the movie actor got up and went to a black-curtained exit at the rear, presumably to use the rest rooms. He hadn't returned in five minutes, and one at a time the other members of his party followed suit. A rear exit? No, they'd have left together.

Finally I got up, left a tip on the bar, and went that way too.

A hallway, too brightly lighted after the room behind me. Doors, labeled Women, Men, Employees Only. And another at the very rear. I moved toward it, saw the box with the glowing red light below the knob—the kind of security lock you find on many hotel rooms. I took the card from my pocket and ran it through; the red light went out and another glowed green. I drew back against the wall and considered.

A private room. Lee D'Silva could be inside. If I blundered in there, she'd flee and odds were I'd never locate her again. But if I didn't go through this door, I might never come face to face with her.

I transferred the card to my left hand, put my right into my little nightclubbing bag, and gripped my .357. Thrust the card into the box and, when the light glowed green, eased the door open.

A concrete stairway led down to well below street level. At its bottom was another door, another security box. I went down, used the card again, and nudged the door slightly open with my foot.

And looked in at Las Vegas.

A large subterranean room, its lighting directed at green felt tables; clots of people gathered around them as dealers sent cards sliding across the felt and croupiers spun their wheels. Smoke clouds rose toward the ceiling; cocktail waitresses circulated. I heard talk and laughter and the occasional exultant gasp. I'd visited many such rooms in the state of Nevada.

But here in the state of California such rooms were illegal.

Nobody was paying attention to me. Quickly I looked around for Lee D'Silva. My breath caught when I glimpsed her, over by the roulette table—

But, no, that wasn't D'Silva. Merely a blond woman who now held her teal-blue wrap over her arm. Who really didn't resemble D'Silva at all.

Disappointment dealt my stomach the kind of weightless, hollow feeling as when an updraft slammed the Citabria. Desperately I scanned the faces of the other players. The movie actor, the writer, and their party were there. Two other people I recognized from their frequent appearances in the society pages of the local papers; another was a well-known local politician, still another a state senator.

But no D'Silva; no Auerbach, either. Of course, they could be in an office somewhere—

A hand grasped my upper arm. I looked around, tried to jerk free. The hand held. It belonged to the doorman who had earlier admitted me.

"Ms. D'Silva," he said with icy politeness, "you'd better come with me."

Russ Auerbach was leaning over a table in a small office, hands flat on either side of a computerized spreadsheet—studying the night's take, no doubt. Up close he looked older and more tired than he had from a distance: just another overextended small businessman at the end of a hard day. He kept his eyes on the sheet and sighed heavily.

"Jesus, Lee," he said, "what're you doing here—and why're you wearing that stupid disguise again? Grow up, will you?"

The doorman had thrust me into the room and withdrawn without relieving me of the key card or attempting to search my purse. Now I reached behind my back and shot the dead bolt while bringing out the .357.

"Wrong woman, Mr. Auerbach."

Slowly he straightened, small eyes narrowing as he focused first on the gun and then on my face. He licked dry lips before he asked, "Who're you? And what is this?"

"My name's Sharon McCone. Does that mean anything to you?"

". . . You're the woman Lee wanted to work for. Did she give you her key card? If that crazy bitch sent you to threaten me—"

"I'm here about Lee, not on her behalf."

"And the card? Where'd you get it?"

"I found it among some of her things."

"I should've taken it away from her, but instead I just canceled it. When you settled your drink tab, it was rejected, and the bartender recognized the name that came up on the account and called me. I told him to let her drink her wine and then ask her to leave."

"He didn't, though."

"No, you headed back too fast for him. He called me again, I said to pass you—her—through and get Danny to bring her to me. Then we'd have it out once and for all." He paused, eyes on the .357 again. "Why the gun?"

"I don't know you, don't know what your relationship with Lee D'Silva is. If you're a friend of hers, we've got problems."

"I'm not her friend. And there isn't any relationship—not since a couple, three weeks ago."

I studied him for a moment, then slipped the gun back into my bag and took out one of my cards. "Mr. Auerbach, why don't we sit down. It's in our best interests to talk."

Russ Auerbach had met Lee D'Silva at the bar of Club Turk the previous November. She told him she frequented a number of the establishments on the slope of Nob Hill. "Likes her nightlife kind of off center and gritty," he said, "same as she likes her sex life."

"Meaning?"

"I don't talk about my women, past or present."

"Come on, Russ. You know you want to tell me."

He smiled, showing small, pointed teeth. "Maybe I do. Broad put me through hell. Lee likes her sex rough—and plentiful. When I started with her, I knew it was a nonexclusive. She goes with a lot of guys."

"She take you home?" I was wondering if he'd seen her collections, and what he thought of them.

"Never. She said she had a flat on Potrero Hill, but it was off limits. One place that was hers alone. I thought that meant she was married or had a live-in, though when she'd've had time for either I couldn't imagine. Anyway, she usually came to my place, or we did it here in the office."

I looked around the little room.

Auerbach said, "She wasn't into comfort."

"Apparently not."

"Wasn't even a relationship, really. I didn't take her to dinner; we didn't go anyplace together. All we did was fuck and talk, mainly about her. She fascinated me, but I didn't really like her."

"What fascinated you, aside from the obvious?"

"Before we go any further with this, tell me why you're interested in her. Did you hire her and get screwed over?"

"I didn't hire her, and because of that she screwed me over."

"Welcome to the club—no pun intended."

"Let's get back to what fascinated you—and what she did to you."

"Okay. Lee's a very driven person, probably the most driven I've ever met. Flat-out perfectionist. Everything she does, she has to do it right; she doesn't cut herself any slack, ever. And she has these mood swings from one extreme to the other, with absolutely no middle ground. When she's down, she's really harsh on herself, and when she's up . . . Well, then it's like she's a completely different person. She flies an airplane, you know that?"

I nodded.

"Well, that's one example. She can fly a fuckin' *airplane*, for Christ's sake, but it's not good enough because it's the wrong kind of plane. The one she wants to fly is more difficult to learn to land, and she's got it into her head that that's what she's got to do, and right away. I ask her why. She says she's got to be better. Better than what? I ask. Just better, she says."

Better than me.

Auerbach shook his head. "Jesus, I can't even get on a *jumbo jet* without slugging down about six drinks, but she thinks she's not good enough because she hasn't learned to fly this little tiny plane yet!"

"Did you ever give her money?"

"What the hell kind of a question is that? I don't have to pay for it!"

"Sorry, I didn't mean to imply that you do. But while you were talking about her flying, I started wondering where she got the money to pay for it. I know her salary history, and I also know what her flat rents for. There wouldn't be much left over for flying lessons."

"Well, I never gave her a cent, but somebody must've. She was one well-financed broad."

"Why d'you say that?"

"Her clothes, her grooming. And I met a guy at one of my other clubs who'd gone with her; he said she'd taken him home. He couldn't remember exactly where—she drove, and he was pretty drunk—but it was some little studio, not the flat on Potrero Hill. So she was paying rent on two places."

"Or has a place she can borrow. This guy—who is he?"

"Regular customer at Napoli. Jim something. I don't know his whole name."

"Next time you see him, will you call me?"

"Sure."

"Thanks. Okay, you've told me why Lee fascinated you. Now, what did she do to you?"

"Call it a betrayal of confidence."

"How?"

"I can't go into it. There're other people involved, and, like you said earlier, I don't know you. Or trust you."

"In my business, I have to be discreet."

"About your clients' affairs, yes. But I'm nothing to you."

She'd threatened to betray his confidence about the gambling club or some other illegal activity, no doubt. And she'd probably threatened to expose his associates, too. I needed to know exactly what had happened, and there was a way to work around this snag.

After a moment I said, "I assume you have an attorney on retainer."

"Twenty-four hours a day, three hundred and sixty-five days a year."

"Get him on the phone. Tell him to hire me to investigate Lee D'Silva."

"The hell I will! I took care of her personally; she's history."

"Have him hire me to investigate her—for a dollar. Which I will loan to you." I took one from my bag and laid it on the table between us.

A slow smile spread across Auerbach's face as he picked it up. Then he reached for the phone.

"I was thinking with my balls," Auerbach told me. "For Christmas I gave her a membership in the casino—that key card. She'd noticed something was going on, was at me to tell her about it. So I thought, Why not humor the crazy kid? Maybe she'd stick around more. After that she was around plenty, but not because of me."

"She's a gambler?"

"Hell, no." He shook his head. "I never once saw her at the tables. She'd just watch. We get a lot of important people in here, and they interested her. At least that's what I thought at first."

"And later?"

"Lee fancies herself a hot-shot private eye like you. I guess you know that. But, shit, the woman works for a bunch of alarm installers; uses a computer good, but so what? If you ask me, she couldn't detect her way out of a paper bag."

He was underestimating D'Silva—but, then, so had I. "Go on."

"Well, what she was really doing here—and with me—was gathering evidence on me and my associates. Them I'm not gonna say anything about, except that we got a pretty good cooperative arrangement in various lucrative areas, and I made the mistake of talking to Lee about it. So she decided she was gonna make a name for herself by exposing us and our important clients. Get her face in the papers, ensure she got the job with your agency. She'd sneak around in this stupid disguise that didn't fool anybody, and she'd photograph and tape stuff. Finally somebody noticed what she was doing and tipped me."

"This disguise—I take it she looked somewhat like me in it."

"Yeah. The bartender—he's new, never knew Lee—described you when he called back here. I was sure you were her."

"Did you ever ask her why she wore it?"

"Sure. All she would say was that she liked to live different lives, and it was part of the fantasy."

"The fantasy?"

Auerbach shrugged. "That's all she'd say."

"Okay—somebody tipped you to the picture-taking and taping. Then what?"

"I had my condo swept for bugs, the club, too. They were there, and in most cases the circumstances were such that she was the only one who could've planted them."

"So you . . . ?"

"Confronted her. Bitch actually bragged about what she'd done, said she had the evidence in a safe place and was going to go to the police and the D.A.'s office with it. I laughed at her."

"Why?"

"Let's just say I got those angles covered, and the little fool was too naive to figure that out."

Payoffs or holds over people at high levels? "What was her reaction?"

"She didn't believe me. It didn't fit her perfect plan. She kept coming at me, wouldn't back off."

"And?"

"Maybe you don't want to hear this."

"Look, we have a deal."

"Christ! All right, what I did: We were here in the office. She got more and more out of control. Shouting, screaming, taunting me. So I took her by the throat and slammed her against the wall. Started choking her. Real quiet, I told her that if I ever saw her in any of my clubs again, or anywhere near my home or my associates, I'd kill her with my bare hands."

The flesh on my arms rippled unpleasantly.

"I kept on choking her till she almost passed out. Then she peed in her pants and skulked out of here like a whipped dog. And I've never seen or heard from her again. Not a pretty story, is it?" He tried to put on a regretful face, but his eyes shone defiantly, almost proudly.

I watched him for a moment, keeping my emotions to myself.

I asked, "Exactly when was this?"

"You mean the date?" He reached for a calendar, flipped it backwards. "A Tuesday, February four."

Tuesday, February 4. On Wednesday D'Silva had gone to work at Carver Security and tossed the key card that she'd never be able to use again into her desk. That night she'd gone home to find the turndown letter from me. And the combination of the two events had sent her—the perfectionist, overachiever, would-be private investigator and pilot—into her crazy emotional tailspin.

Tonight I'm dreaming—I must be dreaming—that I'm flying the Citabria over high-tension wires that have been severed by a storm. They spark and crackle and writhe like huge snakes in the violent wind, lashing at the plane. I make S-turns among them as I sometimes do between billowing coastal clouds.

Hy's not with me. My connection with him is cut as surely as those wires. There's an occasional spark, yes, but mainly I don't feel anything. Nothing but this lonesomeness and a panic that makes my breath come short. I want to ask him how to avoid the crackling wires, but he's out of reach.

I continue making S-turns as I try to spot a landmark on the ground below.

There it is—the safe and familiar. A triangulation of lights against the blackness. Something's important about those lights and what they represent—something I ought to remember.

One of the wires arcs above the plane's nose, almost tangles in the prop. I dive to escape it. When I'm clear, I put in full throttle and outrun the storm.

friday

I knew it was going to be a peculiar day when I spilled coffee on the cat.

I was leaning down to pat Ralph and the mug tipped and there he was, sodden and singed. "Oh, Jesus!" I exclaimed and reached for him, but he escaped my grasp and ran down the hall to where the pet door used to be before his sister returned one night with an enormous rat that later died behind the refrigerator. Ralph's head connected solidly with the closed-up space on the wall, and he staggered back, shaking it. I hurried to him, but he cringed and yowled to be let out. As he stalked away across the deck, he flashed me a look of betrayal. I retreated to the sitting room to make some calls, feeling guilty as hell.

According to the man who answered the phone at RKI's Buenos Aires office, Mr. Ripinsky and Mr. Rivera were still out in the field and unavailable. La Jolla told me Gage Renshaw and Dan Kessell were similarly occupied. In Dan's case, that was an outright lie, since he seldom left his office, preferring the company of a dozen or so stuffed portions of animals that he'd personally slaughtered to that of his fellow humans.

About the only thing that was cooperating this morning was the weather, which had turned colder and beautifully clear.

I was partway through the comics when the phone rang:

Hy's friend from the FAA. He gave me the name of the examiner who had signed off on Lee D'Silva's private license, a Novato cop named Joe Bartlett. I reached Bartlett at home and told him I was thinking of hiring D'Silva and paying for her to get her commercial license so she could fly for the agency; what did he think of her skills?

"Skills're fine. She's great under pressure. We went up for the check ride in a Cessna 150, and . . . You fly?"

"I learned in a 150."

"Well, then, you know how sometimes the doors can pop open in flight if you haven't closed them with the windows open?"

"Uh-huh." It had scared the hell out of me the first time it happened.

"Well, that's what D'Silva's door did on takeoff, but it didn't faze her. She put on flaps, opened the window, tried to slam the door shut. Didn't work. So, cool as can be, she said to me the way a seasoned pilot would to a nervous passenger, 'I'm having a little trouble with this door, so I'm going to go around and make a full-stop landing. I'll secure the door, and then we'll start over.' "

"Pretty impressive, on a check ride where you're nervous anyway." What was it Stacey Nizibian, the SFPD expert on stalkers, had said? Something about them remaining cool under conditions that would have the rest of us climbing the walls. "Just out of curiosity, who was her flight instructor and where did she train?"

"Woman named Sara Grimly—"

"I know her. She's at Petaluma Municipal."

"Not anymore. She got married, moved to Los Alegres."

Los Alegres, where I'd also trained with a woman flight instructor. D'Silva had replicated my flight-training experience.

After Bartlett and I ended our conversation, I got out a rumpled and torn sectional chart—my instructor had often joked that they were called sectionals because they came apart in sections—and located Paradise, where D'Silva had grown up. Los Alegres was only a short detour from a direct course there, so I called the fixed-base operator—flight school, sales, rentals, and repairs—and asked if Sara Grimly was teaching today. She was, had gone out on an early flight and would be back at ten. I left a message asking her to meet me at the Seven Niner Diner, the airport restaurant, and hurried to get dressed. On the way to Oakland I tried not to obsess about Hy, but failed to the point that I nearly rear-ended a pickup on the Bay Bridge.

As I preflighted the Citabria, I realized my dream last night had proved to me how totally our connection had broken down. I missed him more than ever, felt myself sinking further into depression and near panic. But once I was out of Class C airspace, the bad feelings lifted; in this place, the cockpit where we'd flown together for so many hours, it was impossible not to feel some optimism. There's something about physically cutting loose from the earth and all its problems that creates hope.

And at this point, hope was all I could count on.

Sara Grimly was in her mid-twenties, dark haired and petite. She seemed even smaller than when I'd first met her, probably because she was dwarfed by the 1600-pound Cessna that she and her student were pushing into its tie-down—him guiding with the tow bar, but Grimly doing most of the work.

I walked toward them as he secured the chains and she collected her booster seat—in spite of the growing number of women pilots, planes are still designed for tall men—and headset case and purse. She turned, saw me, and waved.

"Bob Cuda relayed your message on the unicom," she called. "Nice to see you again."

"You too." I glanced toward the gas pumps, where a familiar gray-haired lineman in a hooded jacket was fueling an Aztec. "Cuda get his license yet?"

"No, but he's soloed." Grimly turned to the student. "I'll sign your logbook tomorrow, okay?"

He nodded and she touched my arm. "Onward to the diner."

The Seven Niner Diner held many memories for me, some of them bittersweet, and it seemed strange to be sitting down in a booth with Grimly rather than with my former flight instructor, Matty Wildress. Briefly I thought of how Matty would approve of my new take-charge attitude toward D'Silva—much as she would have disapproved of my earlier inability to deal with the situation.

We ordered—tea for Grimly, coffee for me. As she waved aside the offered menu, I spotted the substantial diamond engagement and wedding rings on her left hand.

"I heard you got married," I said. "Lovely rings."

She held her hand up so the light caught the stones. "Yeah. Do you remember when I told you the only way I was going to be able to buy my own plane was either to build up enough hours to get on with the airlines or to marry well?"

"Uh-huh."

"Well, I managed the latter. He's an architect, very much in demand. Now I can instruct for the pleasure of it, and that Mooney over there in the tie-downs is mine. And you know what? On top of all that, I'm crazy about him."

"Congratulations."

"Thanks. So what's happening with you? Your message said you wanted to ask about one of my former students."

"Yes—Lee D'Silva."

"May I ask why?"

"She's applied for a job with me, but something about her strikes me as not right. I can't put my finger on it, and I thought you might be able to shed some light on it."

Grimly considered, squeezing lemon into her tea. "Well, you know my policy of not talking about my students—and you also know I'll violate it for a good reason. Your feeling's correct. At first I couldn't analyze it either. She came into the

FBO last July, insisted on a woman instructor. She learned fast, was very intense—driven, actually—but I couldn't get at her reasons for wanting to fly."

"I'm not sure I understand."

"I don't think she really likes to fly. She found the details—learning the regs, preflighting, flight planning—annoying. And she never relaxed in the cockpit. It's natural to be tense at first, we all go through it; but most students, at least when they start doing cross-countries, soon realize that flying's fun and start to experience the sheer pleasure of being up there above it all. D'Silva didn't."

"Interesting, in light of the fact she was so cool on her check ride."

"You must've talked with Joe Bartlett. Yes, she was cool, but in a situation that had happened before. And I had an earlier student who handled the door-opening problem on a check ride in the same way; I'd told Lee about him."

"That explains it. What else about her?"

"She had mood swings; if I had to put a name to it, I'd say she was borderline manic-depressive. And she was fixated on mastering the difficult stuff before she mastered the ABC's. For instance, she wanted to train in a tail-dragger. I suggested she wait till she had the license, then I'd give her some instruction in the Citabria." She motioned at the red-and-white plane parked near the FBO's entrance.

"Did you?"

"No. I haven't spoken with her since her check ride."

"I wonder why she didn't come back."

"Who knows? Money problems, maybe."

Or maybe she'd been too busy harassing me.

Grimly glanced at her watch. "I've got a lesson in ten minutes."

"And I've got to be off too."

"Where?"

"Paradise."

She stared at me for a few seconds, then laughed. "Oh, the

town! You'll love the airport—it's on a bluff. You land uphill, slows you down nicely. And when you leave, you take off downhill, soar right off the edge of the bluff. If you run into Bulldog, say hey for me."

"Bulldog? Who on earth is that?"

"One of the guys. You'll know when you see him, and he's sure to find *you*."

The Sacramento Valley lay below me, flat and checkerboarded, with the occasional renegade road disturbing the otherwise regular pattern. Ahead and to my right was Sutter Butte, the 1000-foot landmark that made getting lost out here virtually impossible. From 5500 feet I tracked my course by the small towns and huge farms, grain elevators and rivers—and planned what I'd do when I arrived in Lee D'Silva's hometown.

But other thoughts kept intruding: She'd gotten basic details about me from the interview I'd found tucked into her paperback book. She'd taken flying lessons from a woman instructor at the same airport I had. She'd displayed a near-obsession with flying a tail-dragger. But all of this had happened *before* my turndown letter triggered the harassment.

Had the woman been trying to *be* me? What would have happened if she'd come to work at my agency? The possibilities were too awful to contemplate.

The city of Oroville sprawled to my right now; beyond it was the big dam, the lake silvery in the sun. For a moment I let my eyes sweep the clear sky, looking for other traffic. Then I took the airport facilities directory from the side pocket, thumbed it open to Paradise, and spread it on the sectional on my knee.

Unicom, 122.8. I tuned the radio to it. Elevation, 1300 MSL. Runway, 2700 x 40. Land uphill runway 35; take off 17.

I was over the campus of Butte College now, and the land was beginning to rise. The mesa was dead ahead, the town nestled in pine-covered hills beyond it. And there was the steep drop-off at the foot of the runway.

This *was* going to be fun. A few minutes of fun, anyway.

As I was taxiing along the runway I spotted "the guys." Every small airport has them: three or four weather-beaten men who probably learned to fly during World War II, leaning up against a hangar and watching the planes land and take off. From the deserted look of the field, they'd had a long wait between arrivals. I raised a hand as I went by, and they stared— "What's a *girl* doing alone in one of those?"—before they waved in return. There's sometimes a generation gap in the world of aviation, but in the end it doesn't matter; I knew I'd already earned the guys' respect by making a good landing.

Beyond the row of hangars I saw a limited number of tie-downs, all occupied. I parked in front of a Cherokee that would never see the skies again unless somebody bought it a new prop, got out, and wedged a couple of chocks under the Citabria's wheels. When I glanced back at the hangars, the guys had moved into a circle and were holding a conference.

I looked the other way, saw an office with a pay phone and a sign: FLIGHT INSTRUCTOR ON DUTY. When I went over there, though, I found it closed. Other than that, there was nothing but a weathered picnic bench under a tree and a small building containing the rest rooms. I headed back to the plane to check the facilities directory, which had given a number for a taxi service in Paradise.

A pickup truck—once cream-colored but now speckled reddish brown by rust—was coming slowly toward me, one of the guys at its wheel. It stopped by the Citabria, and he got out: the short, beer-bellied one, whose face, on closer look, bore a startling resemblance to that of a bulldog. Apparently Grimly's pal had been elected to check out the strange woman.

"Morning," he said in a twang straight out of a western movie.

"Morning. Okay to leave it there?"

"Piper's not going anyplace; owner's broke, and it is, too. You're fine there. Where you coming from?"

"Oakland, by way of Los Alegres."

"The wife and I fly down to Los Alegres sometimes, have lunch at the diner. Oakland—it's gotten too crowded. I go by Bulldog, by the way."

"I'm Sharon. And I've got a message for you: Sara Grimly says hey."

Thus far he'd avoided eye contact—shy, I supposed. But when I mentioned Grimly, his face lit up and he looked directly at me. "Little Sara. Haven't seen her in a year now. She used to fly up here with her students, have a picnic lunch under the tree, then show them what it feels like to soar off the end of the bluff." He laughed gruffly. "We always questioned the wisdom of feeding them *before* the demonstration. She at Los Alegres now?"

"Yes. Married, still instructing, and she bought herself a Mooney."

"Good for her. You need transportation to town?"

"Actually, I do. Is there a rental-car agency in Paradise?"

"Couple of them. Tell you what—I've got to get home for lunch. The wife's making grilled cheese sandwiches, my favorite. I'll give you a lift, and you can fill me in on little Sara."

My rental car was called an Aspire: ghastly purple with two missing hubcaps and well named, in that it made one aspire to a better vehicle. Not that I cared how it looked; it ran, and the agency staff had been friendly and helpful, providing both a map and use of a phone book and recommending a good motel and restaurant, in case I decided to stay over.

D'Silva was an unusual spelling, and there was only one listed—Harold, on Valley View Drive. I turned off Skyway, the wide commercial strip, and followed a winding road into a residential area where the homes sat on large lots, sheltered by tall ponderosa pines. The D'Silva place was a square two-story yellow frame house set far back at the end of a dirt driveway; unpruned rosebushes pushed their barren branches up all around it, and the house itself had a similar appearance of neglect; the lawn had gone to weeds. I parked and climbed up onto the deep front porch, but received no reply to my repeated knocks.

What now? Butte College, where D'Silva had earned her degree in police science.

I'd seen the college as I approached the airport, but at altitude hadn't been able to fully appreciate its pastoral setting. Tree-shaded, with plenty of open space covered in long wintergreen grass, it centered around a core of low brown buildings, some of graceful design with gently peaked copper roofs, others of the prefab variety. Signs along its roads advised of horse crossings. This was the new breed of California campus, and the students who moved unhurriedly about it seemed as relaxed as their surroundings.

D'Silva had given her former faculty adviser, Robert Fieldstone, as a reference on her job application, and I'd spoken briefly with him to check it out. Now I located him in one of the prefabs at the south end of the campus and told him the same story I'd told Misty Tyree: Lee had come to work for me, gone out on an assignment, and failed to keep in contact.

Fieldstone—a tall man with wavy white hair who must have been approaching retirement age—looked so concerned that I immediately felt guilty for lying. He took off his pale-rimmed glasses, rubbed his eyes, and said, "Lee is so competent. I can't imagine why she'd lose contact with you—unless something very bad has happened to her."

"That's why we're doing everything we can to trace her. Is the Harold D'Silva on Valley View Drive in Paradise her father?"

"Yes."

"I stopped there, but no one was home. D'you know where he works?"

"I'm fairly sure he sold the family business and retired. At least, D'Silva Supplies—the big building-supply place on Clark Road—changed names several years ago."

"Do you know Mr. D'Silva?"

"No, but a friend of mine lives across the street from him."

"In case I can't contact Mr. D'Silva, may I have your friend's name?"

"Certainly—Ken Parrish. It's the cedar A-frame. His wife's name is Beth."

I noted both, then said, "We talked about Lee a while back, but I wonder if there's anything more you can tell me."

Fieldstone thought, replacing his glasses. "You know about her academic record—excellent. Everyone here thought highly of her; we were sure she'd go far. Do you know about her mother?"

"Only that Lee nursed her in her final illness."

"Yes. The circumstances were so unfortunate. Lee was about to start a job with the county sheriff's department in Chico when her father begged her to stay home and help him with both her mother and the business. By the time her mother died, the department had put on a hiring freeze. Lee was devastated and decided to leave Paradise."

"When was that?"

"Seven years ago. Maybe eight. Before the building-supply company changed hands, but not long before."

"Did she keep in touch?"

"Not with anyone here at the college. Your call asking for a reference was the first I'd heard of her since she left. She had a best friend, though." He thought, shook his head. "Sorry, I can't remember her name, but I've seen her recently. She has a business—Spin a Yarn, on Skyway. It's in a little strip mall north of the Ponderosa Pines Motel."

I noted that too. "During the time Lee was helping out her father, did you see her?"

"A couple of times, in town. She seemed a very sad young woman."

"Yet she stayed to the end."

"Of course. Lee D'Silva was what in my day we called a good girl. A very good girl. She always did the right thing. Always."

The tall, gray-haired man who answered the door at the D'Silva house seemed composed entirely of angles, some of them so sharp that the bone looked in danger of perforating his pale skin. His eyes were sunk deep in their sockets, and around his mouth were carved deep lines of discontent. When he acknowledged that he was Harold D'Silva, I showed him my identification and began relating the story about his daughter that now—by virtue of retelling—I halfway believed myself. But D'Silva quickly cut me off in midsentence.

"I have no daughter named Lee," he said. "I have no children."

"Her former faculty adviser at the college told me—"

"He's mistaken."

I studied D'Silva, noted the tic at the corner of his right eye. Most people have a telltale physical reaction when they're lying about an emotionally charged subject.

"You *are* the Harold D'Silva who used to own the building supply company?"

The tic became more pronounced. " . . . Yes."

"Perhaps you don't understand the seriousness of the situation, sir. Your daughter's in danger, perhaps of losing her life."

He looked at me for a long moment, then shut the door. Through it I heard a dry, rasping cry of anguish.

Ken Parrish, D'Silva's neighbor, was chopping wood in the side yard of his A-frame. When he saw me, he anchored the ax in a stump and flashed me a smile of welcome. "You must be Ms. McCone. Bob Fieldstone said you might stop by. The old man turn you away?" He motioned at the house across the street.

"Yes. He claims he has no daughter."

"Bitter old bastard." Parrish took off his plaid cap and ran his hand through perspiration-soaked red hair.

"Why is he bitter?" I asked.

"Why? Who knows? Probably because Lee decided to have a life and moved away after her mother died. She put up with a lot—a *whole* lot—all those years."

"Can you be more specific?"

Parrish hesitated, keen blue eyes moving toward the house across the road. "Raking up old dirt—will that really help you find her?"

"In a situation like this, any detail may lead to a solution."

"Well, all right, then. I was the one who opened that line of inquiry, anyway." He grinned. "Now I've gone and done it— revealed myself as a lawyer."

"I work for lawyers a lot of the time."

"Where?"

"San Francisco, among other places."

"I was an assistant D.A. in Oakland for fifteen years. Now I've got a private practice here. Wills, even divorces, they're a lot cleaner than the cases I used to try, and the air's cleaner too."

"About Lee . . ."

"I know, I talk too much. Chop a lot of wood, too—anything to keep from going to the office on a beautiful day like this. Okay, I'll put it plainly: what Lee put up with was a drunken mother and a father who wouldn't acknowledge and deal with the problem. Ladies weren't supposed to drink all day and pass out in front of their favorite soap opera, so it couldn't be happening in his household. Hal was a successful businessman, president of Rotary, pillar of the church and community. Old story: he covered up, made Lee cover up too. Her function in that family was to calm the turmoil, run the household, and tend to Mommy when she was too stewed to take care of herself, which was most of the time."

"She didn't rebel against that?"

"She did her job. I don't know about the inside of the house—nobody got that far—but the outside was perfection. Those rosebushes weren't always the way they are now. And

Lee was perfection: well dressed, well groomed, always had a smile for everybody. She covered damned well."

"But you knew what was going on."

"Well, sure. Beth and I have a good view of that house. And in a quiet area like this, voices carry. We'd hear Marge screaming and slurring, Hal muttering and avoiding, and Lee always soothing them. When we first moved here, Lee was in tenth grade. We saw what was happening and tried to be good neighbors. Then one day Beth found Marge passed out in the yard. She hauled her inside, put her to bed, waited to talk with Hal. He told her that Marge—who reeked of gin—had a hypoglycemic condition that caused her occasionally to go into shock. Beth used to be a nurse; she wasn't buying that. So Hal showed her the door and never spoke to either of us again."

"And Lee?"

"She acted the same, down to the home-baked cookies at Christmastime, but her smile was brittle. Mom's secret was not to be shared."

"Do you remember when Lee left Paradise?"

"Oh, yes. Big commotion over there. This was maybe a week after Marge's funeral. Lee slipped out early one morning, didn't leave a note, didn't take anything with her but her car and the clothes on her back. Hal had the town police there, sheriff's department too. Was convinced something terrible had happened to her. They expedited the search in spite of the seventy-two-hour requirement—Hal was important, and Lee had been set to go to work for the sheriff before Hal decided he needed her at home. They located her VW in a used-car lot in Oroville."

"But they never located Lee?"

"Three days later Hal called off the search. This I got from a poker buddy at the sheriff's department. Hal told them she was a grown woman, had a right to take off if she wanted, and canceled the missing-persons report. Later he claimed he'd heard from her; she was living in Phoenix. And then he sold the business, withdrew into that house except for the neces-

sary errands, and started the 'I have no daughter' bullshit."
Parrish scowled at the D'Silva house, shaking his head. "Bitter old bastard couldn't stand for her to slip out from under his thumb. Possessiveness I can understand, but to flat-out deny a daughter's existence . . ."

He looked down at the ground, scuffed at wood chips with the toe of one boot. "Beth and I had a daughter, Amy. She died at seventeen—boating accident on Clear Lake. If I could bring her back, I'd trade places with her in a millisecond. No matter what she'd done to me."

Carolyn Alpert's hands were slender and long fingered, and they slipped the colorful skeins of yarn into the honeycomb shelving on the back wall of her store deftly and quickly. Spin a Yarn had no customers at three in the afternoon, although Alpert had warned me that she had a class of advanced crocheters coming at four.

"Yes," she said as she sorted mohair and angora, "Ken Parrish was right about Lee's life—but he doesn't know the half of it."

"You were her best friend."

"Kindergarten through college." She gave up on her shelving and turned—a willowy blonde in a long blue dress and boots. The delicacy of her features was enhanced by wisps of hair that curled softly against her high forehead. "Lee and I were instant friends the day Tommy Guest wouldn't let me take my turn on the rocking horse. My response was to cry; Lee preached a little sermon about fairness at him and damned if he didn't actually get off the horse and help me on." She smiled. "Of course, in high school we found out he'd only done it because he was already smitten with her. His crush was consummated the night of the junior prom."

"What happened to Tommy?"

Alpert began picking at the ball of soft apricot wool she held. "He was killed by a drunk driver the week after graduation. It cemented Lee's decision to go into law enforcement."

"If it won't throw your schedule off too much, I'd appreciate it if you'd tell me about Lee. Anything at all may help me locate her."

She nodded and motioned at a pair of white wicker chairs with pink flowered cushions. As soon as we sat down, she reached into a basket and pulled out a half-finished garment of fine-spun pale yellow. "I knit sweaters to order," she explained. "And I think better when my hands are occupied, particularly when I'm talking about something that upsets me."

"And the subject of Lee upsets you?"

"Makes me sad, more than anything. Where should I start?"

"Wherever you'd like to."

"Well, we covered our meeting. Grade school, we did the usual kid things together, only it was always at my house or some of our other friends'. Lee never even had a birthday party. She explained it by saying, 'My mother is very nervous, and she has a serious medical condition.' "

"Sounds like her father told her what to say. That's not kid language."

"I always thought he did."

"I've heard Lee described as a perfect child and teenager."

"Well . . . yes and no. All A's. All the Brownie and Girl Scout badges. President of the church youth group. High school class secretary. The small-town stuff that makes you shine in parents' and teachers' eyes. But, at least in the early years, she had her other side. She liked to play harmless practical jokes. She'd climb higher and swim in deeper water than anybody. One time she got up on the very peak of my parents' house, and the fire department had to get her down. Nobody ever reported the incident to her folks; most people knew what was going on with them, and they didn't want to make things more difficult."

"You say that was Lee in the early years. What changed her?"

"Her mother got worse, was drinking more and more, and

began behaving outrageously. Lee's response was to become obsessed with perfection and to try to ignore both her mother's drinking and her father's distress and denial. It couldn't have been easy."

Carolyn Alpert's fingers fumbled with her knitting. She bit her lip and pulled out a wrong stitch. "Lee never invited anybody to the house, not even Tommy Guest, and by then they were going steady. But on Thanksgiving of our sophomore year, my parents were away on a free trip they'd won to Hawaii, and Mrs. D'Silva actually told Lee to invite my older brother and me to dinner. Lee was nervous about it, but happy too. Maybe she thought her life was changing.

"Mrs. D'Silva seemed fine when we got there. She'd been drinking, but was in control. But by the time dinner was on the table she was drunk—had been sipping the whole time she was cooking. She started to carp about everybody's table manners, including Mr. D'Silva's, and to complain that nobody appreciated her efforts. She drank a lot more, pushing her food around on her plate, and then passed out with her nose in her mashed potatoes."

"What did Mr. D'Silva and Lee do?"

"He got up and retreated into the den. My brother and I offered to help Lee with her mom and with the mess in the kitchen, but she insisted on sending us home with a generous portion of the leftovers. The next day she told me it wasn't as bad as some of their holiday meals."

"So she could confide in you."

"Up to a point. But that Thanksgiving was a real humiliation for her; afterward we were never as close. And she began pushing harder and harder: she was a cheerleader, student council president, the lead in the senior play, valedictorian, most likely to succeed. The same in college: Ms. Perfect."

"Let's fast-forward to the time when Lee was nursing her mother. Did you see much of her then?"

"No. I was working long hours for the phone company. Lee's mom was more than a full-time job, plus she handled all the bookkeeping for D'Silva Supplies. Right before I was married we had lunch a few times—she was my maid of honor—and I could tell the strain was weighing on her and that she was heartbroken about losing out on her chance to join the sheriff's department. The day of my wedding she couldn't even stay for the reception because her mom and dad needed her."

"What about when her mother died?"

"My husband and I went to the funeral. Lee was like stone; she barely acknowledged anybody's presence."

"And when she left town, did she tell you her plans?"

Alpert made another wrong stitch. Her mouth twitched, and she wrapped the half-finished sweater around the needles and yarn, returned it to the basket. "Not her specific plans, no."

"But you did know she was leaving."

"Not until she actually did." Her gaze became remote, re- membering, and she smoothed her long skirt over her thighs. "I was up early that morning; my husband works construction and he'd had to drive to a job site in Glenn County. I was drinking coffee in my kitchen at four-thirty when Lee's old VW pulled into the driveway and she rushed inside. She looked tired but excited—better than I'd seen her in years. She told me she couldn't leave without saying good-bye, but she was getting out for good.

"Well, I was thrilled for her. Where was she going? I asked. She couldn't say. Why not? She didn't want her father to trace her. Why? I'd know in a few days when everything came out. And then she took both my hands in hers and looked into my eyes, very sad. She said, 'Please don't judge me too harshly for what I've done. I know if anybody can understand, it's you.' We'd been friends all those years, and I'd never been able to make her tell me anything she didn't want to, so I gave her a thermos filled with coffee and watched her drive away."

"Did you ever hear from her?"

Alpert's eyes were now filmed with tears. "No, I kept wait- ing for a letter or a postcard, but none ever came."

"And nothing ever came out about what she'd done, either?"

"Nothing. I've always assumed it was something she did to her father, because a couple of days later he called off the search for her, and since then he's claimed she never existed. Frankly, I've had my suspicions, but I've never wanted to know." She hesitated, lips compressed. "If your finding out might save Lee from whatever danger she's into . . ."

"Yes?"

"I think I know who can tell you."

Roberta Tuggle was reading the riot act to a forklift operator who, from the looks of things, had dropped a load of cartons containing toilets on the warehouse floor at Tuggle—née D'Silva—Supplies. The burly six-footer hung his head as the wiry five-footer described his negligence in terms that lacerated even my none-too-tender ears. After he slunk off, she noticed me and demanded, "What the hell're *you* looking at?"

Calling forth my most conciliatory smile, I extended my ID and said, "Carolyn Alpert phoned you—"

"Ah, shit!" Tuggle ran her hand through close-cropped gray hair. "Sorry. Come on to the office."

I followed her up an iron stairway to a glass-walled cage that overlooked the warehouse floor. Tuggle poured herself a cup of muddy stuff that must have been brewed that morning, raised a questioning eyebrow at me. I shook my head, and she motioned to one of the folding chairs in front of the invoice-littered desk, taking the other for herself.

"So you've seen my bad side," she said. "I shouldn't've reamed the guy out like that—he's new. But, dammit, those crappers're *expensive*. Now, what was it Carolyn said . . . ? Oh, yeah, you want to know about Hal and Lee D'Silva."

"You bought the business from Mr. D'Silva?"

"My husband Dave and I, yeah. Two years later, old Dave—sly thing that he is—ran off with the widow Tyler. I stuck him with a good but fair settlement, took the company, and left him the house, the boats, and the bad-tempered family dog. Now I'm getting rich on all these wealthy retirees who're moving up here, but I'm too damn busy to think about retiring myself. Hell of a note, huh?" She winked, took a swig of the silty-looking coffee, and didn't even flinch.

"Carolyn said your husband worked for D'Silva before you bought him out."

"Yeah, as a salesman. Dave was one hell of a good salesman. Sold me a great line of b.s. for years. Me, I was an accountant, had set up my own kitchen-table firm while our boys were little, which was how we ended up getting our hands on this gold mine."

"How was that?"

"What happened, the D'Silva girl, she was running the office, handling the accounts, before she ran off. It was coming up on tax time, and Hal needed somebody fast, so he called me in. Right away I found out about it."

"It?"

She smiled, stuck her Birkenstock-clad feet up on the desk, enjoying keeping me in suspense.

I hid my impatience. "Must've been something good."

"For Dave and me, yeah." Her smile faded. "For Hal D'Silva, it was pretty damn devastating. Seems his beloved daughter had been embezzling for at least a year, to the tune of nearly a hundred thou. While Hal was watching his wife die, Lee was cooking the books. The business was nearly bankrupt, so Dave and I offered to take it off Hal's hands." She paused, added defensively, "We made him a fair price, considering."

"I'm sure you did. Mr. D'Silva didn't report the embezzlement to the police?"

"Honey, that man is proud. His reputation around town had already taken a beating, given his wife's drinking. D'you think he wanted his perfect daughter exposed as a thief?" She sipped more of her dreadful brew, her round face troubled. "The man was shattered and wanted out. When we made our deal, one of the conditions was that we never tell what Lee had done. You're the first person I've ever told."

"Why me?"

"Because Carolyn said Lee is in danger. And, in a real peculiar way, I couldn't blame her for taking the money and running. She tried so hard, she gave so much, but nothing was ever enough. The more she did, the more Hal and Marge demanded. I guess she just finally snapped."

"Snapped, began embezzling, and continued it for at least a year before she disappeared? I don't buy that."

"Honey, it looked to me that the embezzlements started almost to the day that the sheriff's department announced a hiring freeze. Lee must've realized her father had made her lose her chance at her dream. Maybe she thought she was just taking compensation for her services. Poor kid."

Poor kid.

So I should feel sorry for her? Yes, she had a terrible life, but lots of people have terrible lives, and they don't use them as an excuse to embezzle from their own fathers. They don't use them as an excuse to invade and destroy someone else's life. Not if they're decent human beings.

I sat in the Citabria in the run-up area at the foot of runway 17, checking the mags and carburetor heat, rechecking the oil pressure, the other instruments, the controls.

And fuming. Fuming, because after having heard the story of little Ms. Perfect's terrible life, I felt a twinge or two. And I didn't like that one bit.

"Paradise traffic, Citabria seven-seven-two-eight-niner, departing one-seven, straight out."

It's okay to have empathy for the woman; that way you can anticipate her next moves. But for God's sake don't sympathize; it'll weaken you when the final confrontation comes.

And it will *come—soon.*

I turned onto the runway, eased in the throttle, put in right rudder. The plane sped downhill, the sheer drop-off at the strip's end ever closer. When the Citabria wanted to fly, I pulled back on the stick, and we soared off the edge of the mesa into the clear winter sky. I looked out the side window, watched the land suddenly fall away, and felt a rush of elation.

Here you are, McCone—the one place where no one and nothing can get at you.

Friday Night

It was dark and cold when I got home, and still no word from Hy or anyone at RKI. For comfort, I lighted a fire, microwaved a frozen lasagna, and later curled up on the sofa with a glass of brandy and my files on Lee D'Silva. I'd focus on this investigation, I decided, resist the impulse to panic and begin another session of pointless phoning.

The psychology behind D'Silva's behavior was now becoming clearer: A pattern of obsessive striving for perfection brought on by a difficult home life. Then a snap triggered by her realization that she would not be able to pick up where she left off and fulfill her dream of joining the Butte County Sheriff's Department. A reaction way out of proportion to its trigger, one might argue, but to a rigid, obsessively focused personality any snag in a plan can have devastating consequences. D'Silva's outward appearance and manner remained intact, but she began living the secret life of an embezzler. Once she fled to San Francisco she continued to maintain appearances as far as her work went, but she began leading a different sort of secret life in the city's bars and clubs.

I reached for the file containing her employment application and our background check. Paged through it and saw that her first job here had been with a very low level security firm.

Why, given her excellent academic record? If she'd been going by a false identity, it would have been explainable. But she hadn't. Why not?

Well, for one thing, she'd probably known her father well enough to realize he'd cover up her crime and make no attempt to trace her. But she wouldn't have wanted to risk applying for a job with the SFPD, county sheriff, or any of the better private agencies; their rigorous background checks might turn up the truth about her departure from Paradise. I knew the outfit she'd started with; they would hire anybody who was reasonably sober and breathing. After being there for a while, she'd undoubtedly networked within the business and made contacts who helped her work her way through a series of progressively better jobs.

But then she became aware of me.

In all likelihood she started out simply admiring me; I was a career role model. Possibly she was a bit of a romantic where private investigators were concerned; the paperbacks in her office effects had featured female P.I.'s. But what had triggered her intense fixation? Not meeting me at her job interview; she'd started the flying lessons in early July, six months before I advertised for an operative.

July. What had I been doing then?

The case I investigated for Ricky, of course. The situation had been well documented in the gossip columns and tabloids, and its denouement made a nationwide splash in newspapers and on TV.

But no, that couldn't be it. Ricky had come to me with his problem on July 21—I'd never be likely to forget that date or what followed—and D'Silva had started her lessons early that month.

June, then. We'd been moving our offices from All Souls to the pier, getting set up while also servicing clients. It was a crazy time, what with phone installers and electricians and painters, and on top of it all, I had to give a speech at . . .

There it was: the dinner meeting of the local chapter of the

National Society of Investigators. I flipped to the second page of D'Silva's application; she'd listed the society under "memberships."

What had I said in the speech? Mainly I'd talked about the joys and pitfalls of establishing one's own agency. It was an informal talk with a lengthy question-and-answer session, because I hadn't the time or the inclination to prepare a real speech. And during the Q&A, a former boss of mine, Bob Stern, decided to liven things up by asking about the flying; he drew anecdote after anecdote out of me.

D'Silva must have been there. I might even have spoken briefly with her.

The randomness of the circumstances put a chill on me in spite of the fire's warmth. What if D'Silva had been ill that night or scheduled to work? What if I'd been ill or never accepted the invitation to speak in the first place? Would she eventually have fixated on somebody else—or nobody at all? Or, given our individual makeups, was this whole mess destined to happen?

It wasn't a question that had an answer, or one I was comfortable contemplating. Instead I turned my thoughts to D'Silva's present whereabouts.

I'd had no message from Tamara Corbin, so D'Silva hadn't returned to her Mariposa Street flat. But she had another place in the city, where she'd taken the man she picked up at one of Russ Auerbach's clubs. Auerbach had said he'd contact me if the man put in an appearance, but would he? Nothing to do but wait and see.

I hate to wait. Besides, the house's emptiness and the phone's silence had begun to play with my nerves. Better to get out of there, take action of one sort or another.

I looked at my watch: a little after nine. If Auerbach followed the same schedule every night, he should now be at Napoli in North Beach. I called Information, got the number, called, and asked for the club owner.

"Hey," Auerbach said, "great minds think alike. I was about

to get in touch with you. The guy you want to talk to about Lee just walked through the door. For the price of a drink he'll talk all you want; seems he's pissed at her because she didn't show up for their second date."

"I'll be there as fast as traffic allows."

Fast was what traffic didn't allow. Broadway was jammed between the tunnel and Columbus. I inched along till I came to a motel where, unknown to most people, public parking was available. There I made a quick turn into the underground garage, tossed the keys and outrageous fee to the attendant. A zigzagging course brought me to the block of Kearny where Napoli was located.

A long line of hiply dressed clubgoers snaked down the sidewalk; in my jeans and flight jacket I skirted it and showed my ID to the carder. He motioned me through the door. "Mr. Auerbach's waiting for you at the bar."

Behind me a man said, "Hey, who the hell does she think she is?"

The carder replied, "That's the mayor—he's in drag and whiteface tonight."

Behind me, the door closed on laughter. His Williness, as a local cartoonist had dubbed him, was always good for a chuckle.

Napoli was very different from Club Turk: Italian-campy, with plaster of Paris busts and dusty wine bottles in niches in the brick walls; lots of red plush upholstery, and ornate gold frames around mirrors and dark oil portraits of guys who all looked like Lorenzo de' Medici. The jazz combo ought to have been singing opera.

I turned to my left into the bar area, spotted Auerbach through the smoky gloom; a man in a red silk shirt and a blond ponytail sat next to him. They rose as I came up, and Auerbach introduced his companion as Jim.

"Just Jim," the man said. "No last name; I'm married."

I nodded and shook his hand.

Auerbach excused himself, and I slid onto the stool he'd vacated. "Drink?" Jim asked.

I didn't really want one, but apparently he'd had several, and his manner told me he wouldn't be comfortable drinking alone. "Chardonnay, please," I said, and remained silent while he ordered and the bartender poured.

Jim raised his glass to me. "Cheers."

I touched mine to his. "So," I said, "you know Lee D'Silva."

"Yeah. God, what a bitch. We made a date, I made excuses at home, she never showed."

"You saw her how many times?"

"Just once. Hot number."

"She took you home?"

"Yeah—terrible place. Woman must put all her money on her back."

"Russ says you can't remember where the apartment is."

Jim leaned closer, breathing a mixture of Scotch and garlic into my face. "That's what Lee told me to tell him. Russ wasn't supposed to know about the place."

"Why?"

He shrugged.

"Will you take me there?"

"Sure."

"Good. We'll go in my car."

"No, I wanna drive—"

"I need you to navigate."

He hesitated, glanced at the nearly full drink in his hand. "Okay, I'll take this with me."

I stood, put a bill on the bar. "What part of the city are we going to?"

"Mission. Funny, old Russ doesn't know it, but his sometimes sweetie lives right across the street from one of his clubs."

And suddenly I knew in what building. Christ, she'd done it to me again!

"Yeah, that's the one," Jim said.

The building in whose entryway I'd sheltered the night before. The building where I'd lived during my early years in the city.

"Which unit?" I asked.

"Don't know the number. Lobby floor, left rear."

My old studio.

"Rotten little place," he added. "Has a fridge looks like an old icebox, works off a compressor. Thought those went out with the Edsel. Or maybe the Model T."

Suddenly I felt a fierce protectiveness toward the apartment that—while not luxurious—had been my home and that now, apparently, had been invaded by D'Silva. A protectiveness that was augmented by my serious dislike of this man. "Look, Jim," I said, "why don't you go over to Bohemia, have a few rounds on me?"

"Wondered when you'd offer."

"Hey, enjoy yourself. The night's young. And when you want to go home, take a cab." I thrust a couple of twenties into his hand. He stared at them as if he'd won the lottery, mumbled a few words that might have been thanks, and lurched off toward the crosswalk.

With malice which, I like to think, is totally uncharacteristic of me, I wished he'd get run over by a signal jumper.

Jim walked into the club, and I went to the corner, turned left, and walked along Twenty-second Street to the alley that ran behind the buildings. When you've lived in a place for a number of years, you know the points of ingress and egress; this apartment house had many, all insecure in my day. Time changes places, but if my old-fashioned fridge was still extant, some other things must have remained the same.

The rear windows of the studio—located over the ground-floor garage—were dark, and the one that opened onto the fire escape was shut. I considered climbing up there to see if the window was latched, but decided against it; if D'Silva was home, I didn't want to alert her.

The garage doors were lowered and locked. The building had room for only four cars, and those tenants who paid extra for the spaces guarded them jealously. The door to the narrow hallway that led to the manager's apartment next to the furnace room had always been a weak point, but now I saw it was blocked by an iron security gate. Well, there was still the fire escape to the roof. Tenants used to sun themselves and plant vegetables and flowers in containers up there; the roof door was seldom locked.

I started climbing.

The metal ladder shook perilously under my weight, the landings at the individual floors only slightly less. I wondered how recently it had passed the fire department's inspection. Probably not in years; the SFFD, like our other city agencies, was understaffed and overburdened, and they'd probably given this neighborhood low priority.

On the roof now, not daring to use even my small flashlight. After a moment my eyes acclimated. Over to the right was the door to the stairs; the wooden platform where sunbathers and gardeners had congregated was gone. The deteriorating composition surface crunched under my feet; I accidentally kicked an aluminum can, heard it bounce off the concrete wall. Came to the door, but found it locked.

What next?

Skylight above the stairway. I peered toward it, saw the two-by-four that propped it open.

I gripped the edges of the skylight's opening with my hands, lowered myself slowly. Swung my feet toward the window ledge that I knew to be halfway down the right-hand wall. And missed.

I'm too old for gymnastics, dammit!

I swung again, and my feet touched the sill. The trick now was to let go of the skylight's frame one hand at a time, easing my whole weight onto the sill and planting myself firmly, then drop the remaining distance to the floor. And I'd better do it soon, because my palms were sweating and my fingers were in danger of slipping.

This afternoon I shot off that runway over a sheer drop-off and thought nothing of it. Why am I sweating this?

Well, it helps to have the aid of wings and an internal combustion engine.

I let go of the skylight's frame and transferred one hand to the window's. My fingers started to slip, then held.

Here goes!

I let go with the other hand, grasped the opposite side of the window frame. Crouched unsteadily there, pressing into the small space, breathing hard. Then I maneuvered into a semi-sitting position and pushed off, landing with a thud and staggering into the stair rail.

I was in the upper-story hallway, two pairs of closed doors to either side. I listened, heard nothing, saw no light under them. Quickly I started down the stairs, hand resting on the .357 in my jacket pocket. The overhead fixture in the next hallway was half burned out; salsa music came from one of the front apartments. I hurried through the gloom to the flight of stairs leading to the lobby, one floor up from street level. Below me lights burned—also dim. I stopped on the bottom step and looked around. Down here nothing much had changed.

The lobby floor was covered in something that resembled worn and stained AstroTurf; at its far side was a brick-edged bed of blue pebbles with plastic flowers stuck into it. During my tenancy, the flowers had been geraniums; now they were a peculiar mixture of tulips and poinsettias, with a few orchids thrown in for good measure. Probably this meant that Tim O'Riley still managed the building. He'd always had atrocious taste.

The doors to the apartments on this floor had pebbled-glass insets—a security problem, and it was a wonder they hadn't been smashed by thieves years before. The one at the front glowed with soft light, but both at the rear were dark. I slipped into the space under the staircase and took a closer look at the door that had once been mine.

It stood slightly ajar.

A trap? Probably not. Another game? Most likely.

I moved over there, nudged the door with my foot. Took out my gun as I slipped inside. To my left the bathroom doorway was outlined by the glow of a night-light; beyond that was the dark opening to the kitchen. I inched along the hallway against the opposite wall, noting the empty old-fashioned telephone niche that was about halfway to the main room.

I stopped in its archway. Darkness beyond, and no sounds, not even the soft breathing of a sleeper. Nothing but that familiar nobody-lives-here-anymore atmosphere.

After a moment I reached for the light switch. My fingers encountered it as if I'd moved away this morning instead of years ago.

And that might very well have been the case. So little had changed.

Directly ahead stood the two Salvation Army easy chairs and the coffee table that I'd abandoned when I moved; somebody had taken good care of them, removed stains that I'd assumed would never come out. A mattress, its sheets and comforter rumpled and twisted, stood in the window bay where my own bed had been. My old brick-and-board bookcases, empty now, leaned against the far wall.

I went to the walk-in closet and looked inside. It was a deep one, containing a built-in chest of drawers. Nothing hung there, and the drawers were empty, but a red silk robe hung on a peg behind the door.

My robe: I recognized it by the initials embroidered on one cuff. A gift from my sister Charlene, who is a connoisseur when it comes to pretty lingerie. D'Silva must have taken it from my house; I wore it so seldom that I hadn't missed it.

I took the robe down, breathed in the scent of Dark Secrets. Replaced it on the peg.

An alcove connected the main room with the kitchen. The small dining table and two chairs that had been there when I moved in still crowded the space. On the table sat a corkscrew and a wineglass. I moved into the kitchen, toward the old fridge mounted in the wall, knowing what I'd find.

Deer Hill Chardonnay. By my standards, D'Silva was spending a fortune on wine that went undrunk. I regarded the chilled bottle with distaste, then remembered a line from an old country song—something about drinking the devil's beer for free but not giving in to him—and took the bottle.

In spite of appearances, I knew I wasn't alone. D'Silva would have the place wired for sound. I went back to the main room, looked around again, spoke loudly and clearly.

"Thanks for the wine, Lee. This time I'll accept it, but I don't find it amusing that you stole my robe and brought your men back to my old apartment. Let me ask you this: did you pay the rent with the money you embezzled from your father?"

Tim O'Riley was not happy to see me. Not at this late hour.

He wore a faded plaid bathrobe, a day's worth of stubble, and the scent of beer. His complexion was ruddier than I remembered it, and he'd lost most of his hair. When he saw me staring at his bald pate, he ran a hand over it as if to reassure himself that it wasn't unsightly, then growled, "What the hell d'you want?"

"Nice greeting after all these years." I moved past him into the small apartment. The once green cinder-block walls had been painted white, and his hideous paintings-on-velvet had been replaced by serapes and a huge gilded sombrero, but the furnishings were the same. I held out the bottle of Deer Hill to him, plunked myself on the shabby Naugahyde couch, and smiled.

Tim regarded the bottle as if it were full of cod-liver oil and handed it back to me, then pulled his robe more tightly around his considerable girth. "Shit, you move away, don't keep in touch, and then you think you can barge in here in the middle of the night?"

I kept smiling. He'd always scolded me for various and sundry misdeeds, but in his gruff way he'd also liked me.

"Yeah, grin. You think you're big stuff now, I bet. I seen you on the TV, talking about your new agency."

"Then you know I haven't changed. That TV show was terrible, and besides, I'm still the same person who annoyed you by not bagging her garbage right."

"Still don't, huh?"

"Nope."

"You don't want that swill." He motioned at the wine bottle. "How's about a beer?"

"Thanks."

"Coming up."

He went to the kitchen and came back with a couple of Buds, thrust one into my hand; turned a straight-backed chair around and straddled it. "So what'd you do—break in? All the locks've been changed about a dozen times since you left. Building's supposed to be secure now."

"You'd better check the skylight above the stairs tomorrow."

"Christ!" He swigged beer, dribbling some on his chin and wiping it off with his sleeve. I tried to remember when I'd seen Tim without a beer can in his hand, but couldn't. He was one of those steady drinkers who maintain the same level of high from morning to midnight and still manage to function.

"Whyn't you ring the bell like a normal person?" he asked. "You could've broke a leg and sued the owners, and then it'd've been my ass on the line."

"I hardly think I'd sue over an accident that happened while I was making an illegal entry."

"Oh, yeah? Burglars sue all the time. It helps pay their lawyers' fees."

On the surface, an absurd statement—rendered more absurd because it was true.

Tim asked, "So what happened? You get a yen to visit your old stomping grounds?"

I sipped a little of the beer. "Actually, I'm interested in the present tenant of my old apartment."

"Aha!" He smiled knowingly. "Somebody's caught on to Ms. Elizabeth and her cottage industry."

"Ms. Elizabeth?"

"The tenant."

Elizabeth is my seldom-used middle name. "What cottage industry?"

"To put it delicately, the woman's a whore, and your old place is her crib. She's only there when she's got a john in tow."

"How often is that?"

"Three, four times a week."

"Not a very successful whore, then."

"Okay, high-priced call girl whose johns aren't picky about their surroundings."

"How come you rented to her?"

"I didn't know about her at first. She seemed respectable enough, but even if she hadn't . . . Shit, Shar, things've changed here. Ms. Elizabeth pays her rent in cash, on time. Doesn't do drugs, puke in the lobby, or have noisy fights in the middle of the night—which is more than I can say for most of the other tenants."

"How long has she had the studio?"

He thought. "September? October? I'm not sure. For years after you moved, a nice Vietnamese couple rented it. Last April the wife got mugged walking from her car to the building, and they up and moved to be near some relatives in Modesto. After that the owner—new one, doesn't give a shit about the building or his tenants—he decided to raise the rent so high that there weren't any takers. Finally Ms. Elizabeth came along asking about it."

"She asked about that specific apartment?"

"Well, sure. I had a sign on the front of the building—studio for rent. September, I'm pretty sure it was."

So this obsession had been building to an alarming level as long as six months ago. "What can you tell me about her?"

Tim finished his beer, went to get another. "Okay, she brings guys here during the week, sometimes on the weekend. No sleazes, though. They look like professional people."

"Different men or repeats?"

"Some repeats, but not many."

"You sound as if you've been watching her."

"Who wouldn't? She's not like other hookers."

"How?"

He frowned in concentration, rolling his beer can between his palms. "Well, she's smart. You can see that in her eyes. Has got education. You can tell that from how she talks. But it's the way she acts that's got me. Sometimes it's like she's not really here. Like she's far away, in some dream world. Maybe like she's somebody else."

Somebody else? *Me.*

"You ever check out her apartment?"

"I wouldn't do that!" He sat up straighter, tried to look injured.

"Come on, Tim, I know you. And don't forget—you're talking with somebody who just entered this building illegally."

A rueful smile. "Okay, yeah, I checked it out."

"And?"

"Nothing interesting. No personal stuff that would tell me anything about who she is or where she came from. Not even many clothes. Just booze and snacks in the kitchen, the usual woman stuff in the bathroom. No phone, and she never gets any mail here. Like I said, the studio's just her crib."

"When's the last time you saw her?"

"Earlier tonight, maybe around seven."

Damn! I'd come close again, only to miss her. Had she engineered that?

If she had the Mariposa Street flat wired, as I assumed she must, she knew I'd discovered her identity. She might even know I'd spoken with Russ Auerbach. But I'd flown to Paradise VFR, without having to file a flight plan; she couldn't know I'd spoken to the people from her past there. Unless she was in contact with one of them . . .

"Tim," I said, "what was . . . Ms. Elizabeth doing when you saw her?"

"Leaving alone, with a little suitcase. I said hello, asked if she was going away for the weekend. She said yes, and it was gonna be a great one because she just loves the beach."

"Can you think of anything else about her? Anything at all?"

He considered, arms resting on the top of the chair's back. "The reason you're asking—has she done something bad?"

I nodded.

"Hurt people?"

"Yes."

"Okay, then, let me tell you my personal opinion of our Ms. Elizabeth: There's something spooky about her. Something scary. Anybody that crosses her, they better watch their ass."

Tonight I feel restless. It's well after two in the morning, yet I don't want to go home. The house seems violated, even though it's been nearly two weeks since Lee D'Silva invaded it. So I'm driving south from the city.

Besides, how can I go home to a phone that never rings with the call I so badly need? I'll drive till I'm exhausted.

Past the county line on Skyline Boulevard, where it

angles close to the sea. Down there are the old riding stables, where a friend's little girl used to take lessons. Sometimes I'd drive her there when her mom couldn't, and on one of those days I heard on the car radio that the stables had caught fire and many of the horses had died. She came running out of school—happy little girl in her jaunty riding habit—and I had to break the news. I'll never forget the heartbroken look on her face as her first realization that the world can be a sad, brutal place sank in.

Turned out the fire was set by a developer who wanted the land. A guy with an agenda, and to hell with other people.

An agenda—just like Lee D'Silva has.

Now I'm speeding through the slumbering suburb of Pacifica. Winding through the inland valley toward the still-wild San Mateo County coastline. Hugging the dangerous curves of Devil's Slide—going much too fast, and I don't care. Half Moon Bay goes by in a blur of closed businesses and darkened homes, and now I know where I'm headed.

The state beach at San Gregorio. I park in the deserted lot, zip up my flight jacket, and hit the sand.

There are caves hollowed out of the cliffs here, hollowed by the sea waves. Just like at Bootleggers Cove below Touchstone. I guess that's what drew me—the closest approximation to the place I love more than any on earth. Because I share it with Hy.

Share. Not shared.

The sand's cold and wet, and the hard moonlight makes the surf shimmer. Tide's out, but the waves still pound, tearing away at the edge of the continent. After half a mile or so, I begin to feel at peace, because I'm in my element.

Water: as much my element as the air.

Ever since childhood, I've headed for water when I'm upset. Not because it's beautiful or placid, but because it so mirrors the nature of life itself: shifting currents, eddies, waves, and—at times—violence. Tonight it makes me realize what I've learned in the past couple of weeks.

Everybody acts upon a certain given that provides the illusion of personal safety. For some it's that the job is secure, the doors and windows locked, the kids tucked in bed. For others, it's that they have money and power and can buy or sell anything or anyone. For still others, it's that they have a relatively warm and dry place to shelter till sunrise.

But for me, it's my connection to Hy—that, and a largely false assumption.

The assumption, I now know, is that people—no matter who they are—act on understandable, although sometimes obscure, motives. That they want identifiable things and act in a manner that is consistent with getting them.

That belief is at the basis of the problem I'm having

understanding Lee D'Silva. She wants something from me, she's performing all these acts to get it, she's leaving me messages right and left. But they're messages in a psychological language that's different from any I've ever encountered.

What do they mean?

What the hell does she want from me?

Saturday

When I crawled into bed shortly before four, I hadn't expected to sleep at all, but I dozed off toward sunrise and when I woke, it was after ten. Exhaustion, both physical and emotional, had finally caught up with me. Now I felt rested and clearheaded, except for a nagging sense that I'd overlooked something important. I tried to identify it while showering and dressing, then gave up on it as a lost cause. There were more important items on my schedule, such as sitting down with Greg Marcus to see if I had enough on D'Silva for the SFPD to put out a pickup order on her. If so, Greg could steer me to an officer who would handle the matter quickly and discreetly.

Greg was on duty but couldn't see me till two that afternoon, so in the meantime I made phone calls. To Tamara Corbin, telling her to drop the surveillance on D'Silva's Potrero Hill flat. To Rae, asking how things had been going at the office and finding out that the place seemed to function beautifully without my presence. To Russ Auerbach and Misty Tyree, with whom I went over much the same ground as in our previous conversations. And I called RKI's La Jolla headquarters and Buenos Aires office.

Gage Renshaw and Dan Kessell were either away from

headquarters or ducking my calls—and I suspected the latter. Nobody there or in Buenos Aires would tell me anything about Hy's situation, much less acknowledge that a situation existed. Possibly they were ignorant of what was going on; at RKI information was shared on a strict need-to-know basis— an operational policy rooted in the backgrounds of the principals.

Renshaw had spent years with the DEA, the last few on an elite and now defunct special task force; Kessell had owned an air charter service that undertook delicate and not totally aboveboard transport missions in Southeast Asia. And Hy had flown many of those missions, had returned from Asia with enough guilt and nightmares to last several lifetimes. Pseudo–spy games came naturally to all three, but they were not my favorite form of recreation. Now I chafed at having become an unwilling player.

It was a relief when one-thirty rolled around. I gathered my files into my briefcase and headed for the door. And the phone rang.

"Dammit!" I looked over my shoulder at the instrument, tempted to let the call go on the machine. But it might be important . . .

"Sharon?" Gage Renshaw's voice.

"It's about time!"

"What d'you mean? I've left five, six messages on your machine."

"When?"

"Yesterday, day before."

Oh, hell, now she was erasing not only Hy's messages but Renshaw's as well! After the last incident, I'd changed the remote access code for the machine, but there were only a limited number of combinations, and someone with D'Silva's skills could easily figure out the new code.

"Sharon, I can't talk long, so listen carefully. Where're you going to be this afternoon and evening?"

". . . I'm not sure. Probably away from home. Let me give

you my cell-phone number." I repeated it twice for him.
"Why—"

"No time for explanations. During the next, say, six hours
you'll receive a call. Either from Ripinsky or me." He hung
up.

I stared at the receiver, then banged it down. God, how I
hated his cryptic talk! What Gage meant was that the situation—probably a hostage negotiation or ransom delivery—
was about to be resolved. If positively, Hy would phone. If
negatively, I'd hear from Gage. And if I heard from Gage, it
might mean—

My vision blurred and for a second I lost my equilibrium. I
grasped the back of the armchair next to me, shook my head
to clear it. Pushed aside the impulse to panic.

I *would* hear from Hy. Sometime during the next six hours.
Believing that was the only way it was humanly possible to
go on.

Greg said, "You don't have enough on her for us to take official action."

"I was afraid of that." I got up and began to pace around his
cubicle off the Narcotics detail squad room, stopping to tap on
the windowpane at a pigeon that was crapping on the ledge
outside. It ignored me.

"Anything unofficial you can do?" I asked.

"I can request that our people keep an eye out for her, relay
the information to you if she's spotted."

"I'd appreciate it." I continued to pace.

Greg made a phone call, passed on the details about
D'Silva and her car. Then he said, "Shar, sit down. You've got
to relax."

I sat.

"I've never seen you so wound up—not even during cases
where you had a large personal stake."

"Well, it doesn't get more personal than this, does it?"

He frowned at the edge in my voice. "Something else is wrong. What?"

I shrugged, looking away from him.

"Come on, Shar. This is me you're talking to."

After a moment I looked back, feeling a familiar rush of gratitude that we'd somehow been able to move from a smashed love affair to a friendship. His wry, answering smile cut through my defenses, and I bit my lip, afraid I'd cry. Then I poured out the whole story of Hy's silence from South America and Gage Renshaw's phone call. "And on top of all that," I went on, "I'm trying to deal with this D'Silva situation. The hell of it is, I feel as if I'm ignoring something important."

"Well, about Hy—you're just going to have to wait it out, like Renshaw said. I know that's poor comfort. About the other—why don't you give it a rest? Do something relaxing instead."

I stared at him. "What, this woman is trashing my life, and I'm supposed to go to the movies? Or curl up with a book?"

He held up a hand. "Now, don't get testy on me. What I meant is do something mindless that'll free up your thoughts and allow whatever it is to percolate up from wherever it's lodged. You used to walk on the beach when you were thinking something through."

"I already tried that. San Gregorio in the middle of the night. It's a lot like Touchstone's beach, and I thought—*Jesus Christ!*"

"What?"

"That's it!" I yanked my cell phone from my bag and began punching in the Point Arena number of Ray Huddleston, the caretaker who periodically checked on our property. As it rang I said to Greg, "D'Silva told the manager of my old building that she was going to the beach."

He frowned, then nodded, comprehension flooding his eyes.

"Come on, Ray," I muttered. "Come *on!*"

Ray answered on the ninth ring, sounding out of breath. "Sharon! Sorry; I was outside getting some wood."

"No problem. Will you do me a favor—right away?"

"Sure. What?"

"Take a drive down to our property and see if everything's okay there. Then call me at this number." I read off the cell-phone number to him.

"Half an hour," he said. "I'll get back to you."

As I stuffed the phone into my purse and stood, Greg asked, "You really think she's there?"

"There, or close by. It's the only part of my life she hasn't invaded—and the most precious." I whirled and started for the door.

"Hey, wait! You don't know for sure."

"I know—I should've known last night. She's demonstrated she can read my mind. Now, by God, I'm reading hers."

Before I left town, I stopped by an outfit on Third Street where I often rented equipment that was too expensive and too infrequently used for the agency to own, and picked up a device I thought might come in handy at Touchstone. Then, from the car, I called the FBO at North Field and asked that they have someone fuel Two-eight-niner. Next I phoned the Oakland Automated Flight Service Station and listened to a taped weather briefing for the Mendocino County Airport at Little River. Hy and I had put in our own dirt strip on our property, but if conditions were bad at the airport, which lay inland, they'd be even worse at Touchstone.

The weather sounded good, with winds at three knots and unlimited visibility, but the tape was several hours old, so I stayed on the line to talk with a briefer. He said a front was forecast for midnight which would bring high-velocity winds and rain. To verify his information, I called the airport and spoke with a woman employee whom I knew personally; her visual take on the outlook was that the front would arrive earlier.

"If conditions start to look dicey," she added, "you're better off landing here, rather than at that strip you guys've got down there on the cliffs."

I'd just ended the call when the phone buzzed. Ray Huddleston. "Sharon, I checked the property over, and nobody's there, but the security system's been tampered with and it's not functioning. I went through the cottage and the sheds, and covered the grounds pretty good. Nothing's been damaged, nothing looks disturbed, but there's a strange car in the shed with your truck—blue Honda Civic."

D'Silva's. Ray hadn't seen her but she was there—possibly hiding in one of the caves in the cliffs below. The driveway in from Route 1 was long, and she'd had plenty of time to get clear of the cottage after she saw him coming.

"Thanks for checking, Ray."

"A pleasure. You want me to see about getting the system repaired?"

"Not necessary. I'm on my way up there."

"I could stay here till you arrive, just in case."

"No, thanks, you've done enough."

It would be just D'Silva and me. Just the two of us, alone.

The Citabria was fueled and waiting. I took the time to do a more thorough preflight than usual, checking both the gas and oil for contaminants I couldn't see by actually feeling for them with my fingers. There were no granular particles that suggested they had been sugared or otherwise tampered with, and I felt a sense of relief as I climbed into the cockpit.

The finer points of detecting sabotage had been taught to me by a seventy-something pilot friend. Erlene didn't fly by herself anymore, but frequently she and I took spins around northern California, sampling the haute cuisine at airport diners, and occasionally she liberated the controls from me. It was on one of our jaunts that she told me about flying transport as a civilian for the military during World War II, ferrying aircraft to the locations where they were needed. Some of the male pilots felt so threatened by women in the cockpit that they sugared the planes' fuel and oil—a little known and less than proud moment in our military history—but the women quickly caught on and learned lifesaving detecting techniques. I'd asked Erlene to pass them along to me, never imagining I'd have real need of them.

"Clear!" I turned the key. The engine caught and sent the prop spinning into a silvery blur. After switching on the beacon and radio equipment and adjusting my headset, I contacted Ground Control.

Here I come, D'Silva. Now we find out which of us is the better McCone.

Saturday Night

"Little River unicom, Citabria seven-seven-two-eight-niner, request area weather advisory."

"Hey, McCone." The voice belonged to Sonny West, the man who managed the terminal building; Hy and I used to catch rides up and down the coast with him when we tied at the airport and were without the truck we kept at Touchstone. "Wind's picking up, around fifteen, sixteen knots from the west, and there's a mean-looking fogbank offshore. Your destination your own strip?"

"Affirmative."

"Mind the crosswind on the clifftop."

"Will do. Two-eight-niner."

It was after six-thirty and a very dark night. Below and to my right lay the scattered lights of the little town of Boonville in the Anderson Valley, roughly 15 miles southeast of Touchstone. I watched them recede, noted the position lights of another plane some 2000 feet above me, then pulled back on power to begin a gradual descent on a direct 45-degree angle to our strip.

The fog was out there, all right—big gray billows sitting menacingly at sea. It could come in fast here on the coast, but not fast enough to prevent me from reaching my destination.

Familiar landmarks now: the lights of three ranches lying in a triangle—

My God! That dream I had the night after I first talked with Russ Auerbach! I was flying through a storm amid out-of-control high-tension wires, looking for a landmark. A triangulation of lights.

I believe in the usefulness of dreams. They often carry messages from the subconscious that, if properly interpreted, can serve us well. But I'd paid scant attention to that important message, hadn't realized my subconscious was trying to tell me what I'd forgotten.

D'Silva, according to Glenna Stanleigh, had known about our stone cottage by the sea. Had even known that we called it Touchstone. Shouldn't I have realized that it would all end on this remote stretch of coastline?

But how had she known about it?

I thought back to the day she had come to the pier for her job interview. Pictured her sitting tense and eager to please across the desk from me. It was a Thursday, and I'd promised the use of the cottage to Mick and Charlotte so they could get away for a long romantic weekend. Keim had stuck her head through my office doorway, seen I was busy, and started to withdraw. I excused myself to D'Silva, asked, "Charlotte, what is it?"

"Mick and I are ready to leave for Touchstone."

"Keys're in my bag on the coatrack—the ring with the seagull medallion."

"Appropriate, for your beach cottage."

"Maybe, but you know what? I hate seagulls. They're nasty, voracious birds; I once saw one eat a dollar left as a tip in an outdoor restaurant."

"So why d'you have the ring?"

"Same reason Hy has a gull painted on his plane—it's the emblem of the Friends of Tufa Lake, his environmental foundation."

D'Silva had sat through the conversation looking out the

window at the bay, politely pretending a lack of interest. But in reality she'd been making mental notes of our every word. And from there it was a short step to the public records that gave her the address of the property.

I adjusted my course a few degrees to the north of the ranch on the coastline. Pulled back some more on power and began looking for the security lights that marked the perimeter of our property. They were operational; D'Silva hadn't disabled them, and I knew why: she *wanted* me to arrive here.

Our runway lighting was a simple and relatively inexpensive one; I activated it by keying the radio's mike, and the strip's outline appeared in white. I turned downwind, noting the strong crosswind, pulled on the carburetor heat, slowed the plane some more.

She's heard the engine by now. She's waiting for me.

As I turned base, I slipped the plane with aileron and opposite rudder to lose altitude.

Somewhere down there she's watching.

On final now, the crosswind from the west very strong. The Citabria drifted slightly off its flight path, but I slipped into the wind and corrected it.

She's—

You can't think about her now. Concentrate on making the strip.

Airspeed good. Altitude good. At around 300 feet I switched off the landing lights so they wouldn't make the ground seem to rush up at me.

Ten feet, level off. Feel the sink as the plane starts to settle. Use your feet, keep it centered. Feel where the wheels are, only inches off the ground. Hold it off now . . .

Well, what do you know! A perfect three-point. Good omen.

I taxied along, braked, turned off toward the tie-down chains that were embedded in the concrete pad to the side of

the strip. Shut the plane down and, before I got out, took the
.357 from my bag and turned my cell phone back on. It had
pained me to have to leave it off during flight, in case the
promised call came from either Hy or Renshaw, but cellular
phones can't be used in planes because they interfere with the
radios.

For a moment I sat in the cockpit, staring into the darkness
and seeing nothing. Then, before the runway lights could automatically shut off, I got out and chained the Citabria tightly.
The wind was blowing more strongly than the 15 or 16 knots
Sonny West had estimated. The fogbank held stationary, but
stray wisps drifted high against the sky. Down below, the sea
crashed on the rocks.

The runway lights switched off, leaving me in total darkness.

So where is she?

The phone buzzed.

I snatched it from my bag, flipped it open. Before I could
speak, a familiar voice said, "Guess where I'm calling from."

I stared at the dark stone cottage.

"Anytime, McCone. Any old time."

Even though I'd known where she was, I began shaking
with near uncontrollable rage. She'd violated Hy's and my
sanctuary, the place we shared with no one but those for
whom we cared the most. She'd walked through our rooms,
examined every object. She'd sat by our windows, looking
out at our sea view. She'd used our phone. She'd slept in our
bed.

The enormity of what she'd done fueled my resolve. This
was the absolute *last* incursion she would make into my life.

*Okay, McCone, think. Get inside her head. What does she
expect you to do?*

Call the law? Certainly not. She knows this is just between
us.

Lead her away from there, thinking to confuse her in the

dark on unfamiliar terrain? Possibly, so she's studied the lay of the land.

Create a diversion and then take her while she's distracted? Also possible, so she'll be on her guard.

Charge into the cottage, gun drawn? That's probably what she's angling for—a duel to the finish, for God's sake. Which means she's well armed.

This isn't leading anyplace. Go about it another way: what does she not *expect you to do?*

She doesn't expect me to do nothing.

If you were in her place, and she did nothing, what would your response be?

Right: I'd try to force her to take action.

I turned my back on the cottage and got into the Citabria. Closed the door and reached for the night-vision goggles that I'd rented from the equipment firm in the city. Developed by the military for pilots on night flight, they transform total darkness into clear daylight while leaving the wearer's hands free for the controls—or for combat. All of that, plus a nifty price tag of $8,000.

After slipping the cumbersome scope over my head, adjusting the strap, and settling it none too comfortably on my nose, I looked around. The cottage and details of the surrounding terrain appeared as they did on a cloudy day. I adjusted the focus and sat back to wait D'Silva out.

The night was growing colder, but my body heat soon warmed the small cockpit. I glanced at the sky, saw high-flying shreds of fog backlit by a near-full moon. The strong wind buffeted the plane, moved its ailerons and elevator; the tiedown chains groaned as it strained against them.

For half an hour nothing happened. Then my phone buzzed. I hesitated before flipping it open; if it was D'Silva, I'd prefer to up the tension by ignoring her. But if it was Hy . . .

"What's the matter, McCone? You afraid of me?"

I broke the connection.

Another half hour. And another call: "If you've set the county sheriff's department after me, they must be having trouble finding the place."

I broke the connection, smiling. There'd been an edge of anxiety in D'Silva's voice this time. Things were not going according to her plan. Sooner or later she wouldn't be able to resist my unspoken challenge.

I placed the phone on the dashboard, wishing it would ring with the call I really wanted. When he phoned at one-thirty, Renshaw had said I'd hear within six hours; the promised call was now more than an hour and a half overdue. True, he or Hy could have tried to reach me while I was in flight, but wouldn't either have tried again by now? The silence worried me; Gage seldom underestimated a situation or time frame.

It was forty minutes before the phone rang again. I waited till the third ring to answer.

"McCone, I know what you want. You want me to show myself. That's it, isn't it?"

I hung up.

Edginess had been plain in her voice. I was getting to her, all right. I watched the cottage carefully, allowed myself to feel her tension. She'd been pacing the two rooms, stopping frequently to look out at the Citabria. Her eyes would search the grounds to see if I'd somehow slipped out of the plane and was creeping up on the cottage. She'd wonder what to do if I'd made no move by morning.

I loved having the tables turned. I'd put her through the same kind of agony she'd caused me.

Another hour. No more calls. No sign of movement in or near the cottage. The wind blew steadily; the fogbank crept closer. The cockpit grew overly warm, so I opened the window and sea air rushed in at me. The surf smashed violently against the cliffs, and beyond the cottage spray was thrown high.

Twenty minutes more, and a figure in jeans and a down jacket ran from behind the cottage and into the cypress trees surrounding it. For a moment I lost her, but then she sprinted across bare ground to the platform above the staircase that scaled the cliff face to Bootleggers Cove. Her light hair blew wildly as she started down the stairs and disappeared.

Where the hell did she think she was going? It was high tide; she had to be able to see that. At best she'd get halfway down before she'd have to turn back—or be swept out to sea.

Two possible scenarios here: She planned to stay on the stairway till I gave up my vigil and came after her, then take me by surprise. After all, she had no way of knowing I could observe her every move through the night-vision goggles. Or she hoped I'd seen her climb down the stairs and would begin to fear for her, then rush to her rescue. The latter seemed more in tune with what I now understood about her; she'd bonded with me in a strange way, and if I tried to help her, it would prove I'd bonded too.

But I hadn't.

Twenty minutes now. Twenty-five.

And then she reappeared, ran hunched over toward the cottage. She was heading back to get warm, regroup, make a new plan. To try to figure out what I would do next.

What am *I going to do?*

Nothing. Let her pace, speculate wildly, hone her tension. I'd drive her as crazy as she'd driven me.

Midnight. One o'clock. Two.

No further calls from D'Silva. No call from Renshaw or Hy. The expected front hadn't blown in and the fog was dissipating, although the wind was still very strong. Not surprising—the weather was nearly impossible to predict on this wild north coast. You could be experiencing a beautiful blue-sky day one moment and be mired in gray the next, or just the opposite.

Two-thirty. Three. Three-thirty.

Possibly she'd gone to sleep. Stress wearied most people to the point of total exhaustion, although I wouldn't have expected it to affect D'Silva that way. It certainly didn't exhaust me; if anything, it made me more alert, heightened my sense of being alive. And this kind of stress—being on the raw edge of danger—made me higher than I'd ever flown. When Hy first saw me in the grips of it, he'd accused me of having a death wish; now he knew it was an addiction. One he shared.

Four o'clock. God, I was starving!

I rooted around in my purse, found one of those health bars they're always passing out in the supermarkets in hope of luring new customers. When I bit into it, I decided that this particular company was not one to buy stock in. I ate the bar anyway, lusting after a bacon cheeseburger.

At five o'clock, on the off chance that Gage Renshaw had forgotten I'd said to call me at the cell-phone number, I dialed my house and accessed my messages. One from Mick, asking if I'd be needing his services this weekend, and a hang-up. It didn't surprise me; if anything important had come in, D'Silva had probably accessed and erased it. I stuffed the phone into my bag, convinced it would never ring again.

The night-vision goggles weighed heavily on the bridge of my nose, so I took them off and massaged it. Darkness still lay upon the land and sea; this time of year the sun didn't rise here till around seven. After a moment I put the goggles back on and peered at the cottage. She must be awake, because she'd lighted a fire, and smoke came from—

The roof, not the chimney! A thick, oily stream that quickly expanded into billows.

"Oh, no, not fire!"

But it was. She'd done the one thing that would make me come to her.

I tore off the cumbersome goggles and dumped them on the rear seat, tossed my purse after them, and grabbed my gun from the dash. Then I was out of the plane and running in a crouch toward the shelter of the cypress grove. I dodged and weaved through the trees toward the ocean side of the cottage.

The smoke was thick there, tainted with oil, and when I reached the grove's edge I saw the leap of orange flames.

I stopped, coughing from the noxious fumes, gun extended in both hands. The flames shot higher—but not from the cottage.

Where?

A 50-gallon oil drum, over there by one of the sheds. Hy had brought it here for disposal of waste when he changed the oil on the plane and the pickup. Directly behind it was—

"Oh, Christ! The propane tank!"

The main house that once stood on this property had been destroyed by explosion and fire. I couldn't let that happen to our cottage.

I started to rush toward the drum, then realized that was exactly what D'Silva wanted me to do. She was out there, armed and waiting.

Or was she? Would she really stay close by, risk dying in an explosion? No. Her recent behavior had been self-destructive, but deep down she was as much of a survivor as I. She'd lured me from the plane, and now she would bide her time, keep her distance from the fire. Then—

No time to think about that now.

I edged out of the grove, gun extended, and swept the surrounding terrain with it as I ran toward the fire. The drum sat dangerously close to the propane tank, and the heat of the fire had already charred what vegetation clung to the sandy ground nearby. I could feel it on my face and hands.

I looked around, spotted a length of two-by-four leaning against the far side of the shed. Ran over, stuffing the .357 into my waistband, and grabbed it. Dragged it back to the propane tank and shoved its end into the sand under the drum. Worked the piece of wood deeper, deeper, then laid my whole weight on it and pushed down.

The drum tipped slightly, only to settle back and force the two-by-four up so it smacked my midsection. I grunted in pain, pushed it back down. Straddled it like a seesaw and tipped the drum over.

The two-by-four came loose; I fell to the ground on top of it. When I started up, I saw the drum spurting flame and rolling toward the cottage.

I caught the two-by-four, scrambled around, and jammed it into the drum's side. Its momentum made me stagger, but I got it stopped in time. I leaned hard into the two-by-four and started rolling the drum up the slight incline toward the cliff's edge. My eyes and lungs burned from the toxic smoke, my face felt seared by the heat; sweat and tears combined to blur my vision. Flames still spurted from the drum, smoldered when they touched the sand.

Another yard and I'd have the cliff made—but then I stepped on a patch of slippery, fat-leaved ice plant, and my feet went out from under me. As the drum started to roll back, I got to my knees, straining against the two-by-four; the drum stayed where it was. I eased into a crouch, the two-by-four anchored against my shoulder, and gave it a final shove.

For a moment it teetered on the cliff's edge, flames flaring in the offshore wind. Then it pitched forward, the two-by-four flying from my grasp and pitching me forward too. I half crawled the remaining distance and watched as the drum banged off a high ledge and plummeted like a dying Roman candle to the waves below. There was a huge splash, a hiss, and then no sound but the crash of the surf.

I sank into the cool ice plant, panting and wiping my hot face against it.

And behind me I heard an engine start up.

The Citabria!

I pushed to my feet, reaching into my jacket pocket for the plane's key; it was there. Over on the tie-down pad, the Citabria's beacon and position lights flashed on.

I began running.

How did she start it? Oh, right—extra keys on the hook in the cottage's closet.

The plane began to taxi, turned nose into the wind. I kept running, yelling for her to stop, even though I knew she couldn't hear me.

She didn't do a run-up! She's never flown a tail-dragger!

D'Silva put in full throttle. The plane gained momentum. Veered briefly, as if she was in danger of losing directional control in the strong crosswind. Recovered and continued straight.

Maybe she does *have a death wish. Or maybe she's just stupid and arrogant.*

The Citabria was near takeoff speed. It began to bounce—it wanted to fly. I stopped halfway to the strip and watched, my hands clenched into fists at my sides.

The plane lifted off, tipping and teetering in the crosswind. I held my breath, unsure whether to expect a stall or a spin—both fatal at such low altitude. But she got it under control, dipping the left wing into the wind and using right rudder. It climbed out and disappeared into the darkness.

Shaking with a combination of rage and delayed terror, I changed direction and ran to the cottage to use the phone.

Sunday

Sonny West looked pasty-faced and unkempt when I pulled up to the small beige terminal building at Little River. As I stepped down from the truck and hurried toward him, he yawned widely. "McCone, why'd you have to call up and get me over here at the ass end of a night when me and my buddies closed the Buckhorn?"

"It's an emergency. I need to use the unicom. Somebody's hijacked Two-eight-niner."

He paused, keys to the terminal in hand. "The hell you say! Who?"

"No time to go into it now." I waited impatiently while he discovered he was using the wrong key and fished through the others for the right one.

"You call the sheriff's department?" Sonny asked.

"Deputies are meeting me here."

"What about the FAA?"

"Not yet. Maybe you can handle that?"

He got the door open and flicked on the fluorescents; I pushed past him into the cluttered waiting room and headed toward the high counter where the unicom sat on a shelf. Although the airport wasn't attended at this hour, the unit was always on so air traffic in the vicinity could communicate with one another. I turned the volume up.

Sonny asked, "What're you gonna try to do—raise the hijacker?"

"Yeah. She's still within range. New pilot who's never flown a tail-dragger before. I'm going to try to talk her down here before she wrecks the plane or injures or kills innocent people." I'd had the radio set to Little River's frequency when I landed. If D'Silva turned it on—and I had no reason to doubt he would—I'd be able to get through to her.

"Christ," Sonny muttered, "we'd better have a fire truck and ambulance standing by." He headed for the phone on the other side of the waiting room.

I keyed the unicom's mike. "Citabria seven-seven-two-eight-niner, McCone at Little River. Request your position."

Nothing.

"Two-eight-niner, acknowledge."

Still nothing.

Sonny hung up the phone, gave me a thumbs-up gesture.

"Two-eight-niner, acknowledge."

"What else can I do?" Sonny asked.

"Give me a sectional."

He took one from a rack at the far end of the counter, handed it to me. I opened it, thinking to check other area frequencies that she might have switched to. As I rattled the chart, a moth-eaten blanket bunched in a corner of the broken-down red Naugahyde couch began to ripple; a black nose poked out, swiftly followed by the long snout and bleary eyes of a small black-and-white terrier. Gilda, the airport dog, somewhat stunned by our early arrival and confusing the sectional's rattle with that of the wrappers of sandwiches which transient pilots frequently shared with her. She assessed the situation, flashed me a reproachful look, and burrowed back under the blanket.

Little River's frequency was 122.7, the same as Los Alegres's and Petaluma's. Ocean Ridge, down the coast near Gualala, was

122.6. If she'd gone inland to avoid the high-velocity winds here, her closest choices were Willits, Ukiah, and Boonville.

But after her near-disastrous takeoff, had she the presence of mind to make a plan, reset the frequency? I didn't think so; flying the plane would be enough of a task.

"Citabria seven-seven-two-eight-niner, request your position," I repeated.

Silence.

"Two-eight-niner, acknowledge. *Please* acknowledge."

"Two-eight-niner." The familiar voice was weak and shaky.

I sucked in my breath, let it out slowly. Warned myself to proceed with extreme caution. Enraged as I was with her, I couldn't let anger communicate itself. Couldn't let her hear how much I wanted revenge.

"Two-eight-niner, what's your position?"

No reply.

I couldn't lose her now! "Position, Two-eight-niner?"

". . . I don't *know!*" Close to panic.

Reassure her. Calm her down. Save the plane and—more important—the lives of the people she might encounter in the air or when she hits the ground.

"That's okay, Lee."

"It's *not* okay!"

"Everybody gets lost now and then."

". . . Even you?"

Hating myself for doing it, I tried to force warmth into my voice. If I wanted to talk her down, I'd need to build a rapport. "Even me."

Silence. It wasn't working.

I thought back to the acting class I'd taken as an elective in college, remembered the instructor's words: "Make yourself the character; *fuse* yourself with the character's psyche." Okay, right now I was an air traffic controller, bringing in a frightened pilot with whom I'd never before had contact. There was no bad history between us; this was a job—a delicate and important one—but only that.

"Lee, on my first solo cross-country I was going to Lincoln Regional, transversing Class C airspace at Sacramento. I'm looking for the airport, and I'm looking, but I can't spot it. So I finally break down and contact their unicom, say I'm a student pilot who's lost. The guy laughs and says, 'Well, maybe you can't find us, but we've got you. Look down.' "

Silence for a few seconds, then, "You're not making that up?"

"Nope. You can imagine how I felt after I landed and trudged in to get my logbook signed."

She laughed—a fluttery sound edged with relief.

Good. I had relaxed her some. Now I'd bring her down, one step at a time. Bring her down in more ways than one.

"Okay, Lee, listen to me. You've got plenty of fuel, and the wind velocity is decreasing. You . . . no, *we* are going to land the plane at Little River. Got that?"

". . . Yes."

"Okay, Lee, look down. What do you see?"

Silence. Behind me the door opened, and two sheriff's deputies came in. I held up my hand before either could speak, waved them toward Sonny.

"Lee, what do you see?"

"The coast. It bulges out here, and there's a flashing light at the tip. And a string of lights a little bit inland, along the coast highway, I think."

Point Arena Lighthouse and the town of Albion. I placed my thumb on the sectional, measured with my forefinger. Roughly twenty nautical miles, and a good thing too, because I'd lied to her about having plenty of fuel.

"You're at Point Arena, Lee, only twenty nautical miles away. We'll have you on the ground in no time. Now, what's your altitude?"

"Um, twenty-five hundred."

"That's good. And your heading?"

"Three-one."

I grabbed a straightedge, laid it on one of the chart's compass roses. If she continued on that course, she'd be over the open sea soon. I adjusted the straightedge for Little River. "Lee, steer it to three-four."

More silence. I glanced outside, saw the ambulance and fire truck that Sonny had requested pull onto the field. He and the deputies went outside to meet their drivers.

D'Silva said, "Okay, I'm on three-four."

"Hold it there. How're you feeling?"

". . . Scared."

Had to be a big admission for her. Now the question was, would fear make her more cautious, or make her lose it?

"Well, that's natural. That solo cross-country I was telling you about? I was an idiot to plot a course through Class C, but my instructor okayed it. Said she knew I could handle it and that I'd learn a valuable lesson."

". . . What?"

"Sacramento kept advising me of jet traffic, and I'd bob my head around like one of those ornaments you see on car dashboards, and I still couldn't spot those huge heavies. I was sure I'd cause some horrible midair and hundreds of innocent people would die because of my overconfidence. Going home I deviated all the way north to the Maxwell VOR and slunk over the hills to Los Alegres—if one can slink in a Cessna 150. And I never got overly ambitious again."

She was silent, probably realizing the relevance of what I'd told her to the present situation.

"Lee?"

"Other traffic! What if—"

"You don't have to worry about that, not at this hour." And not strictly true. But by now anybody who'd been monitoring this unicom would have split for safer parts or be holding at a distance. "Still on three-four?" I asked.

"Yes."

"Tell me what you see to your right."

"Not much. A few lights."

The hamlet of Elk. "And directly ahead?"

"Some lights on a point, and inland—oh!"

"You have the airport."

"I have it! God, the way it just appears out of all those dark trees!"

"Not too hard to spot, huh? Okay, traffic here is left, for runway two-niner. The lights on the point are Mendocino; avoid flying over them, but if for some reason you can't, stay above two thousand feet. When you're at the right position relative to the airport, make your turn and come in on the forty-five like you would anyplace else, gradually losing altitude till you're at a thousand feet."

"Sharon, I don't think I can do it. Not in the dark, in a strange plane."

For a second I wanted to step out of my air traffic controller's role, to scream that she should have thought of the consequences before she stole the "strange plane." I bit my lip, held it in.

"Sharon?"

God, how I hated to further encourage her identification with me! But it had to be done.

"You aren't going to land the plane alone, Lee. *We're* going to do it together."

More silence. Then in a calmer tone, "Maybe we can."

"We can. Let's bring you down now."

"Citabria Two-eight-niner, on the forty-five for two-niner."

She was back in her pilot's mode, secure in correct radio-speak. I also switched to the language of the airwaves. "Two-eight-niner, what's your altitude?"

"Twelve hundred feet."

"Descend to one thousand and maintain till you turn base."

"Two-eight-niner."

I'd moved over to the window so I could both talk and monitor her progress; now I saw the Citabria's position lights. Sonny came in from the field, stood silently beside me. Waves of tension radiated back and forth between us; even Gilda had come back out from under her blanket and sat nervously alert on the couch.

"Two-eight-niner, turning downwind for two-niner."

"Altitude?"

"One thousand. Oh!"

Through the predawn murk I saw the plane veer sharply off course. "Lee, what is it?"

"The crosswind! You said it'd died down!"

"I said it had decreased. You're still going to have to contend with it. Use rudder, crab it."

"I can't! The wind's too strong!"

Don't panic now! "It's not nearly as strong as when you took off. You crabbed it then, you can do it now."

Silence, but she was doing what I'd told her to, because her ground track straightened.

"Sharon—did you mean what you said? We'll land this plane together?"

"I meant it."

"Why're you trying to save me, after all the things I've done?"

"We're not going to talk about that now. We're going to concentrate on making a good landing." She'd reached midfield. "Pull on the carburetor heat."

"It's not me you want to save, is it? It's the plane."

"The plane isn't the main issue. I don't want anybody hurt or killed. Have you pulled on the carburetor heat?"

"Yes. But maybe I *want* to die. Did you ever think of that?"

No no no, not this, not now! "That's not you talking, Lee. You're made to survive, just as the Citabria's made to fly. Bring back the power now, and slip it."

"Slip it?"

"It doesn't have flaps; slipping it serves the same function."

". . . Okay."

When you're piloting, the process of landing seems to take a long time, but when you're watching and worrying, it goes by in a flash. It seemed only a second before I said, "Turn base, Lee."

"I'm turning . . . Oh, God, this wind, I'm being blown clear out of the pattern!"

"Crab it again." I watched the position lights as the plane changed direction and it counteracted the wind. "Now, don't worry about other traffic, Lee. Just look over at the runway. You're ready to turn final."

"Two-eight-niner, turning final."

"Okay, let's us land the plane."

"Airspeed looks good, Lee. Keep the nose right where it is. Keep it straight. *That's* right. A little left aileron now. Not too much . . . Good!"

As a pilot, she's talented. Too bad—after this fiasco she'll never fly again.

"Now look at the runway. Look at the two-niner. Don't let the numbers move up or down on the windshield from where they are right now. This is old stuff to you; you know what to do. A little more left aileron. That's it!"

Her father let her get away with embezzling from him, but she's not going to get away with stealing that plane.

"Glide path looks good. *Everything* looks good. You've got the airport made."

She's going to find out that she can't go through life hurting people and then not taking responsibility for what she's done.

"Level off now. Eyes on the end of the runway. Feel the sink. Feel it."

Now for the tricky part. Can she handle a three-point landing?

"Okay, ease back on the stick. That's right—ease it back and hold it off. Hold it . . ."

The Citabria touched down on the runway—hard, but down.

"Keep it straight, Lee!"

Oh, hell, she's losing it!

"Don't freeze! Keep it straight!"

The plane looped out of control.

"Christ, no!" I dropped the mike and ran for the door.

The plane was sliding sideways along the runway at close to 60 miles an hour. Tires shrieking, it spun around and tipped onto one wheel; I sucked in my breath, smelled burning rubber. Heard metal shearing as the landing gear gave way and bent at a crazy angle. The plane plowed toward the shoulder, and then there was a hideous, gut-wrenching crunch—the wing slamming into the ground. And a millisecond of silence before the fire truck and ambulance rushed to the scene.

It had happened so fast, but that's all it takes. An instant of inattention, carelessness, or, in this case, arrogance giving way to sheer terror.

Hands on my shoulders, restraining me as I was about to run over there. Sonny. "Let them do their jobs," he said.

I looked up at him, nodded, my lips pressed together.

"Didn't catch fire," he added. "That's a blessing."

A blessing? Of sorts, but cold comfort.

"You going to be okay, McCone?"

I nodded again, numb clear through.

"Good. I need to get on to the FAA. Hope they can come out and look over the wreckage soon." He let go of me and loped back toward the terminal.

Business as usual. And why not? He wasn't intimately involved, and besides, he had an airport to run.

I remained where I was, watching the paramedics and firemen. They pried the door open and one of the medics climbed up and leaned inside. He shouted something, and the other ran back to the ambulance, returned a minute later. When I started over, he saw me and called, "She's alive. We've ordered a medevac chopper to take her to the trauma unit at Fort Bragg."

I waved and nodded, feeling nothing. No relief that she hadn't died. No anger, at least none for the moment; that had all been wrung out of me. Only sorrow, because of the wreckage that lay beside the runway. And a sense of regret because I'd been cheated out of confronting her.

I'd been cheated out of proving which of us was the better McCone.

Sunday Morning—Later

Odd, I thought, how the midmorning sun made the crumpled contours of the Citabria look like an abstract sculpture: startling, thought-provoking, even; white marble, the cracks and fissures dark veins. Maybe Hy and I should mount it on a pedestal in the entry of the house our contractor was scheduled to begin building at Touchstone once the danger of the winter rains had passed.

And you, McCone, have a sick sense of humor.

They say if you can't laugh, you'll cry.

Then I realized I was already crying; tears leaked from the corners of my eyes and washed over my face. My hair, blown by the wind, stuck to my wet cheeks. My shoulders and chest heaved.

What a sorry, awful mess! D'Silva was being operated on at the trauma unit in Fort Bragg, her injuries numerous but not life threatening. The Citabria would never fly again. And now it was up to me to break the news to Hy.

Except I had no clue as to his whereabouts. When I'd called RKI's headquarters an hour ago, the operator told me she thought he'd left São Paulo for San Francisco yesterday. He'd been in Argentina, I argued, not Brazil. No, she replied, she was sure Mr. Renshaw said Brazil. Was Mr. Renshaw there? Sorry, everyone had left for the weekend.

RKI, the organization that routinely put in 168-hour weeks, had chosen this, of all times, to knock off and relax.

Behind me, the airport was operating as usual. Because the Citabria had slid well off the tarmac onto the median strip between it and the taxiway, runway 29 was clear; planes landed and took off, their occupants casting cautionary looks at the wreckage. After the FAA investigators came out, it would be removed, and it would seem as if the disaster had never happened.

Except it would replay vividly in my mind for the rest of my life. And I'd never fly the little white plane again. Would never occupy the backseat while Hy piloted. With a stab of pain I remembered our first flight together, how scared I'd been. I remembered the first time he'd put the plane into a precision spin, and how, in that moment, I'd decided to become a pilot.

How many hours had I logged in the Citabria? How many takeoffs and landings—

"Don't cry, McCone. It's only a plane."

I whirled at the sound of his voice. "Ripinsky!"

He held out his arms to me.

I ran to him, burrowed into them. My joy and relief were short lived, extinguished by a wrenching pang of guilt. I began to cry harder.

"Sssh." He smoothed my hair against the back of my head, pulled me closer.

"Where *were* you?" I asked, hating the plaintive note in my voice.

"Hostage negotiation in São Paulo. CEO of one of our big multinationals down there was snatched; fortunately I wasn't far away and could take charge quickly."

"It turn out okay?" Hy was RKI's best man for such negotiations, but even in the most talented of hands they often go badly—for all concerned.

"Yeah, but it took a long time. Too long. Later I'll tell you all about it."

I stepped back, wiping my eyes, and looked him over. His chin was stubbled, and weariness showed in his eyes. "Gage called me yesterday afternoon."

"I know." His lips twisted. "The things that must've been going through your mind when neither of us got back to you . . . All I wanted was to make my flight, catch some sleep, and get on home to you; Gage told me it sounded as though you'd be on the move, so I asked him to let you know when I was getting in. He got sidetracked, forgot to call you. Classic screwup."

Or was it a deliberate lapse on Renshaw's part? Although we'd forged an uneasy truce in recent years, the relationship was a problematical one. I'd once bested him in a professional situation, and he'd never forgotten it.

"When I got back to the city," Hy went on, "I took a cab to your house. There was a message on your answering machine from Greg Marcus—something about having information on somebody named D'Silva and being concerned because you'd flown up here alone. I tried both the cottage and your cell phone and got no answer, so I rented a 172 and was on my way within the hour."

"My cell phone's on." I pulled it from my bag, which one of the firemen had retrieved from the Citabria, and flipped it open. The digital display didn't light. "Oh, hell! Dead battery pack. Did you land at Touchstone?"

"No. When I tuned to Little River, I heard Sonny advising of wreckage on the median strip, so I got on to him, found out what had happened, and came directly here. Was it that woman who was hassling you?"

"Yes. Lee D'Silva. Job applicant I turned down." I glanced at what was left of the Citabria, quickly looked away. "God, I feel terrible about the plane."

"Don't. Frankly, Two-eight-niner was getting to be a pain in the ass. The radios've never worked right, and it's too small and uncomfortable for long trips. We're overdue for a new plane."

"But the expense—"

"Insurance'll cover some of it, and the rest we can afford."

"You loved the Citabria."

"So did you, but it's not like it was a person. I can take its loss. What I couldn't face would be losing you—and for a moment when I heard about the wreckage, I thought I had."

"And I'd been thinking I'd lost *you*." Quickly I returned to the security of his arms.

After a bit he asked, "You know what shopping for a plane's like, McCone?"

"Uh-uh."

"Well, be prepared for a lot of pushy salespeople who won't take no for an answer. But also be prepared to test-fly any number of aircraft before we make our decision. I don't know about you, but I'm thinking high-performance. I'm thinking comfort. I'm thinking *sexy*."

I tipped my head back and smiled at him. "Funny," I said, "I thought you'd been thinking sexy ever since I met you."

Monday

I hung up the phone and looked across the desk at Rae. Wearing a new blue sweater that matched her eyes, she seemed exceptionally cheerful; successfully managing the agency during the past week had given her confidence yet another boost.

"So what was Greg's information about D'Silva?" she asked.

"It wasn't so much information as a rumor. On Saturday evening he spoke with a former SFPD inspector who's currently on the Paradise force. The guy told him that at the time of D'Silva's mother's death there was some speculation that it had been an assisted suicide—or murder. And Lee was the only person with her the day she died."

"They look into it?"

"Not very thoroughly; Lee had the reputation of little Ms. Perfect, and her father was highly regarded in the community. Besides, Mrs. D'Silva would've died within a matter of days anyway."

"So maybe Lee got away with murder."

"And maybe she thought she could get away with murdering me."

"You really think she lured you up to Touchstone to kill you?"

"I don't know what she intended—or what she wanted from me. Maybe she doesn't know, either." She was in the hospital in Fort Bragg, under police guard, and remained on the critical list.

Rae glanced at her watch. "Fifteen minutes till the meeting between Anne-Marie and Hank and Bud Larsen's attorney. You attending?"

"Yes. Ted, Neal, and Larsen'll be there too. As well as Glenna Stanleigh."

"Wish *I'd* been invited."

"No, you don't. It's likely to get ugly."

She nodded absently. "Shar," she said after a moment, "I need to ask you something."

"Sure, what?"

"Well, the wedding . . ."

"Have you set a date?"

"Tentatively we're thinking May, but it's not firm yet. The whole thing's complicated by Ricky having some surprise in store for me that's taking time to arrange. God, I wish he'd get it settled, whatever it is! He doesn't realize that even for the small kind of ceremony we want, there's stuff I've got to get started on."

"Such as what to wear."

"And flowers and food. And what the best man and woman're going to wear."

"Who are they?"

"Well, Mick for him, of course. And for me . . . what I want to ask is—would you?"

"Stand up for you?"

"Give me away, too, if you want. I'm sure you've been dying to do that for years."

She phrased it lightly, but I knew my answer was important to her. I'd been both her mentor and her friend for a long time, but she was also marrying my sister's former husband and, given my past behavior, she must have been afraid I'd decline.

I got up, went around the desk, and hugged her. "I'd love to stand up, give away, *and* help with the arrangements. Just don't make me wear something pink and frilly."

"That'd be like me wearing something white and frilly. We'll be coolly sophisticated instead." She struck a fashion model's pose, and we both began to giggle at the concept. Sophistication was no more us than frills were.

I perched on the edge of the desk. "So what d'you suppose Ricky's surprise is?"

"I haven't a clue—and usually I can read his mind."

"Well, it's bound to be an interesting one."

"Yeah, it will. Between my job and Ricky, life's never boring."

"Let me see if I have your offer straight," Alan Symons said. He was a portly, bald man in a shiny blue suit who affected folksy mannerisms that masked a sly shrewdness. "My client gives up his job at the Plum Alley building and agrees never to come within a hundred yards of your clients, their residence, cars, or places of business?"

Anne-Marie, who had assumed a power position in the seating area of the law firm's office—a high desk chair facing the sofa where Symons and Bud Larsen sat—nodded. "That's correct. In return, Ms. Stanleigh will not use the footage of Mr. Larsen in her documentary on hate crimes." There was no such documentary in the works, but Symons had neglected to ask for proof.

"This is coercion," he said.

"No, counselor, it's negotiation. You viewed the footage—you know we could take it to the police. But my clients don't care to put Mr. Larsen behind bars; they simply want to put this behind them and ensure that they're left alone in the future."

I glanced at Bud Larsen. He was slumped in the corner of

the sofa; occasionally he'd glare at Ted and Neal, but mainly he stared down at his lap.

"Ms. Altman," Symons said, "I may be dense, but—"

Hank muttered, "I'll stipulate to that."

Anne-Marie frowned at him, while the rest of us did our best not to laugh. Symons appeared unruffled by the remark; probably he'd fielded many similar ones. "I may be dense," he repeated, "but what you're doing is actionable. My client will file suit—"

"Fine. And we will take the footage of your client to the SFPD. Where Ms. McCone has high-level contacts."

Symons was silent, looking at Larsen. Finally Larsen met his gaze and shrugged. "Job doesn't pay much anyway," he said. "Be good to get away from those faggots."

Symons sighed, a trace of a sneer tugging at his lips, and I began to think better of him. He'd been hired to strike a deal, he'd done it, but that didn't mean he had to like or approve of his client.

God, I was glad I'd never had the urge to become a lawyer! I truly didn't understand how good people like Anne-Marie and Hank could continue practicing without becoming hopelessly jaded. Or maybe I did. Maybe sessions like this were what kept them going.

They discussed an agreement, set a date and time for it to be signed by all concerned parties. Then Symons stood and motioned to his client. Larsen followed him partway to the door, but detoured at the last second and went to loom over Ted and Neal, who were seated next to each other.

He said, "Nothing's changed. You're still filthy perverts."

They exchanged glances and, without moving, became a unit, putting up an invisible wall between themselves and his hatred. They'd been having problems, both had told me, since Neal had found out about Ted's deception, but they were determined to try to work them out. Now I knew that time and their commitment to each other would see them through.

Larsen sensed he couldn't get to them. His face reddened

and he said, "I know your kind, all right. Uncle Nick, the nicest man on the block, took care of kids so their folks could get away. Always punched them on the arm and called them buddy—just like you, Osborn."

Symons said, "All right, Bud, that's enough."

Larsen ignored him. "Good old Uncle Nick—that wasn't all he was punching down in his basement while his wife thought the kids were helping out in his woodworking shop. And afterward he'd say they'd be sorry if they told, and then he'd act like nothing happened."

Now we all exchanged glances. Larsen had used the impersonal plural pronoun, but obliquely he'd explained the roots of his rage.

He added, "All this crap about genetic programming and your fuckin' rights—the hell with it. You're sick, that's what it comes down to."

Slowly Ted stood, faced him squarely. "No, Bud," he said, "you're wrong. Uncle Nick was sick; he preyed on children. Men like that *are* called perverts. Neal and I are healthy men who love each other. *We're* called gays."

Larsen blinked, swallowed. Then he muttered to his attorney, "Get me out of this hole."

We all watched them go in silence.

Half an hour later, I faced my staff in the conference room and saw the unease that I felt mirrored in their eyes.

Now was the time to address the issue that was on all our minds.

"What's happened to us?" I asked.

Headshakes. Shrugs.

"We used to be a team," I said. "Remember last fall? When we all pulled together to solve the Seabrook case? Why weren't we together on this?"

Rae said, "Ted didn't trust us. And you didn't give us a chance either, Shar."

"But why?"

"Maybe we're all too independent minded for our own good."

"So what do we do about it in the future?"

Ted said, "Try harder," and Neal nodded.

"Well, you guys ought to know about that," I told them.

"Try harder," Rae repeated, "and remember that there's too much . . . bad stuff out there for people to take things into their own hands."

"And," Charlotte said, "remember that we're lucky we *can* trust each other."

"And," Mick added, "remember that sometimes the boss can act like a horse's ass."

"And," I finished, "remember that at least one of our people can sometimes act like a *smart* horse's ass. Now let's adjourn to Miranda's—burgers and beer on me."

friday

Propped against the headboard of her hospital bed, Lee D'Silva looked smaller than the woman I'd interviewed for a job last month. Her honey-blond hair was stringy, both eyes were blackened, and there was a strip of adhesive tape across her nose. Her right arm was in a cast, and her doctor had told me that she'd sustained three broken ribs and substantial internal damage, including a collapsed lung and a ruptured spleen. Much of this could have been avoided had she been wearing a seat belt when she put the Citabria into the ground loop.

Although her eyes were focused on the small TV mounted high on the wall, they had a lifeless sheen that told me she wasn't really seeing the talk show it was tuned to. Her left hand toyed with the remote control, caressing its contours in a repetitive pattern. But when she saw me, her face became animated and she switched off the TV.

"Sharon! I knew you'd come. It's all a big mistake, isn't it?"

In her situation, I'd have been summoning the police guard to remove me from the room. But D'Silva had identified with me before we'd even met, and she probably still entertained the delusion that landing the Citabria together had been a bonding experience for both of us.

Without responding, I shut the door and went to stand at the foot of her bed. My fingers found the rail, gripped it hard. In spite of the rage and revulsion she inspired, I wasn't about to let my feelings spin out of control; I'd come here for two purposes, and I wanted to accomplish them with as much calm and dignity as I could muster.

D'Silva looked puzzled because I didn't speak. She said, "Sharon, they arraigned me on felony charges this morning, right here in the hospital."

"I know."

"Isn't there something you can do?"

"I wouldn't if I could."

"But—"

"What did you expect, Lee? You broke into my cottage. You set a fire. You stole my friend's airplane. You endangered the lives and safety of people in the air and on the ground. What *did* you expect?"

". . . You're really going to press charges?"

"Damned right I am—both here and in San Francisco. For once in your life you're going to learn that you can't escape the consequences of your actions."

She stared at me. Her stunned expression confirmed that up until now she'd been in denial about those consequences.

I said, "I came here to tell you that. And to ask why you did all those things to me."

Silence.

"So why *did* you do them, Lee?"

No reply.

"You did them. You must've had your reasons."

She looked down, began toying with the remote again.

"Was it my letter turning you down for the operative's job? Is that what decided you?"

"I didn't *decide* to do anything. It just happened."

It just happened. You hear the phrase all the time these

days. Half the population, from inefficient employees to mass murderers, use it to excuse their transgressions.

It just happened that your order got lost.

It just happened that I blew them all away.

"You made a lot of preparations and went to great lengths for something that just happened."

Shrug.

"What did you hope to gain from your actions? My approval? My friendship?"

". . . Maybe."

"I don't think so. Where was all this supposed to lead?"

Silence. Her fingers gripped the remote, the knuckles going white.

"*Where*, Lee?"

She looked up, eyes flaring and then going stony. She raised her hand and hurled the remote against the wall below the TV. Suddenly I was seeing the real Lee D'Silva.

"I didn't know—all right? I was just . . . doing things."

"No, you had a plan. You're not the sort of person who operates without one. Remember when your mother was dying and you were working at your father's company? For two years you carried out your plan—embezzling that money and hoarding those morphine pills. And then you put it into effect. And it worked."

She lay pale and still; for a moment she actually stopped breathing. It was as if she'd died too, and maybe in a way she had, because when she spoke again her voice was flat and emotionless, her expression blank.

"You don't know anything about those years," she said. "You don't know anything about that day. Or what kind of a person I am. Why should you? You're too wrapped up in being you, in living your glamorous life."

"What's that supposed to mean?"

"Valentine's Day? I went to your office late, when I thought you'd have time to sit down and talk. I planned to beg you to give me another chance at the job. But you weren't there, so

I took a long walk along the Embarcadero, trying to figure out how to convince you to take me on. I'd had a horrible experience a few days before—"

"With Russ Auerbach."

"You *know* about that?"

"I spoke with him."

"God." She closed her eyes for a moment before she went on. "I can't talk about him—now or ever. So anyway, Valentine's Day. I was coming back from my walk, and I saw you and some other people getting out of a limo in front of Hills Plaza. I was there to beg, and you were getting out of a limo, all dressed up in red, surrounded by beautiful people. I followed you into the restaurant and watched you having a good time and hated you because I knew my life would never, never be that way, unless . . ."

"Unless what?"

She whispered something I couldn't hear.

"What, Lee?"

No reply.

"Unless you dismantled *my* life piece by piece? What did you think that would accomplish?"

"Just go away. Please go away. You've betrayed me enough, don't add to it."

"*I* betrayed *you?*"

"You said we'd land Two-eight-niner together, and look what happened."

I stared at her in amazement. "Lee, we *did* land the plane. *You* lost control of it on the ground."

Her eyes became slits and her jaw clenched; I sensed she was fighting down a scream. Little Ms. Perfect was getting a foretaste of what she'd be in for in court; there, the facts behind her fantasy would be all that counted.

After a moment she spoke. "Sharon?" she said in a soft little-girl voice. "You think you know everything about me, but you don't. The day my mother died? It wasn't me."

What next? I waited.

"It was my dad. He gave Mom morphine he'd saved up. I found out about it and was going to tell the police, so he gave me the money to cover up for him and go away."

No way. The embezzlement had started long before her mother's death—at a time when Lee was in charge of the books. "You'll do anything to get sympathy, won't you?" I said. "Anything, including framing your own father for something you did. You're a very sick woman, and I hope that in prison you'll get the help you need to come to terms with your past and cope with your future."

"Prison!" The little-girl mask fell away, and her eyes flared. "You fucking bitch!" she exclaimed.

"Ah, that's more like it." I leaned across the bed rail, looked straight into her eyes. "Show that side of yourself to the jury, why don't you? Won't make any difference: the evidence is plain."

"You can't do this to me!"

"I can and I will." I turned my back on her and walked out the door.

On the sidewalk I paused for a bit, taking in the brilliantly clear day—one of those that make our wild north coast a paradise. The sun was already sinking toward the sea; the smoke from the stacks at the Georgia Pacific lumber mill along the shore drifted in the light breeze. Hy was over at Ace Hardware, buying supplies for some repairs he wanted to make at Touchstone tomorrow. I'd meet him there, and then we'd drive south, stopping at a favorite fish market in Mendocino for the catch of the day before we continued home.

Home. D'Silva had violated but not destroyed it. This weekend we'd reclaim it.

The hours while other people sleep are peaceful now.

Hy is one of the slumberers; he lies in our bed, half tuned to danger, but less so than when I met him years ago. Then he was always on the alert—the legacy of living too long on society's dangerous fringes. Tonight when I left his side he didn't stir, and it pleased me that he's secure in this home we share.

I'm sitting on the platform above Bootleggers Cove. It's a mild night for this time of year, and anyway, I'm wrapped in one of seven long terry-cloth robes he gave me for Christmas. Seven, in various colors! Because, he claims, I turn him on even more than usual when I wear this particular style, and he was afraid the mail-order company would stop making them.

The man's a lunatic at times. I love him.

I keep thinking about D'Silva. I'm still angry, even though on some level I feel sorry for her. I guess in time the rage will fade. I guess.

But the randomness of being singled out like that—it's what gets to me. That, and my total lack of control over the situation. How it could happen again anytime, and I wouldn't even know until it was too late to stop it.

Don't dwell on it, McCone. Think of tomorrow. Think of next weekend when, weather permitting, you and Hy will start to look at and test-fly aircraft. Think of the new plane, the hours you'll log in it. The house you'll have built here, the years you'll live in it.

Let life go on. In time this habit of fear will be broken. You'll stop jumping at every ring of the phone, every creak of the floorboards. You'll let go of this nightmare.

But the randomness . . .

April 1
San Francisco

11:50 a.m.

"I feel like a goddamn fool."

"What?" I hadn't been paying proper attention to what Hy was saying over the phone because I was trying to decipher the hand signals my nephew and computer expert, Mick Savage, was flashing at me from my office door. I waved him off.

"A goddamn fool." Hy Ripinsky's tone was injured; my lover and best friend knew better than anyone, and had radar for those rare occasions when I didn't listen to him.

"Why?"

"Because I should've known better than to trust Virgil. What kind of name for a contractor is that, anyway—Virgil? The jerk called me at my ranch and asked if I could come over here to the coast so he could dig a hole."

"A hole."

"Yeah, by the foundation of the old house." Hy was currently at the property we jointly owned in Mendocino County, where we were trying to get construction of a house underway, and where the unseasonably rainy weather was doing its best to thwart our efforts.

"And?"

Mick reappeared in the door, somewhat wild-eyed, his blond hair standing up in stiff points that defied gravity. Again I waved him away.

Hy said, "What d'you think? Virgil never showed. Plus it started storming like a bastard fifteen minutes ago, so now I'm stuck here and I can't find any matches to light a fire."

"Stuck there? Don't tell me you flew?"

"Borrowed that Cessna we're thinking of buying."

"*You're* thinking of buying." The Cessna, in my opinion, was a piece of junk.

He ignored the comment. "So now I'm stuck here. No way I'm flying in this storm, and— What the hell did you do with the matches?"

"What did *I* do with them?" I realized I sounded sharp, but it had been an awful morning for me too.

"McCone, you made the fire last time we were here. Think."

That was true, and I couldn't blame him for being irritated. The stone cottage on the cliff's edge above Bootleggers Cove must be cold, damp, and miserable.

"Did you check the kindling basket?"

"First place I looked."

Mick reappeared, rolling his eyes in alarm.

"What about that blue bowl on the kitchen counter?"

"Nope."

2

"Well . . . " My nephew was hopping around now, as if he badly needed to pee. "Try the dirty-clothes hamper."

"Why the hell—"

"Because the jeans I was wearing that last time're in there. The matches're probably in their pocket."

"And women think we men are strange creatures."

"Just look. I've got to go now." I recradled the receiver and said to Mick, "What, for God's sake?"

"Come on. Hurry!" He turned and rushed from the room. I heaved a sigh, got up, and followed him onto the iron catwalk that fronted McCone Investigations' suite of offices, high above the concrete floor of Pier 24½.

Three of my five staff members stood around the desk in Mick's office when he and I came in, staring at the brand-new computer—something he called a Wintel—that he'd coaxed me into spending a small fortune for. Ted, my slender, bespectacled office manager, fingered his goatee nervously and kept at a distance. Craig Morland, in sweats and running shoes looking nothing at all like a former buttoned-down FBI field agent, had his arms folded across his chest; his expression suggested that he feared the machine might attack him.

Charlotte Keim, on the other hand, was very much on the attack. She advanced aggressively toward the desk, her petite features set in stern lines. "You varmint!" she exclaimed, her Texas accent more pronounced than usual. "When I get through with you, you're gonna be road kill!"

At that instant a sickening thump came from under the desk. "Hell and damnation!" Rae Kelleher's voice shouted. She backed out of the kneehole, rubbing the crown of her curly red-gold head, a smudge of dirt across her freckled nose.

"I *told* you it was plugged in," Mick said to her.

A cold sense of foreboding washed over me. "What's going on here?"

"Uh . . ." Mick looked down at his shoes.

"*What?*"

"I . . . don't know. I mean, I must've done something wrong."

"Why?"

"Well, you asked me to print out the report on the McPhail case. And I tried to. But it's . . . like gone."

"*Like gone?*"

"It's gone."

There were no hard copies of the report on a major industrial espionage investigation, due to be delivered to the client this afternoon.

"So's everything else," Mick added in a small voice, still hanging his head. It seemed to me that his shoulders were shaking slightly. Well, if he wasn't already crying, I would—in the well-remembered words of my father— give him something to cry about.

"Mick," I said, "you are supposed to be a computer genius. You got suspended from high school for breaking into the board of education's confidential files. You smashed the security code at Bank of America and very nearly got yourself arrested. Last week—against my explicit instructions—you obtained federal information that even Craig couldn't call in markers for. So how in hell could you lose all your files?"

He shrugged.

"I don't believe this!"

4

"See for yourself." He motioned at the machine.

I went over to the desk, narrowing my eyes against the unholy light that I—one of the top two or three techno phobes in San Francisco—am convinced is evidence computers are a creation of the devil.

A message was displayed there. White letters on the blue background:

APRIL FOOL! I'VE ALREADY ORDERED THE PIZZAS!

I blinked. Relief welled up, and I staggered back, laughing and letting Ted catch me. Belatedly I'd remembered my promise that if Mick could trick me this April Fool's Day, I'd treat the entire office to pizza.

1:33 p.m.

"Shar," Ted said through the intercom, "Glenna Stanleigh's on line two."

"Calling from Hawaii?" Glenna Stanleigh was a documentary filmmaker who had offices on the ground floor of the pier. For the past two weeks she and her crew had been shooting a film on the island of Kauai.

I depressed the button. "Hey, Glenna. What's happening?"

"Nothing good." Her Australian-accented voice was strained. "Sharon, d'you think you could come over here? As soon as possible?"

"To Kauai? Why?"

"I want to hire you. My backer on this film agrees it would be a good move, so I can pay your usual rate and cover all expenses. And there's plenty of room in this lovely house I've got on loan. You could bring Hy along, make it a vacation of sorts."

I hesitated, thrown off stride by the unexpected re-

5

quest, as well as by Glenna's tone. Even at the worst of times she displayed a sunny disposition that could be offputting to us curmudgeonly types, but now she sounded miserable.

I said, "You'd better tell me what's wrong."

"Can't. Not now. Somebody might overhear."

"When, then?"

"When you get here. Please, Sharon."

An undercurrent of panic in her voice made me sit up straighter. "Glenna, I can't drop everything and fly over there without knowing why. Besides, I'm not licensed in Hawaii. I'm not sure I could arrange it so I could work there. I could refer you to an agency in Honolulu—"

"No! I need somebody I can trust. It could be . . . well, a life-and-death situation."

"Are you serious?"

"Never more so. I think somebody's trying to kill me—or kill someone else on my crew."

"What! Why d'you think that?"

"Something happened this morning. I really can't go into it now. And there've been other incidents. Please, Sharon, I don't know what I'll do if you won't help me."

I was silent, considering. On the other end of the line I heard Glenna breathing hard, as if she was about to hyperventilate. "Just a minute." I reached for my calendar, paged through it, noting appointments that could be rescheduled and work that could be shifted to staff members. My personal caseload was light this month, and recently Rae had demonstrated she could handle the day-to-day operations of the agency as well, if not better, than I. Besides, Hy and I had been talking about getting away to someplace warm and sunny.

"Give me a couple of hours," I told Glenna. "I'll see what I can do."

"Ripinsky, it's me. Did you find the machines?"

"Right where you said they'd be."

"Good. Listen, Glenna Stanleigh called. She wants me to fly over to Kauai as soon as possible."

"Oh? Trouble?"

"Big trouble, according to her. She claims somebody's trying to kill her or one of her crew members."

"Claims? You don't believe her?"

"I don't know what to believe. She sounds panicky, wouldn't go into details on the phone. Anyway, I think it's worth checking out. She's got a house on loan, and she suggested you come along, as sort of a vacation."

"Hmmm. Tempting, but you know what'll happen. I'll get sucked into this thing as well, and that'll be the end of the vacation."

"Would that be so bad? We've worked well together in the past."

"That we have. You're not licensed in Hawaii, though."

"Yes, but I've been thinking: Your company has a Honolulu office. I could probably work under RKI's umbrella."

"Most likely you could. I can set it up. And I may as well go along; I haven't met any of our people in the Islands yet. You want to make the travel arrangements, or should I?"

"I will. How soon can you get down here?"

"Storm's letting up some. I'll fly down later, meet you at your house this evening."

"What about the Cessna?"

7

"It's on long-term loan."

"Well, don't take any chances with this weather."

"Not to worry, McCone. I've flown reckless in my time, but that was before I had you to come home to."

3:42 p.m.

"Hawaii?" Rae said. "When d'you leave?"

"There's a flight at eight-forty tomorrow morning. Hy and I will be on it if you'll agree to take over here."

We were seated in a booth at Miranda's, our favorite waterfront diner, enjoying a mid afternoon break. Rain streaked the already salt-grimed windows and turned San Francisco Bay to a gray blur. Inside, the diner was warm and cozy, redolent of freshly brewed coffee and fried food.

Rae didn't reply. Instead she stared at the window, a frown creasing her forehead.

I added, "I'm sure this trip won't last long enough to interfere with your wedding plans." Rae and my former brother-in-law, country music star Ricky Savage, were to be married in May.

"Better not, since you're to be my best person." The frown deepened.

I felt a stirring of unease. Ricky's marriage to my sister Charlene had hardly been one to instill confidence in his regard for the sanctity of that institution, and ever since he and Rae had announced their engagement on Valentine's Day, I'd had my fingers crossed against him doing something to shatter her happiness.

She sensed what I was thinking and made a hand motion to minimize the problem. "Don't mind me. I'm

8

grumpy today. The thing is, we'll be lucky if we're married by Thanksgiving."

"Why?"

"This new album of his is taking a long time to pull together. He and the band're down in Arizona at the studio this week, and their sessions haven't been going well. And then there's the surprise wedding gift he's promised me: it's working out about as well as the album. By the time everything's settled, there won't be time to plan a May wedding."

"So you'll be a June bride instead."

She scowled. "No way! I refuse to become a stereotype at this point in life. And July is out—that's when I married my first husband. And August is when Ricky married your sister."

I shook my head at the complexities contemporary society breeds. Rae and Ricky had any number of anniversaries they didn't want to be reminded of, plus the difficulties of dealing diplomatically with my sister, the six children he'd had be her, and her new husband. Of course, complexities are more easily surmounted when one, like Ricky, is reputed to have earned upwards of forty million dollars the previous year. . . .

I said, "September's a nice month for a wedding."

"By then the kids're back into their school-year routine. Charlene's already informed Ricky that she doesn't want them to miss their weekend soccer meets and gymnastics lessons."

"This is their *father's wedding* we're talking about, for God's sake!"

She shrugged. "Well, you know Charlene. I suppose we could always settle for Thanksgiving." But she smiled when she said it. Rae, I knew, didn't care when or how she married Ricky; in a sense they were already husband and wife, had been since a few days after they met.

"Anyway," she added, "I've got no problem with taking over the agency. It'll give me something to do while Ricky's in Arizona. I do envy you Hawaii. This wet season's gone on too damn long."

"Well, don't envy me too much. It's a working trip."

"At least you'll be working warm and dry. You really think somebody's trying to kill Glenna?"

"I won't be able to form any opinion till I hear the facts. Whatever's going on there, it sounds serious."

6:11 p.m.

"Swimsuit. T-shirts. Shorts. Couple of dress-up outfits. Wonder if I should take my Magnum? Hassle, filling out the declaration forms for the airline—"

"Jesus, McCone, when did you start talking to yourself?"

I turned, saw Hy standing in the bedroom door, and felt a rush of pleasure. With this tall, lean, hawk-nosed man I shared a life, the cottage on the coast, a love of flying, and—upon occasion—certain risky ventures. He was loving, generous, sentimental, and strong. He could at times be enigmatic, mercurial, bullheaded, and downright dangerous. Right now he was just plain wet and weary.

"So how was your flight?" I asked.

He crossed the room and flopped on the bed next to the clothes I'd piled there, running long fingers through touseled dark-blond hair and smoothing his luxuriant mustache. "Grim. You're right about the Cessna—it's a piece of crap. Altimeter went out on me, magnetic compass was whirling around like a mouse in a Mixmaster,

10

and coming into Oakland the radio started up like a banshee wail. So when *did* you start talking to yourself?"

"I always have, when I'm home alone, and neither of the cats is around to talk at. Anyway, I'm glad you finally agree with me about the Cessna." Hy's old Citabria had been totaled a month before in an incident for which I still felt partially responsible. We'd been trying to replace it, but hadn't found a used plane we mutually liked.

"You know," he said, "after tonight I'm leaning more toward that Warrior we test-flew last weekend. I'd forgotten how much I like a low wing."

"Low wing's fine with me, but that Warrior's got its drawbacks." I sent a lacy bra sailing toward the pile on the bed.

He caught it, looked it over speculatively. "Pretty sexy. I thought this was supposed to be a working trip. What's wrong with the Warrior?"

"I don't like the rudders. And the interior's kind of grungy. There's no reason we can't work in a little romance over there."

"A little—or a lot—suits me fine. I know what you mean about the interior. It'd take over ten grand to bring it up to snuff. But what's wrong with the rudders?"

"Too stiff for my liking. Catch!"

"You *are* thinking of romance. Yeah, you do have to kind of animal the controls around. And it really could do with a prop overhaul, maybe a fire-wall forward treatment, too."

"So what're we looking at beyond the purchase price?"

"Thirty, forty grand. You know what, maybe we should be considering a new plane. When you factor in the expense of making a used one right, there's not a hell of a lot of difference."

11

"There's a difference. And new planes depreciate very rapidly. Should I take my gun along?"

"Nope. I checked with our Honolulu office, and it's okay for you to work under our umbrella, but they tell me carry permits there are as rare as hens' molars. If I registered the plane to RKI, they could insure it under the company policy and take the depreciation in exchange. That would defray some of the expense."

"I could've sworn it was molars. I'll do that when we get back."

"Good. And it *is* teeth."

"I'm always right."

"Most always. C'mere, McCone. Why wait for Hawaii for the romance?"